pig

sbr martin

The Artists' Orchard, LLC

This book is a work of fiction. Any references to historical events, real people, or real locales are used fictitiously. Other names, characters, places, and incidents are the product of the author's imagination, and any resemblance to actual events or locales or persons, living or dead, is entirely coincidental.

*Publisher's Weekly is an independent organization. The review on the back cover was written based on a manuscript version of the book and not a published version.

Copyright © 2012 Sarah Beth Martin

Edited by Sherry Linger Kaier

Cover art, *Catwoman,* by Jenn Wertz

Cover Photography and Author Photo by PicChick Photography by Lizzy Bittner

The Artists' Orchard, LLC
P.O. Box 113317
Pittsburgh, PA 15241
www.theartistsorchard.com

ISBN 13: 978-0-9857014-2-0
ISBN 10: 0-9857014-2-0

Library of Congress Control Number: 2012913717

Produced and Printed in the United States of America

read it. live it. love it.
sbr martin

pig

~ 0 ~

In the corner of a cool, well-lit room, a troubled woman sits alone on a small couch. She is wearing a black dress, which covers her thin body like a tent held in place by the pitches of her swollen, aching joints. Underneath the garment, her breasts are sagging, just like the rest of her skin. Her hair is light brown, with a few random streaks of silver, and her face is pursed with increasingly noticeable fine lines and wrinkles.

She's somewhere in her mid-50s, though she feels much older. She'd stopped paying attention to her age years ago, when she started measuring time not by the turn of calendar pages but by the progress, and decline, of the people around her.

Some of those people whose lives she used to measure time are here in this room with her now. They surround her, dozens of them, packed in this tiny room, adjacent to a larger room which contains scores of more familiar faces.

Among those collected here today are her two daughters. Both ladies are grown women with independent lives of their own, but she still sees them as her babies, her little girls, running around their large house, opening doors and climbing on furniture, breaking all the household rules and flouting their violations of her authority. Her little blonde babies, plump and jovial, smiling and laughing as their mama chases them.

But they aren't laughing today. Today, their faces are solemn and stern. The woman scans the room to locate her girls. Her oldest daughter, her Tina, is standing at the entrance to the room, her head glancing distantly downward, beyond and beneath the carpeting of the showing room floor, chatting with a cluster of acquaintances whose names she can't all recall.

The woman wonders if Tina's lisp has returned, which often it did when she was flustered or scared. That lisp has been a part of Tina's personality for her entire life, something she worked to get rid of before and during elementary school, but something that came back when she wasn't completely cognizant of how she spoke.

Tina's lisp had been amusing at some times and frustrating at others. And now her mother finds herself inappropriately giggling at her recollections of how her Tina had once said words like "eggs" and "juice."

Worried that her grin will catch the attention of those nearby, the woman quickly turns it upside down and sucks at the inside of her lower lip before scanning the room again, this time in search of her youngest daughter, her Robbie.

The woman's eyes cannot find her Robbie in this room, but she knows that Robbie is here, probably in the other room, probably trying to bring cheer to the other unfortunate guests, probably smiling a smile that would be received as a welcome interruption to the austerity of this day.

Robbie's smile had always been a radiant one, one that could brighten even the darkest of days, even a dark day like today. Robbie knew what her smile could do, to her mother and to others, so she frequently used it even when she wasn't happy, just to have it work its magic. Her mother, again, finds herself inappropriately grinning, reflecting on the too many times Robbie had comforted her with her smile.

Still grinning, not letting the judgment of bystanders spoil her thoughts, the woman looks out over the audience for a third time. She is looking for her son, her Fox. She strains her ears to hear a rougher, manly version of her Tina's lisp. She strains her eyes to find a broader, manly version of her Robbie's smile. But, most of all, she strains her common sense to find him, because she knows he isn't here. She knew, well enough, that he wouldn't be here. He couldn't be here. Yet, nonetheless, she looks for him, hoping to find him, perhaps, because she wishes to be where he is rather than here.

The woman holds her purse in her lap with her left hand, her right hand resting on the couch cushion beside her, tightly gripped around a folded piece of paper. This piece of paper is very important to her, and she doesn't want to lose it. Every once in a while, she pumps her fist against the paper, making sure it is still in her grasp, wrinkling it and moistening it with her sweaty palm.

She refuses to let go of this piece of paper. Even when people are gathered around her, she still clings desperately to this scrap. She wants only to hold it, even at the expense of avoiding physical contact with others, which is something she has done all day. Rather than extend her right hand to greet any of her guests, she twirls it around on top of the couch fabric to rudimentarily wave, replacing physical contact with an empty gesture.

Though most everyone makes their way over to the woman, they do little more than bow their heads and offer customary regards under their breath before skirting off to the other, larger room for the main attraction. No one stays with the woman for any significant amount of time; no one sits beside her on the couch; instead, in deference to her state, they allow her to sit here, alone in the corner of this small room, burdened by thoughts that weigh heavily on her mind.

The woman dare not go into the other room herself. She wants only to stay seated here. She's been sitting here for nearly six hours, only occasionally leaving her post to visit the bathroom, the coffee pot, or the small window on the other side of the room. In the entire time that she's been here, she never entered the other room, not once, though no one, not even her daughters, is particularly disturbed by this fact.

Sitting in her lonesome corner, like an untrained rookie keeping guard, she is scared, anxious, and nervous. She looks like she has something to say, like she has a story to tell. But no one around her is asking her to tell her story. They care more about the story of the body lying in the casket. It's that tale they want to hear, not hers.

The man in the casket is her husband. Everyone wants to know exactly how he got there. They want to make sense of the tragic "accident" that befell him. If they'd cared to know her story, they'd inevitably discover crucial elements of his as well. But, alas, nobody is asking her to spin her yarn. And it's probably better that way, as hers is a story she'd prefer to keep to herself.

She wakes from her most recent daze to the faulty British accent of a man with whom she hadn't spoken in years, "Oh, good grief, my sweet, precious Flower, what a horrific nightmare! Such a tragic loss! My Flower, our Bender— gone, left this world!"

The man talking to her is Leo, stage name Leo London, a former bandmate of her late husband. Leo is not, in fact, from London, or from any other part of England or its territories for that matter. His British accent is faked and forced, thinly veiling a Pittsburgh tongue he longs only to conceal—a Pittsburgh tongue, that like her Tina's lisp, still crept out in certain situations and under certain circumstances.

The woman is surprised to see Leo here today, since he'd long ago left town to pursue a musical career in Las Vegas. She is also surprised to hear anyone refer to her husband as "Bender." It had been years since anyone, other than she, called him that, and she had presumed that the rest of the world had long forgotten "Bender" as his name, as most everyone else referred to him as "Ben" or "Benny" these days and had done so for the greater part of the last two decades.

Bender was the name that she had given him early in their courtship, nearly thirty years ago, as an abbreviation for "Ben, dear," which is how she tended to address him when he was irresponsive or when she had to raise more serious, or less playful, questions or topics.

"Ben, dear, can you pick up a box of tampons on your way home?"

"Ben, dear, I don't think we should drink so much anymore."

"Ben, dear, please don't hit me ever again. Ben. Dear. Please?"

She said "Ben, dear" so frequently that the words collided one day and were haphazardly abbreviated to "Bender." As they were both fond of nicknames and words of their own creation, she was amused by her verbal slip and decided that it was a funny, and fitting, name for Ben. Soon, it became the only name she ever called him. It turned out that he liked his new name, so much so that he took it on as his stage name and used it as both parts of the name for the band he fronted.

The band was named Bender's Bender. It was a small market cover band that churned out hair and metal tunes from the 1980's and rocked the local music scene for five years before fading away into oblivion. It was Leo, this Leo London, who had caused the initial break-up of the band. Leo, the lead guitarist, who decided to leave his musical brethren behind and go at it alone in Las Vegas' no-holds-barred jungle of excess, indulgence, and shimmering sequent esteem.

No matter how surprised the woman is to hear Leo refer to her husband by this name, it is Leo's voice, his presence here, that surprises her most. She finds it awkward that Leo would show his face at this "affair."

Bender loathed Leo after his departure dismembered the band, and he loathed Leo even more after what happened a couple years later. Maybe that's why she did what she did, why she chose Leo, Leo London, of all people, as the one person with whom to conduct her one and only extramarital affair. Maybe she wanted to give Bender another reason to hate him, another reason to hate someone other than her.

The woman's eyes lift to meet Leo's, and she is taken back to that night, seventeen years ago, when she and Leo swapped oral sex in the stairwell of his brother's home, where he was staying during a brief visit to his hometown. He had contacted her a few weeks prior to his trip, to ask if she and Bender would like to get together for drinks or a meal. When she told Bender about Leo's call, he laughed in her face. There was no way in hell he was going to meet up with that de facto defector.

For days, Bender ranted and raved about the absurdity of Leo's request. He went on and on about how Leo had betrayed him and now had no place in their lives. Leo was a traitor, and he cursed his wife for even taking his call.

The woman examines Leo's form.

His hair is thin, dry, and short. It had been much fuller and longer, teased and tangled, on that distant night, when he buried his curly head between her legs and devoured her sex as his black painted fingernails clawed at the waist of her raised frill skirt.

The tiny beer belly that he now has wasn't there years ago. Somewhat of an awkward protrusion against his otherwise thin frame, that little belly presses against a leather belt studded with silver spikes, a belt similar to the one he wore on yesteryear's night. She remembers carefully undoing such a belt, so deliberately, before pulling his him out and taking every inch of it that she could into her mouth.

"My Flower," he groaned. "My sweet, precious Flower," he groaned, repeatedly, as she worked him with her mouth. She didn't have to work on him for too long, though. He was spent in no time, a matter of less than five minutes.

But, oh, those five minutes! Those five minutes were on top of years of wanting this woman, on top of the taste of her that still lingered in his mouth.

Those five minutes—those five minutes were the whistling of a boiling pot that had been on the burner for far too long, the violent, hard stirring of fluids that led to a hot and heavy eruption, spurting, spilling, dripping from an already overheated spout. Oh, dear God, those five minutes!

As she looks at him and tries to find something to say in response to his words, she wonders if he still thinks of their encounter, if he'd worn that belt, and greeted her as he did, to jog her memory. She wonders if he still wants her, if he still burns for her the way he once did, even now, now that she is older, wrinkled and greying, now that she is nothing of the she she once was.

The woman feels a flutter in her belly, a tingling sensation. But it isn't a fluttering or tingling of excitement. It is one of disgust—disgust that she thinks these thoughts as her husband lies lifeless in the other room. It's a disgust that reminds her of the disgust she felt those many years ago, after the reality of what she'd done had fully settled in.

When she had met up with Leo on that ancient night, it was purely and completely for one reason: to be with him. From the moment she called him and arranged a meeting without Bender, they both knew what was going to happen. And they both wanted it.

She snuck out of the house well after midnight, after Bender had passed out from having one too many beers, and made her way through darkness to Leo's brother's house, where Leo was standing at the front door, eagerly awaiting her arrival.

He started panting when she stepped onto his brother's porch, opening the door before she could even raise her fist to knock. She stepped in to an immediate embrace which barely left room for the door to shut behind her. Slowly pulling away from the hug, his arm still wrapped around the small of her back, she lightly ran her right hand across his neck, over the hissing snake tattoos mirrored on each of his pronounced collarbones, and down his chest.

She playfully trailed her fingers up and down his lower abdomen, where his beer belly now sits, barely grazing the skin-tight shirt that clung to his inviting skin beneath, and brought her hand to the buckle of that spiked leather belt so like the one he wears now. "Hey," she whispered, opening her mouth to meet his wet kiss.

It was fast and furious after that. They flung their bodies against the hallway walls, knocking pictures off of one wall and tripping over shoes laid in front of another. Before they could make it past the hallway, they landed on the nearby steps to carry out their lustful intentions.

After they finished on the steps, they shared more of themselves with each other in the home's proper interior, through both the additional bodily fluids and the naked words they exchanged.

When the cock had crowed and the sun began to inch up on the horizon, they both realized that their time together was at an end. It had been over two years since they last saw each other, and there was so much more they could have shared. But now was not the time.

Indeed, the time would never come, because, when they parted ways, they both accepted the silent understanding that this would be the last time they would ever be together, as lovers, friends, acquaintances, or anything else that they could ever imagine.

But today is something neither of them had ever imagined, something that, despite the inevitability of death, neither of them had had the foresight to consider. Now, in recognition of her husband's death, he stands before her in blatant disregard of their longstanding understanding.

The woman starts to speak, "I never thought," but she is distracted by the two young women standing beside Leo. One young woman is her daughter, her Tina, and she's shaking Leo's hand.

The other young lady, a girl who couldn't be more than 20 years old, is not her daughter, but she looks more like her than her own daughters do, like the offspring of the woman had she mated herself with herself.

Taking notice of this young lady, who appears to be here with Leo, she changes her mind about her words midsentence. But before she can open her mouth, Tina opens hers, "And is this your daughter?"

Leo smiles, "No, no, dear Tina, she isn't my daughter. She's my wife."

Tina looks flustered. The woman considers speaking up herself, but decides against it, waiting to see if Tina's lisp will now make its debut.

"Don't worry," says the young lady. "We get that all the time.

"My name is Celia, by the way," the young lady says as she extends her hand forward to shake Tina's. "I'm so sorry for your loss."

The woman smiles beneath her lips, a smile as fake as

Leo's accent, and waves her fist at Celia in her familiar salutatory fashion.

Celia only glances at the woman briefly, not looking her in the eye, "It's so nice to meet you. I've heard so much about you. Well, no... No, I don't mean that... Um, I mean... Well, it isn't nice to meet you, given the circumstances... But... You know... Like I said, I've heard so much about you. Yeah, I would have preferred to meet you under different circumstances... but..."

Though Celia is still speaking, the woman no longer listens. She is both flattered and bewildered that Leo has told Celia about her. She wonders what exactly Leo told her. Surely, she thinks, he couldn't, he wouldn't, have told her about that night.

As the woman's mind continues to wander, Celia carries on her one-way conversation, directing her words at Tina, who is having a hard time following the nonsense and looks as if she wants to change the subject.

Slanting his head toward Celia in a sideways glance, squinting his eyes, scrunching his nose, and raising his right eyebrow, Leo mouths a word to his rambling wife. That word is "enough," and his front teeth fall down below his lower lip, causing a puff of air to sweep across his jawline as he labors to articulate the "f" sound at the trail of his inaudible utterance.

At this, Celia's awkward introduction closes.

"Have at it, C. Go," Leo instructs, nodding his head upward and leftward toward the drawing of a cigarette on the white placard sign affixed to an exit door at the back left corner of the room, which leads to a smokers' courtyard.

Celia turns to walk away, and Leo kneels down in front of the woman on the couch. His hands are so close to her body. She fears that he is going to touch her, that he'll put his hand on hers or pat her leg or shoulder.

She does not want Leo to touch her. No, it isn't because she is afraid of offending her dead husband; or, because she is afraid that his touch will awaken some desire deep inside her. No, it isn't because she fears that those around her will be suspicious of her closeness with this man, whom most of these people don't know or remember; or, because she fears that his young wife will be jealous.

It is because she does not want to touch him in return, because, if she does, she might have to let go of that piece of paper in her hand—and under no circumstance is she willing to do that.

Before Celia gets too far away, she turns once again to the corner of this cool, well-lit room and speaks to her husband and the woman before whom he kneels, "So this is your Flower?" she asks. "Very beautiful."

"No," Leo barks. "Don't call her that, C. That's just my pet name for her. Nobody calls her that but me.

"Please refer to her by her name."

~ 1 ~

Though there were some who called her by other names, the woman's name is Lily.

She was born Lilith. Leo called her Flower. Her children called her Mom, Mum, and Mama. A few acquaintances, those happenchance friends here and there, called her Lil. But at the bottom line, her name was Lily.

Her husband had pet names for her, too—dozens, in fact. Some of his favorites included terms of endearment like pig, slimeball, sleazeball, asshole, idiot, slob, bum, and loser. Then there were those that were of the more profane sort: bitch, cunt, whore, and slut.

Sometimes he referred to her by adjectives alone, using words like worthless, lazy, and stupid. Phrases made the cut too: piece of shit, waste of life, and good for nothing.

Every now and then, Bender got a little creative, stringing selections of these words and phrases together for one super-saturated, super-hyphenated insulting nickname.

"You stupid-lazy-piece-of-shit-sleazeball-pig-cunt."

"You're nothing but a worthless-good-for-nothing-loser-whore."

And so on and so forth.

He even once called her a "lump of coal." Lily never quite understood where that one came from. She knew, of course, that the phrase had much to do with Christmas, but she didn't know why he said it in late April.

When he called her that, about fifteen years ago, she laughed.

"Yeah, Bender, I'm a lump of coal. That's right."

Just as the term son-of-a-bitch is not an insult to one's target but rather to one's target's mother, a lump of coal was not an insult to Lily. A lump of coal was what Santa Claus gave to a bad child who didn't deserve anything better. If Lily was the lump of coal, then, it follows, Bender was the bad child.

And even if a lump of coal didn't appear to be anything all that special, even if the bad child didn't want it or tossed it aside, at least it was something that nonetheless had incredible potential. Such a pity it was that that potential could only be realized under pressure or on fire.

The name-calling started a few years into their marriage, before she'd done what she had done with Leo, when Bender decided, after a tragic night in jail, that it was no longer prudent to slap, punch, kick, or hit his wife. Lily, too, preferred this alternative, since Bender's words were easier to ignore than his fists.

Plus, Lily already knew that Bender had a filthy mouth. She'd known it from the first moment she saw him, and was reminded of it nearly every day since.

On that night, 28 years ago, she'd gone out to a local dive bar with her friend Irene. The bar was packed, filled with drunken 20-somethings, sweat, and smoke. A typical line-up of fellows had approached the pair of ladies, offering them drinks, cigarettes, sex, or anything else they'd oblige.

Both women gave the men cold shoulders at first, since the pair had their own reason to be out on the town that night. For Lily, however, that reason became less and less important, and those men's offers became more and more appealing, as the night went on. The pitchers of beer and rounds of shots saw to that.

One man in particular had caught more than her eye.

He was a tall, lean man with long waves of messy dirty-blonde hair. He had been one of the first to approach them that night, flirting with both of them at the same time, to catch whatever fish would nibble at his hook.

When he first sat down at their table, Lily was a little upset by the fact that he'd chosen to squeeze into the booth to sit beside Irene. After a while, though, she was happy with his decision, because it gave her the chance to look at him for the ten or fifteen minutes they allowed him to sit there with them.

Lily liked his grey eyes—at least she thought they were grey in the dimly lit bar. She liked his square chin, the way it jutted out to bend upward and make a hard dimple at the point where his jaw ended.

His tongue was pierced close to its tip. Lily couldn't keep her eyes off of him each time he'd habitually scrape his tongue across his front top teeth, making the bottom of his piercing peek out and flick shiny, round, and wet against the bulge of his lower lip.

The clothing he wore was worn snug to his body. From the high cut of his short-sleeved shirt's short sleeves, and from the low cut of his dark brown corduroy pants, Lily surmised that his clothes were probably women's clothes. But that didn't matter to Lily, or to him, or to anyone else, because he looked damn good in those clothes—though, Lily thought, he probably would look even better without them.

On his right forearm, he had an artist's sleeve of tattoos. Lily worked hard to identify and decipher as many of its components as she could in the brief time he was at her and Irene's table. She saw what looked like a dragon, what was probably a rose, what could have been a skull, and what was definitely some sort of writing.

A tattoo of a crisp star, maybe 2 inches high by 2 inches

wide, was centered on the left side of his neck. Lily wondered where else he might have tattoos, if he had any others that were hiding. She imagined herself searching for them, and licking them when she found them.

Suffice to say, he was definitely Lily's type. If it hadn't been for Irene's need for Lily that night, Lily would have gone home with that guy at the drop of a hat. Actually, she would have gone anywhere with him—his house, her house, the parking lot, the back alley, the women's restroom. Anywhere.

Indeed, by her 22nd or 23rd birthday, it had become Lily's practice to engage in casual, random sex whenever she pleased—and, throughout her mid-20s, she had pleased quite often.

As it was, her sexual promiscuity was a very curious thing. She took to sex like many men did, perhaps pushing the limits to an even more absurd extreme. Men were there to be played with, collected, and achieved. It wasn't necessary to love them or to keep them around.

In her entire life up to this point, Lily had never had a boyfriend or been in any type of committed relationship, other than a few and far between acquaintanceships consisting entirely of nothing more than recurrent sexual acts.

Men were little more to her than the sex they could give. They were the outs to her in, the pluses to her negative, and the bolts to her coaxial cog. Disposable. Interchangeable. A dime a dozen.

Maybe she turned out this way because she was raised only by women. With no dominant or permanent male figure ever-present, or ever present, in her younger years, perhaps she saw no need to have one with her as an adult.

Or maybe she was this way because she'd seen how

fickle both love and life could be, how some people crumbled when others floated in and out of their lives with such tremendous ease. Why attach yourself to someone when everyone, one way or another, only leaves in the end?

No matter why or how she ended up this way, one thing was clear: while she could go without love, whatever that was, she could not go without sex. She had to have her primal needs met.

She usually met those needs by getting drunk and picking up men at bars or parties. Sometimes she could go at it without the booze, but she typically needed it for an edge, to drown her inhibitions and push grain courage through her veins.

She had accumulated 75 partners this way. Seventy-five men who looked largely the same, sharing a common set of physical features and attributes. Seventy-five men, tall and thin, with long hair and some form of ink or metal disrupting their skin.

Though she had gathered these men one-by-one, their images fused together in her mind. Each of them became but one of 75 parts of the only man she'd ever known, 75 anonymous male appendages dangling from a singular male machine like utters from a cow.

The reason that the grey-eyed, dirty-blonde did not become Lily's 76th at the opening of the evening, the reason why Lily had to dedicate her attention only to Irene, was that Irene needed Lily to help her escape reality that night.

About two weeks earlier, Irene had received a phone call from Dr. Banding, of the Center for Psychiatric Treatment and Rehabilitation at St. Helen's Hospital. The call was to tell her that her ex-boyfriend of six years, Marty, with whom she had broken up four months earlier, had been admitted after midnight that morning, for treatment for the modern equivalent of a nervous breakdown.

The doctor was calling at Marty's request, to inform Irene of the reasons for Marty's admission to the hospital. Marty went loopy upon hearing that his, Marty's, ex-boyfriend had recently been diagnosed with advanced HIV. He went to the hospital to get pricked for a blood test and lost all control of his sense when the hospital staff informed him that it would take two weeks for the lab to return the results.

Marty started screaming and pulling at his hair and face, punching himself in his own temple. He kicked at the cabinets in the phlebotomy station and knocked supplies off of a counter. Carrying on that he couldn't live for two weeks without knowing whether or not he was infected, he threatened to kill himself. It was then that the men in white coats came in to sedate him and drag him away to the ambulance which carried him a few miles to St. Helen's.

Once medicated and collected, Marty begged his newfound psychiatrist to call Irene so that she too could get a blood test to see if their carnal knowledge of each other had damned her.

To say that this phone call disturbed Irene or was unsettling is a gross understatement. Irene was terrified that she might have the unstoppable virus, that her life would be cut short because of something as insignificant as sex.

But more than anything, Irene was shocked. She didn't know that Marty had an ex-boyfriend. She didn't know that he was gay, or bisexual, or whatever it was that he was. She'd never known him to have any homosexual inclinations, let alone any homosexual relations.

What Irene didn't know about Marty could have filled a pint-sized volume of homoerotic literature. Sure enough, all the while he and Irene were together, Marty snuck around behind her back to stand behind another man's back.

Prejudice, judgment, and hatred were what caused Marty

to keep his sexual identity a secret from those around him. He didn't want to lose his family or friends over an immutable part of himself, so he covered up his true face with a lovely beard named Irene.

And now his beard was faced with a horrific situation. She turned to her good friend Lily for help and comfort. She assumed that Lily, like any good loose woman worth her salt, must have had moments of her own where she feared that she'd contracted a sexually-transmitted disease, and, for other reasons, she figured that maybe Lily could talk her through some of the shock of discovering the secret homosexual lifestyle of one whom she once considered a loved one.

Lily had been there for Irene over the past two weeks. And, on the night here in question, she was there for Irene again, because Irene needed her now more than ever. The blood test results were to come back the next morning, and Irene needed Lily to sit with her during the eleventh hour as she dulled her nerves and killed a few brain cells with libation.

Irene had been the one to dismiss the men who approached them that evening, so that Lily could continue to coddle her in conversation. Lost in her own anxious need, Irene couldn't see how increasingly distracted Lily got with each sip and with each flirtation.

Eventually, Lily reached a point where she needed to stumble out of the conversation.

"I'll be right back, Irene. I have to go pee."

Lily didn't really have to use the bathroom though. That was just her excuse to leave their table and, truth be told, to look for that man who had so enticed her.

Lily walked the length of the bar to the ladies' room at its rear hallway and stood in line behind a few other women waiting to use the toilet. When it was her turn at the pot, she managed to squeeze a few drops of urine out of her bladder while she readjusted her breasts in her bra, to make them sit higher up and press together like the round bulb peaks of a heart.

As she exited the bathroom, she heard some commotion coming from further down the hallway, near the men's room. A cluster of men stood at the restroom's open door. They were talking and laughing, shouting at times, and sounded like they were haggling out some type of deal.

"No way, man, you've got to be kidding me," said the plump man who stood nearest to where Lily stood listening.

Another voice drifted out from the bathroom interior, "I'm serious, one hundred dollars. But not here—it has to be where everyone else can see it."

A third voice sounded, "Okay, dude. You're on! Let's do this!"

Two men rushed out of the bathroom together—one gliding, the other pouncing, down the hallway.

Lily would have never noticed these men or paid them any mind had it not been for the ruckus they were creating. Neither one of them were all that exceptional in her opinion. Neither one nor the other of them was anything that even faintly resembled the type of man she typically scouted.

The one who was gliding down the hallway was tall, heavy, and stuffy. He looked like the kind of guy who worked as an accountant's accountant or told jokes that relied heavily on preexisting knowledge of calculus-based physics. He was boring and dry. On his body, he wore pleated khaki pants and a maroon long-sleeved button-down shirt with the top two buttons undone; on his head, he wore average-length dark brown hair, thin wire-rimmed glasses, and patches of adult acne.

The other man, the one who pounced down the hallway, wasn't anything incredibly exciting either. He wasn't too tall, maybe 5'11" or so. His body was thick, but cut, probably toned from working construction, landscaping, maintenance, or some other physical gig.

He had a large, round head that was shaved very clean to his scalp and capped off with a black baseball hat worn low on his brow. The plain white T-shirt and department store men's jeans he wore were really quite bland.

As the men passed Lily in the hall, the stuffy one scooped his hand through the air in front of her, smiled, and said, "You'll want to see this honey. C'mon."

Intrigued, Lily jumped on the bandwagon, trailing these two men and the three others who followed them into the main area of the bar. She stopped to stand by one of the backmost booths while the group of men made their way to the approximate center of the room.

The noise of the night drowned out whatever words the stuffy one chose to use to address the preoccupied crowd. One of his followers, a small guy who Lily hadn't even noticed before, stepped up in front of his friend and said, "Listen up everybody! We got a real good wager here."

That small guy had a big voice, which caught the attention of those nearby. In his hand he held a clear disposable cup. Lily hadn't noticed the cup before either, but she noticed it now.

He held the cup up in the air and motioned toward the stuffy man, "My buddy here said he wanted to have some fun tonight."

The small guy's focus shifted to the other main player, the one who'd pounced down the hallway, the one with a large, round, closely-shaved head, "So my buddy told this asshole here that he'd pay him a hundred bucks to put this here urinal cake in his mouth."

The small guy held the small cup up higher in the air, positioning his thumb and middle finger around the rim of the cup, with his other fingers sticking out, so that the misshaped, cratered puck inside was clearly visible.

"And, this asshole's actually gonna do it," he said as he handed the asshole the cup.

The asshole grabbed the cup and reached in to extract the urinal cake. He held it in the grip of his fingers and extended his arm in front of his body, to wave the cake across the panorama of his audience's view. Then, he grinned before opening his mouth wide and shoving the cake in.

When he did that, the crowd—his crowd—went wild. Some people cheered, some cried out words of disgust. Others, like Lily, just watched in awe.

The asshole kept the urinal cake in his mouth for a little while to goad the crowd. He pumped both of his arms in the air like a champion would. The stuffy guy put one hand on the asshole's shoulder and another in front of his face to hold out the cash that was the asshole's prize.

In triumph, the asshole grabbed the money and spit the urinal cake out of his mouth, onto the stuffy man's maroon long-sleeved button-down shirt with the top two buttons undone. The stuffy man jumped back like an alley cat that'd just been sprayed, and the crowd cheered once more.

But not everyone in the bar was entertained by this spectacle. In particular, the management was not pleased. Two burly bouncers came over to break up the group of men.

One of the bouncers ushered the stuffy man and the small guy toward the door, "That's enough for tonight, guys. You're outta here."

The asshole stood there laughing, thinking he was allowed to stay.

When the other bouncer tapped him on the shoulder, he knew that wasn't the case, "That means you too, Ben."

And that's how Lily saw for the first time a man who she would not have otherwise noticed—Ben, the asshole with a filthy mouth.

~ 2 ~

Lily is watching Celia as she makes her way to the parlor door leading to the courtyard. She is still astounded by how much Leo's young wife looks like her. She sniffles to hide a tiny grunt of laughter when she realizes that Leo, just like her, must have also had a type to which he was most attracted—a type into which both she and Celia were cast.

Lily is suddenly overcome by a feeling of lightheadedness. It feels like a rush of hot air is clouding her mind, as if she had sucked that tiny laugh back up hard inside her and sent it straight to her brain. But it isn't air or laughter that makes her feel this way. What is attacking her mind is a series of jumbled realizations, questions, and thoughts.

She wonders whether Leo had been attracted to her because she was his type, or whether he had defined his type based on her.

Back in the heyday of Bender's Bender, Lily had seen Leo with all different sorts of women—girls of different shapes and sizes, from a veritable rainbow of hair colors, eye colors, and skin colors. If he had a type back then, he didn't stick to it. Variety, the spice of life—he seemed to have wanted to slurp up every flavor.

Was it just coincidence that she and Celia looked so much alike? Or had he purposefully sought out someone who looked like her? Was Celia, was Leo's wife, merely a replacement for his Flower?

Lily envisions Leo and Celia in bed together, their bare bodies entwined, clasped together, writhing, pushing, shaking. She imagines that she is the narrator of the scene, a voice emanating from an open eye in the ceiling, a voice that only Leo can hear: "Hey Leo, who is that you're really fucking? Is that your wife? Or is that your Flower?"

She pictures Leo laying there on his back as his wife, that carbon copy of her, rides his lanky body and slaps herself against him. She pictures his face distorting with pleasure, his jaw dropping open as he digs the crown of his head deeper into the pillow behind him. His nostrils flaring. His eyes drawn to focus above and beyond his squirming wife, to look only at the ceiling above them, from where the narrator again sounds: "Come on Leo, tell me. You're imagining me, aren't you? Say it, Leo. Say it!"

Her mind's eye sees him only further flustered by her commanding narration, his enjoyment being pushed up a steep hill toward a not-so-distant peak of ecstasy. Steering his wife's body harder and deeper against his, he looks up to the eye in the ceiling and moans in release as he mouths his reply—his front teeth fall down below his lower lip, causing a puff of air to sweep across his jawline as he labors to articulate the "f" sound at the lead of his inaudible utterance, "Flower."

But, Lily realizes, the Lily who she is in this scenario, if she is any Lily at all, is the Lily who she no longer is, the Lily who Leo had known years ago when they were both younger and firmer. That long-ago Lily might have had something on Celia, but, she concludes, the current Lily surely doesn't—who would want a wilting flower when he could have a replica of its former bloom?

"I've missed you," Leo whispers beneath his breath, not knowing whether or not his exposed Pittsburgh accent will travel the distance between them.

His voice, his words, reach her. This is only the second time she has heard him speak without his Anglo front. The first time, of course, had been the last time she saw him.

Staring straight forward, she delivers her hushed reply, "Me too, Leo."

The room is spinning in fast motion, though each moment is drawn out for Lily—drawn out for Lily and only for Lily, like she's trapped in a bubble, where time has forced itself to stop, sitting pretty as a fixture on the edge of a galaxy busy with action and about to explode.

Before the galaxy can explode, the bubble bursts, pierced through by the voice of a man named Jimmy Hayes, "Whoa, no way, am I seeing a ghost?"

Jimmy Hayes is referring to the unexpected appearance of Leo London here, but, no sooner than he says these words, he realizes how inappropriate the word "ghost" is in the given situation. He looks at Lily, "Oh, geez, I'm so sorry. Poor choice of words! I just meant…"

"It's okay Jimmy, I know what you meant. I understand completely."

And, yes, Lily does understand completely.

Leo rises to his feet and gives Jimmy Hayes a hug. They begin conversing with each other. They talk about many of the things that transpired in their lives since the time Leo blew town—Leo's business, Jimmy Hayes' hobbies, sports, and the volatile political arena. They also share memories of Ben, Bender, and Bender's Bender—grieving the death of all of the above.

Lily only half listens as they converse, grinning or nodding her head every now and then when she hears key words or phrases. Intermittently, she squeezes her hand, or glances at her tight fist to check for signs of the paper she is still grasping. Neither Leo nor Jimmy Hayes seems to register her odd behavior—or if they do neither says anything.

"Man, I can't even imagine life without Benny. I've

known that bastard for almost my whole life, and I don't know what I'm gonna do now that he's gone," Jimmy Hayes says.

Lily isn't sure whether or not Jimmy Hayes' comment was meant for her, but she replies to it just in case: "Me either."

While Lily does not know about the future, she knows about the past. She knows that Jimmy Hayes is, was, Bender's oldest and dearest friend. She knows that they grew up together in rural Pennsylvania and moved out to Pittsburgh around the same time, with similar sets of hopes and dreams.

And she remembers that Jimmy Hayes had been there the first time she met Bender.

That night when Bender, who was just Ben at the time, put the urinal cake in his mouth for $100? That was the first time that Lily saw him, but she didn't meet him that night. It wasn't until three days later that they actually met.

On the night of their actual meeting, Lily and Irene were out at the same bar where they had been only a few nights earlier for Irene's eleventh hour inebriation. This night, the two ladies were at the bar as part of a three-day drinking binge in celebration of the fact that Irene's blood test came back clean. They drank, too, to lament the fact that, when he received his blood test results, Marty, Irene's ex-boyfriend, hadn't been so lucky.

Lily and Irene were slamming down shots of tequila at the bar counter when, out of the corner of her eye, Lily saw Ben enter the establishment. He was with another fellow who looked a little bit like him, only with darker skin and itty bitty nubs of brown hair checkering his head—Jimmy Hayes, though Lily didn't know it just yet. A young Jimmy Hayes.

The men strode up to the bar counter and sat at stools some slight distance from Lily and Irene. They hadn't approached the girls, and perhaps they might never have.

It was Lily who approached them, or, precisely, approached Ben.

Drunk, she slunk over to them, tugging Irene along.

"Why don't you buy me a drink, hero?" she asked Ben, angling herself between the men and inserting herself into whatever conversation they were having.

"Excuse me?" he questioned in reply to her question.

"I said buy me a drink, hot shot. You couldn't have blown through that entire hundred bucks already."

Jimmy Hayes busted out laughing.

Ben closed his eyes, smiled, and shook his head slowly from side to side, "Oh shit, you were here the other night? You saw that? Man, I was wasted. I couldn't turn down that offer!"

Lily thought of another offer Ben wouldn't be able to turn down—but that would come later. And so would he.

"Yeah, you sure know how to make a first impression," Lily said. "Your name's Ben, right?"

"Oh, yeah. Sorry. I'm Ben, and this is my friend Jimmy Hayes."

"Well, Ben, I'm Lily, and this is my friend Irene," she was mocking him with her introduction, talking in a choppy voice to make Ben's matter-of-fact presentation seem juvenile and overly simplistic.

"Hmm, Lily, like the flower," Ben snorted.

"Actually, no. Lily, short for Lilith. Lilith, like the female demon goddess. Lilith, like Rossetti's famed femme fatale. Not Lily like the flower. I hate it when people say that."

Again she was mocking Ben, this time ridiculing his otherwise harmless comment and lording over him her superior knowledge of her name's historical tradition. She was being a demon goddess, a femme fatale, honoring her namesake, by antagonizing and provoking, poking and prodding, her male victim.

She'd done this type of thing before, acted this way with other men, as a way of enticing them—holding herself out as a shrew so that her prey would be tempted to tame her.

But rather than being tempted, Ben was humbled, "Wow, I'm sorry, Lily. Lily, not like the flower. Got it... I'm really batting a thousand here, huh? How 'bout I buy you that drink?"

As Ben motioned to the bartender, to order a round of drinks for the four of them, Lily's mind started to wander. In less than five minutes, Ben had apologized to her twice. Twice.

The man who sat at the bar tonight was meek and meager, not anything like the boasting asshole she'd seen make a fool of himself the other night. Could any one man possibly possess two such dissimilar faces?

Sure, alcohol changed people. Lily knew that all too well. But could alcohol turn a little kitten into a lion?

They swilled their drinks together, and Lily had more of Ben's disposition unfold before her. He was a generally happy man, cheerful, optimistic and appreciative, considerate. Even as he became intoxicated, as his voice got louder and his words slurred together, he was a passive, collected creature.

It was a passivity which, though calming, was nonetheless quite unremarkable, the kind of thing that combined with all of his other features—his appearance, his voice, his name—to make him nothing if not entirely ordinary.

If Lily hadn't seen him dip his fingers into a tin of chewing tobacco and put a sticky lump of short-cut chew inside his lower lip, she would never have been reminded of his filthy mouth, the only thing that made him at all visible to her in the first place.

Lily, Irene, Ben, and Jimmy Hayes sat and drank together for nearly two hours. At some point, they had moved across the room to share a booth together, where they sat separated like shy prepubescent kids at a mandatory school dance—boys on one side and girls on the other.

The bar was going to close soon, so, since she had already invested so much time and energy in talking with Ben, and as the crowd in the bar had tapered down to only the slimmest of pickings, Lily decided that, what the hell, she'd do this guy a favor and take him home with her tonight, even though he wasn't her type and wasn't who she thought he was.

Her initial tame-the-shrew gimmick might not have worked on Ben, but she had a few other tricks up her sleeve, skills she'd honed when achieving all those other men. She knew she'd be able to find something she could do to entice him.

The trick she pulled out from her sleeve was one of her favorites, one that almost always worked.

Right after the bartender announced that it was last call, Lily excused herself, with no explanation, and walked over to the bar, where she purchased a 12-pack of beer to go.

When the transaction was complete, she grabbed the two repurposed grocery bags that held her twelve 16-ounce cans of beer, or "pounders" as most drinkers liked to call them, and returned to the table.

She just sat down where she had been sitting before and jumped back into the conversation, trying to catch up on things. She didn't say anything about her purchase. She didn't even look at the bags or acknowledge them in any meaningful way. She just sat there and carried on as though she'd never left the table at all.

"You girls going to a party or something?" Ben asked, glancing down at the bags of beer that sat by Lily's left foot.

"No," Lily said. "Why do you ask?"

"Well, you got a lot of beer there."

"Oh, this?" Lily questioned, gently tapping her foot against the cans on the floor. "Yeah, it's cheaper when you buy it in a 12-pack here. Plus, I'm feeling a little thirsty."

"No way a little thing like you is gonna drink that whole 12-pack."

Lily chuckled when Ben said that. Though she wasn't big by any measure, she didn't really consider herself a "little thing," especially when compared to someone the size of Ben. Ben was only a few inches taller than her, not several like the men she usually held herself up, and out, to. She was thin, but not a twig, with full, perky breasts of which she was particularly proud.

Regardless of the precise terms he used to refer to her, he had stepped right into the trap she had set for him.

Return the shrew.

"What, Ben? Are you trying to mooch some of my beers off of me? Or, wait, are you trying to get me to go home with you or something?"

"Oh, no, Lily. I'm sorry. I just meant, you know, you have a lot of beers there, that's all."

Another apology! The third of the night. A different guy might have said something like, "Yeah, that's what I'm trying. Did it work?" or "Exactly, let's go." But, no, not Ben.

Exit the shrew.

"No, Ben. I know. I'm just teasing you. It's okay. I'm not gonna drink all these beers, by the way. Just gonna stay up for a while and pound back a few. You're welcome to join me if you like, if you're a night owl too."

"I guess I am a night owl. Sounds fun. Count me in."

Check!

Lily waited out what was left of the night, until the bar was ready to lock up, before telling Ben she was ready to head out. She hugged Irene, as Jimmy Hayes, inconspicuously, beamed a smile of decadent approval and reached out to give Ben a well-hidden, down-low high-five.

Ben and Lily walked through the crisp night air, together making their way back to Lily's home, which was only a few streets away from the bar they'd just exited as a pair.

Their conversation along the way was casual, just as her conversations had been with the many other men with whom she beat this familiar path. Talk of the weather, the neighborhood, the sky.

When they got to Lily's house, she opened the door and welcomed him in, eager to add yet another man to her collection.

She walked Ben into the living room, the room closest to the door, and showed him to the couch, where she invited him to sit while she carried her bags of pounders to the refrigerator in the kitchen.

Ben sat down and looked around the room, waiting for Lily to return. When she reentered, with two tall cans in hand, Ben looked up and said, "You've got a really nice house, Lily. Have you lived here long?"

"Thanks. I grew up here, lived here my whole life. It was my Grandma's house."

As soon as she said that, she realized she'd never said

it before, at least not in this type of situation. There were people who knew this information. But it wasn't something her playthings usually knew, or cared to know, or cared to ask about.

She shrugged it off and handed Ben his beer. Ben was sitting in the middle of the couch, so Lily sat in its right corner. Her back was flush against both sides of the corner, and her legs rested upward and inward on the couch, near to her body, bent at the knee.

The total effect was that Lily's body curled in all the right places to make her appear like a scribbled number "6." Her torso was the 6's sunken back; her neck and head, the 6's thin upward-slanted vein; and her legs, the 6's stomach, an oblong formed by the tops of her thighs, arching to the corners of her knees, and rounded out by the closeness of her heels to the backside of her very same thighs.

She looked over at Ben, biting the inside of her lower lip, and asked him to hand her her beer, which she'd placed on the coffee table in front of them. He quickly obliged and leaned back into the oversized couch, legs open and spread.

"So, Ben, what should we do now?"

Lily reached down toward her stomach. Her shirt had hiked up her body a little because of the way she was sitting, exposing her pierced navel. Finding her little belly hole, Lily played with the piercing, wanting Ben to see her slide the metal around so that it twirled up and down through her skin.

Ben noticed what she was doing and bashfully looked away, eyeing the room some more. Staring at the coffee table in front of them, he said, "I don't know... Wanna play?"

Progress, sweet progress, this all had taken far too long.

"Sure," Lily said. "What exactly did you have in mind?"

Ben looked at her and smiled before he turned away again, leaned forward, and knelt down on the floor. Only he wasn't facing Lily. He was still facing the coffee table. He bent down to explore the contents on the table's lower shelf, "Let's see what you have here. You got Madden™?"

Lily's hand involuntarily flung from her body to hit the arm of the couch beside her, and her eyes blinked in utter disbelief.

What Ben was doing was exploring the Playstation™ games that were stacked on the storage shelf beneath the surface of the coffee table. It was the game console, the joysticks, and the video games—not Lily—with which he wanted to play.

Check, but no check mate.

"Yeah, I think I have Madden™ down there somewhere," Lily said. Defeated. Deflated.

She kneeled down beside Ben on the floor, to help him sort through the games and make sure the console was plugged in appropriately. Once everything was ready to go, they battled each other on the pixelated football field.

And, much to Lily's surprise, she had a lot of fun. Ben would shout, at times in joy, at times in anger, as his pretend players played out the plays he selected. He'd chant popular fight songs to spur the little men on the screen, and egg on Lily's line-up to "ice" the whole team.

She was amazed by some of the ridiculous plays he called from time to time, like when he chose a passing play in place of punting on fourth down, when he ran a play fake from field goal formation, or when he repeatedly attempted offside returns.

Before, whenever Lily played this game, she, and with whomever she played, played according to a commonly accepted player's set of player rules. Players were expected to play a certain way, she thought. And now Ben was playing by a different set of rules, doing things she never even knew could be a viable part of the game.

Lily narrowly won the football feud, though she was fairly certain that Ben had allowed her to—again, something she wasn't used to in this game. Why would a player look out for anyone else but himself?

"Good game, Lily. You really don't play like a girl."

"I know. I've been told that before." Of course, Lily and Ben weren't talking about the same thing.

"I guess I should get going now, it's getting pretty late. We should do this again sometime though... Can I get your number?"

Lily wrote down her phone number, on the back of a grocery receipt that was lying on the coffee table, and handed it to Ben, who put it in his wallet, behind what few dollars of those one-hundred remained. As he began lifting his body up from the couch, Lily stood up to walk him out.

At the door, he spoke again, "Can I give you a hug?"

"Sure, Ben," Lily said. Earlier in the evening, or with some other man, she would have been sure that his request was made with an ulterior motive, that he was throwing a Hail Mary on a fourth down late in the game.

But after getting to know Ben, she knew that what he wanted was just what he'd asked for—a hug. So that's what she gave him. A simple, regular hug, not the kind she was used to giving, the kind where she'd press her chest against her partner's body, play with his hair, breathe thick breaths on his neck, or run her hands over his body. Just a simple, regular hug.

He pulled away from the hug and smiled. As he turned away he said, "I'll call you tomorrow, Lily."

And he did, which didn't surprise Lily, since he said that he would. What did surprise her was that she actually took his call.

~ 3 ~

"What's that in your hand, Lilith?"

"Nuffin."

"Don't lie to me! What's that in your hand?"

"Nuffin. I don't have nuffin in my hand."

"Yes. You do. And I know what it is. Give it to me, Lilith!"

Lily closes her eyes, thinking, if she can't see the woman talking to her, then, maybe, the woman talking to her can't see her either.

The woman talking to Lily is Lily's mother, Carla. She's heavy-set, with a body that's much bigger than it used to be and a hair style that's much shorter.

Carla maneuvers her big body to kneel down on the floor in front of the couch on which Lily sits. She puts her hands on her daughter's bare knees. Looking up at Lily, Carla says, "Honey, I'm so sorry about all of this. But you have to give it to me."

"No," Lily says, shoving her tightly fisted right hand underneath her body so that her mother can't reach what's grasped within.

"Lilith, give it to me."

"No. I don't got nuffin in my hand. I already told ya."

"Lilith! I don't have time for this!"

With that, Carla pulls at her daughter's arm. She yanks it hard so that Lily's hand comes out from beneath her body.

Carla pries Lily's fingers open with her own. What Carla is after is right in front of her now, so she grabs it before Lily can close her hand around it again.

It is a key. A car key.

"Noooooooo! Momma, please. Please don't leave me."

Carla walks out of the room, holding back tears and not speaking.

Lily jumps up to chase her, "No, Momma, don't leave me here all my byself!"

Lily is screaming and crying, inconsolable, out of control.

But Carla keeps on walking.

"Momma! Momma! I love you, Momma! Please don't leave!"

Carla walks out the front door, across the porch, and steps into the passenger seat of a small car. She hands the driver the key. The driver puts the key in the ignition, starts the car, and drives off.

That was the last time Lily ever saw her mother.

She was three years old at the time.

Carla left Lily to live with her grandmother, so that she could run away with her high school sweetheart, a suitor of whom Carla's mother certainly did not approve.

Though it wasn't until much, much later in Lily's life that she would be able to put two and two together, and though her grandmother never admitted or acknowledged it, Lily's mother was a lesbian.

And she was also a teenage mother—before she abandoned her daughter, that is.

Carla had given birth to Lily when she was only 16 years old.

It was not an outlandish fact that Carla was both a lesbian and a mother. But, rather, it was an unfortunate one. While she had always suspected she was one of these things, she never dreamed she'd end up the other.

Carla had come in to her sexuality around age 12 or 13, when she found herself spying on other girls as they changed in the gym locker room, and when she became preoccupied with her own developing breasts not only because they were hers but also because they were breasts.

When she discovered that she liked girls, Carla pretty much concluded that she could never have a child, since children came from men and women, not from women and women. She was too young to understand, let alone appreciate, the equal rights efforts or political movements that would allow her to be both a lesbian and a mother if she so pleased.

In any event, Carla's belief that her sexuality precluded her from ever having a child didn't bother her one bit. As a baby herself, she could never see herself having a baby, at least not any time in the near future.

Carla worked hard to keep her newfound sexual identity a secret from everyone around her, especially her mother. She had watched enough television, heard enough jokes, and seen enough condescending glares to know that lesbianism, homosexuality, wasn't a good thing in a lot of people's eyes.

She didn't want to be teased or hated, or anything worse.

So she hid that part of herself for as long as she could, frequently pretending she had crushes on male classmates, making up names of fake boyfriends, and going to middle school dances and sports games with a male "date."

By the time she got to high school, however, it became harder for Carla to deny who she was. She met a girl named Jill, with whom she had a lot in common. They both liked the same movies and music, and both had a hard time with algebra. They had something else in common, too.

Carla and Jill would make-out with each other whenever

they got the chance, which wasn't all that often. Maybe they'd sneak up to Carla's room while they were studying at her house, or go to the basement and neck while Jill's mom prepared dinner upstairs.

All they ever did, at first, was kiss, perhaps fondle each other over their clothes. They were too afraid to do more than that, mostly because they feared that someone would catch them. Because, if someone caught them, that'd mean they'd probably be forced to stop being friends, to split up, part ways. And neither of them wanted that.

Both Carla and Jill were also scared of the sex itself, that they wouldn't know what they were doing or wouldn't like some of the more vulgar aspects of it. Most novice lovers are scared of their first time, but, they surmised, a novice lesbian faces some, hmm, potentially unsavory prospects.

Summer heat and grain alcohol allowed them to lose some of their inhibitions one night. After nearly a year of being something more than friends, during the summer between their freshman and sophomore years of high school, the girls went to a classmate's house party. The boy's parents were away for the weekend, and he invited anyone and everyone over for a free-for-all night of breaking the rules.

The couple went to the party, as friends on the face. They enjoyed a few plastic cups of homemade jungle juice punch, spiked hard with grain alcohol. Being in a home without parents to catch them, and being drunk, the girls decided to slip away to the upstairs to explore each other in uninterrupted embrace.

They found their way to the master bedroom at the end of the long upstairs hall, where they shut the door behind them and took to being themselves. They were two Sapphic queens on a king-sized bed, enjoying each other in altogether new ways.

Though they were acting on hormones and desires, they were also acting on love. They were sincere and romantic in what they did, soft and gentle. Tender kisses, slow moving tongues. Hands that lovingly caressed, balancing out fingers that furiously flicked.

They found rapture with each other that night. Together, they stumbled into heaven. And then, together, they were cast into hell.

They were lost in each other's bodies when the door flung open. Carla jumped up, her hand still embedded in the mound between Jill's spread legs. There were three teenaged boys standing at the door.

"Oh, damn, look what we found!" said one of the boys, who'd come upstairs with his friends to smoke some pot away from the crowd.

"Hey, Dan, Joe, you guys gotta come see this! There're two dykes in here, messing around," said another boy.

"Guys, just leave us alone," Carla requested as she slid her hand away from Jill's body.

Jill adjusted her body and her clothes, "Come on Carla, let's just leave."

"Ah, don't stop on account of us, ladies. Please, carry on!" It was the boy who'd first spoken to them who said that, but Carla and Jill had lost track of who was saying what anymore.

Two other boys, possibly Dan and Joe, who had been called to the scene, appeared at the door.

"Holy shit, that's hot," one of them said when he saw the girls disheveled and disrupted as they climbed off of the bed.

"No, it's not hot," said the other new guy. "It's disgusting and unnatural."

The speaker turned his attention to the girls, "What's the

matter, Butch and Bitch? Maybe you lesbos need a real man to show you what sex really is?"

He walked across the room toward the girls and started to undo the fly to his pants. Looking at Jill, he raised his voice as he spoke, "I'll show you what it's like to be with a real man, honey."

"Get away from me," Jill screamed as he neared her. She jumped back up on the bed and rolled across it to find safety on its other side. But she didn't make it to the other side. Before she could get there, he jumped on the bed too and grabbed her by her legs.

He pulled her in front of him, lengthwise across the bed, "You're gonna love this. You'll never go back to twat again after having me." Jill tried to squeeze her legs together so that he couldn't reach that part of her she wanted most to reach.

Carla dove onto the bed and started pulling at the boy's body, to remove him from Jill. But she couldn't overpower his built athletic form.

Carla turned to look at the boys who were still collected around the door, who were watching with perplexed looks on their faces, "Please, guys, someone help her. Please, someone help me."

The boy attacking Jill flung Carla away from him and turned to speak to the others as well, "Yeah, guys, someone come over here and help that poor dyke out."

One of the boys, one of the originals who'd happened upon the girls, sprinted across the room to the bed, "Okay, I'll help you out, baby. I'll help you out real good."

Carla was terrified when he got to her. Just like Jill had done, she tried to escape her predator. And just like the other boy had done to Jill, this boy caught her before she could get away. He bent her over the side of the bed, and held her down from behind as he let down his pants and pulled at hers.

The way that he had tackled Carla left her looking forward out onto the bed, laying parallel and slightly away from where Jill was trapped. She could see Jill's body and face as the other boy was forcibly sliding himself in and out of Jill's victimized womanhood.

"See what my friend is doing to your girlfriend? That's called sex. That's what I'm gonna do to you now," he said as pushed her down harder onto the bed.

"No," Carla screamed. "It isn't sex. It's called rape."

"Get off of me," she shouted. "Please, somebody, help me," she cried to the boys at the door.

But her pleas were of no use at this point. The other three boys had shut the door behind them and two of them were rubbing themselves as they watched what was going on.

"I'm gonna wait for my turn with you," said one of the boys at the door. "I'm gonna wait for my turn with both of you," he clarified as his hand stroked inside his bulging pants.

Carla started screaming and tried to fight off the boy who had her pinned down. It was already too late though, as he'd pushed himself hard inside her.

"Stop," she begged. But he wouldn't stop.

Carla looked over at Jill, who was quietly sobbing, "Jill," she cried out. "Jill," she cried out again.

Carla was still trying to fight off her rapist. The more she fought, the more he fought back, and the more he enjoyed it.

"Carla," Jill whispered, flooded with tears. "Carla, listen to me. Just stop fighting. Just stop," she sobbed. "There's nothing we can do. They'll just hurt us more if we fight."

"Just let him do it, Carla," Jill whispered in a crackling voice.

Carla realized that Jill was probably right, so she went limp on the bed. She stopped fighting back as the boy continued to assault her from behind.

Carla and Jill laid there and looked only at each other as they were relentlessly victimized by the group of five young men. Looking only at each other throughout the rest of the disgusting ordeal, they both sobbed the entire time, each crying at what was being done to her as well as at what was being done to the other.

Carla and Jill were grateful for their locked gaze, for their ability to find something to unite them and give them a tiny, miniscule crumb of comfort and hope while their worlds and bodies were being attacked and violently destroyed.

They had each other to look to while they were each being repeatedly raped. They had each other to distract them from the boys who robbed them of their coital virginities and took repeated pleasure at their repeated crime. It was, by no means, a saving grace—but it was better than having nothing or no one in a time of dread.

Carla never knew for sure how many of the boys had unwantedly entered her that night, or how many times any one boy had taken a turn. All she knew was that she was used and abused, tortured, unwillingly stretched and stuffed, for upwards of an hour. And she knew that Jill had endured the same.

When the boys were done with them, they left the girls in the room, like discarded tissues absorbing their spunk. They boasted to each other as they exited, patting each other on the back here and there.

The initial antagonist, the one who had started it all, was

the only one to speak to them when he left the room. "You're welcome," he said.

As soon as the boys were out of sight, Carla crawled over to Jill. They crumbled together, and held each other in a different kind of embrace. They soaked each other with their tears, shaking, bleeding and raw, as Jill kept begging one question over and over again: "Why?"

It wasn't clear who Jill was asking for a reply, whether she was asking herself, Carla, their rapists, or God, if she was even asking anyone at all. But no good answer ever came to her. And no good answer ever would, or ever could.

They slipped out of the party as swiftly as possible, no one noticing their mussed clothing or matted hair. Like thousands of women before them, and thousands of women to come, they decided to keep the incident to themselves, to not tell their parents, their friends, or the police.

It was something, too, that they decided to not tell themselves. They vowed to never speak of it again. Even if it remained unspoken, though, it was still something that bound them together in a way that nothing else in this world ever could.

They'd traveled together through heaven and hell in the course of one night, felt tremendous joy and tremendous pain within a very short period. It was something that not even time could erase. They were forever attached, forever changed.

Two months later, Carla discovered that she was pregnant.

Naturally, Jill was the first person she told. At first, Jill tried to convince Carla that there was some way they could raise the child together. Jill proposed that the two of them run away together and start over as the two moms of one baby. They could imagine, Jill said, that the baby had been created by the love they shared that night, not by the hate committed against them.

It all sounded fine and dandy to Carla, but for one thing: Carla didn't want to have a baby. She didn't want to be a mom, not a single mom on her own or one mom in a pair.

Since she was morally opposed to abortion, Carla decided that she wanted to put the baby up for adoption. But, before she could do that, she had one more obstacle to overcome. She had to tell her mother.

Telling her mother was no easy thing. The age-old story of the pregnant teen was again retold. Her mother called her names, asked her questions, made threats. Carla cried, fought, and made her own threats.

When Carla's mother, Roberta, asked who the father was, Carla told her half of the truth. She said she didn't know who the father was, that she'd been with a few different guys around the time she got pregnant. She left out a crucial fact, though—she never said she'd been raped.

And she never told her mom about her relationship with Jill. She never revealed the truth that she was gay. Carla thought it was better for her mother to think she was a whore than to know she was a lesbian.

A few days after their shouting match, after the waters had calmed as much as they could, Carla told her mother that she intended to put her baby up for adoption once it was born. Roberta was totally against that idea and said she would raise the baby with and for Carla.

As it was, Roberta didn't care much for the idea of adoption because she herself had been an adopted child, adopted late in childhood after years of being passed around in foster care. Roberta spent most of her life wondering why no one ever wanted her—why her birth parents didn't want to keep her; why the different sets of foster parents never adopted her; why no adoptive parents ever selected her until she was just under 9 years old; and why the parents who ultimately adopted her looked at her as nothing more than a child who was a fifth mouth to feed, a necessary addition to their already large family of adopted kids, a necessary addition to get additional welfare benefits from the state.

Roberta did not want her grandchild to go through life with a similar set of questions and a similar low self-esteem. She overlooked the millions of other adopted children out there who had stories far more pleasant than hers, the children who felt special, planned, and very much wanted because their adoptive parents had so wanted a child.

Roberta's low self-esteem, her desire to be wanted, was part of the reason she too was a single mother. She'd slept around to feel wanted and accepted. She didn't know who her daughter's father was either.

So she couldn't criticize Carla for that. Like mother, like daughter, right? Well, of course not! But Roberta didn't know the secrets her daughter kept. What she did know was that Carla had ended up even worse off than she. Carla got pregnant early in high school, at an age more than ten years younger than Roberta had been when she got pregnant.

This too all added up to another reason Roberta wanted Carla to keep her child, why she wanted to help raise her grandbaby. Roberta concluded that she'd messed up in raising Carla. She must have done something wrong. Carla's baby could be Roberta's second chance.

Because Carla had been pregnant during a time when parents still had the ultimate say in the reproductive outcomes of their minor children, Carla had to accept her mother's decision, even though she definitely didn't like it.

Jill was very happy about it though. In many ways, she thought of the baby inside of Carla as not only being Carla's but also her own. She desperately clung to the idea that the baby had been created by their love, not by their rape.

Jill supported and helped Carla during her pregnancy. And Roberta was pleased to see that her daughter had found such a compassionate friend. She did think it was awkward, however, that Carla wanted Jill in the delivery room with her when her baby was born.

When that baby was born she was named Lilith—a name that meant something more to Carla and Jill than it did to anyone else.

Jill had been the one to name the baby, or, in point, to provide the name to Carla for Carla to name her. When they'd learnt that the baby was to be born a girl, Jill fingered through books and did a lot of research to find the perfect name.

The Lilith after whom Lily was named was Lilith from 8th century Jewish folklore, Adam's apocryphal first wife.

As the story goes, Lilith had been created at the same time as Adam, and from the same soil of the same earth. Unlike the biblical Eve, who was created from Adam's rib, Lilith did not come from man's bone.

According to midrashic proverbs, Lilith refused to be subservient to Adam. She wanted to be on top during sex, but Adam wouldn't have it. So she scorned Adam and left him alone in the Garden of Eden.

Thus Lilith turned away from man. She was not a suitable helpmate and did not need him.

Literature and lore throughout the Christian Middle Ages had Lilith returning to the Garden, to take from Adam his seed. She was from then on depicted as an evil temptress of men, taunting them and coming at them only for sex, populating the earth with creatures designed to destroy men.

And, ah, the contemporary interpretations of Lilith! She

had become a modern emblem for women's liberation and freedom from oppression. And handfuls of new age scholars and social reformists had pointed to her as the first lesbian, the mother of all lesbians, back to whom all homosexual persons could trace their genetic roots.

So Lily was named, by Jill, for these select stories of Lilith.

In so naming Carla's baby, her baby, Jill fancied herself setting out a prophetic path for the small infant.

Lilith, in recognition of the ancient woman who scorned Adam and made way for the baby's lesbian mothers.

A name given to an infant baby so that she may grow to never need man, so that she may never be subservient to him in any way or be his subordinate. So that she may never be under his control or be his victim.

A name given to an infant baby so that she may grow to taunt and torment man, to use him only for that which she needs, to see him as nothing more than what he could provide her if, and only if, she wanted it provided. So that man may not come upon her; but rather that she may come upon man, only for her own purposes, and may otherwise seek out to destroy him.

And, yes, a name given to an infant baby so that she may avenge the sins perpetrated against her mothers.

Lilith, because she did not come from man's bone.

Though Jill was not able to help rear the child into Lilith, and was not there to see the child grow into the adult Lily, Lily nonetheless fulfilled much of Jill's prophecy.

Indeed, Lily did grow to exemplify many of the qualities of the fabled woman after whom she had been named. In her young adulthood, she did not need man, and she was not in any way subservient or his subordinate. Throughout her life, she did taunt and torment, tease and torture, man and turn only to him for her needs, seeing him as nothing but the sex he could provide her, the sex she wanted.

Time after time she came upon man, and usually liked to be on top when she did so.

In other ways, however, Lily had failed to live up to the nature of her namesake. Alas, she had become one man's victim. One man had come upon her.

And some might think that it was for these reasons that Lily made her most recent difficult decision. That she had acted to compensate for the fact that she had become one man's victim or to prevent her future victimization; or, that because one man had come upon her, she had acted to destroy that man in further fulfillment of the prophecy she perpetuated.

But, no, it was not for any of these reasons that Lily killed her husband.

Her reasons for doing that were entirely different.

~ 4 ~

Lily's body aches. Her knees, backside, back, and neck are each locked in position, bound and captive, immovable from where and how they now sit.

Her right hand, the hand closed tightly around what it holds, is a club of fused-together flesh, nails, paper, and ink.

Too, Lily's head, as well as her heart, pounds, burdened by the sequence of events leading up to her late husband's early demise.

The aches and pains in her arms are the greatest. Lily does not feel like she has carried the weight of the world on her shoulders; she feels like she held it in her hands and let it slip away because her arms were too weak to lift it.

The only parts of Lily that do not suffer are her feet and toes. They have not moved much this day and, instead, have found rest. Thank God for sensible, soft shoes, a lifetime of them in fact.

Jimmy Hayes and Leo are still talking, and Lily is paying them little, if any, attention. She is more concerned about the aches and pains overcoming her body. She can think only of herself and alleviating the torment that preys upon her.

Too often she has felt this way.

Lily stands to walk and stretch out her body. She does not dismiss herself from the conversation. Mindlessly, she strides away toward the bathroom, leaving her purse on the floor next to Leo's feet but carrying with her that cherished piece of paper.

She finds her way to the small one-toilet bathroom of the funeral parlor, a decorated room of soft colors and sweet fragrances meant to look more home-like than industrial.

Inside the bathroom, Lily carefully opens her right hand and removes the piece of paper, to place it on the counter of the oval sink which is in front of the commode.

Though she does not necessarily want to sit again, Lily perches herself on the toilet to allow a steady stream of urine to escape her body. After she concludes the steps of her potty protocol, she stands to wash her hands in the oval sink, on top of which there is a tall rectangular mirror.

When she unknowingly gazes up at the mirror, her body jolts with a quick, sharp shock. "Who is this old lady in front of me?" she asks, and then realizes the answer to her own question: the old lady is she.

Seeing Celia reminded her so much of herself when she was younger that she somehow thought that she was, in fact, younger. She realizes now, however, that she is not.

As Lily's thoughts turn to Celia, she does not know whether to laugh or to cry. Lily realizes that she is not only old enough to be Celia's mother, but also that Celia is probably younger than her youngest daughter.

Lily can't help but shake her head in light of the tremendous age difference between Leo and Celia. She wonders if it at all impacts their marriage, or if the couple joshes about it like she and Bender used to do about the much smaller age difference between them.

Lily's shaking head stops shaking, to smile a coy smile as she remembers how she first discovered the age difference between her and Bender.

When Ben called Lily the day after he was not added to her collection, the two of them arranged to hang out that evening. Hanging out with a male, with no ulterior objective, was something completely new to Lily.

Her upbringing with her grandmother had been a very

strict one. Roberta sent Lily to an all-girl catholic school for the length of her education as a minor. What's more, she did not allow Lily to date or to keep mixed company with boys on even an irregular basis.

If Roberta saw Lily talking to a young man, she would interrupt the conversation. If Lily asked to go out with a boy, or to go to an event where there would be boys, Roberta would lecture her at length regarding the destructive nature of sex.

"One wrong move into a boy's arms could ruin your whole life, Lily," was the type of thing Roberta told her.

Since Roberta had to worry not just about straight sex but also about the possibility of inherited homosexuality, Roberta was quite restrictive of Lily's socialization with girls as well. Lily was not allowed to have sleepovers at her house, nor was she allowed to attend them at the homes of other girls.

Study sessions at Lily's home were to always be chaperoned and were to always be in the open. Her visits to friends' houses were regulated, and could only last a maximum of two hours.

Needless to say, for the first eighteen years of Lily's life, she was not at all a social being. As a matter of fact, her only friend, the only person with whom she regularly interacted was her grandmother.

But once Lily started college, that all changed. She had a different schedule to follow and was exposed to a tremendous variety of people. Very early in her college career, Lily discovered parties, alcohol, and, yes, young men.

Lily liked her newfangled entertainments and committed to them as often as possible. Even though she continually broke her grandmother's rules and frequently fought with her about them, Lily still yet enjoyed the companionship of her grandmother, her only lifelong friend.

Lily would hit the campus for classes, come home to spend time with her grandmother, and then return to the school property for parties, sex, and whatever else she was after. And, when her fun was done, Lily would return home again. It was a cycle she'd more than seldom spin.

Ingrained with the limited social options available to her in her younger years, and trying to accommodate her new lifestyle with her old one, Lily merely floated through the college scene without ever really taking root. Maybe it was because she didn't know how to socialize any better; or maybe it was because she wanted to stay true to and not let down the only person who had ever been there for her.

Just as Lily didn't have any friends other than her grandmother, her grandmother didn't really have any friends other than Lily. Sure, there were neighbors who stopped by and old acquaintances who would occasionally visit. But no one was a permanent or frequently reoccurring fixture.

Roberta had sacrificed her own social affiliations to raise her granddaughter, her second-chance daughter. She was committed to rearing this one well.

Lily was in college for five years before she graduated. The fifth year was to add a second major to her academic record. When she graduated, she took on jobs here and there but never stayed in any one job, or in the workforce, for too long.

Roberta was able to support herself and Lily through the growth of wise investments she had made in her younger years, most of which had originally been intended to support her daughter Carla. But, with Carla gone, those funds were there for Lily, and both Lily and Roberta saw no need for Lily to work underwhelming jobs in order to augment Roberta's accumulated savings.

Plus, as Roberta got older, she needed Lily for more than companionship. She also needed her for assistance. Lily was largely Roberta's caregiver, until Roberta's health declined to a point where she subscribed to bi-weekly visits from a nursing school student.

That nursing school student was named Irene, and she soon became the only regular outside friend Lily had ever had, even though their friendship started inside Roberta's home.

Roberta was content with Lily's and Irene's friendship, since she had both become attached to Irene herself and trusted that there would be no hanky-panky between the girls since Irene had a serious, long-term boyfriend named Marty.

Irene became Lily's friend as she tended to her grandmother and remained her friend after her grandmother died. She was something that bridged the before and after in Lily's life. She was the only thing that ever crossed over Lily's two different thresholds—a friend who knew Lily's social face as well as her home body, someone with whom Lily could enjoy the present and reflect upon the past.

And even though Lily didn't realize it at the time, Irene was someone who would also bridge her present and her future. Irene was, after all, there the night that Lily met Ben.

And now it was Irene who Lily immediately called after speaking with Ben and arranging to hang out. Lily was giggling when she called Irene, laughing as she explained that nothing had happened with Ben the night before and, she expected, nothing would happen that night either.

Lily asked Irene for tips on how to hang out with a fellow, since she'd never before done so.

"Geez, Lily, I don't know what to tell you. I mean, you just have fun. Talk about stuff, ask questions, find out more about him, things like that," Irene advised her.

When Ben arrived at Lily's house that night, they settled in on the couch and Lily got to following Irene's advice. The first awkward question Lily asked Ben was how old he was.

"30," he said, which would put him at just four years older than Lily.

"Really? I would have thought you were older," Lily said before realizing her insult.

"Thanks, Lily. Thanks a lot," Ben sarcastically said.

It was quite obvious that, for the first time ever, Lily had no idea what she was doing with the man before her.

But Ben wasn't bothered by her novelty to conversation. He tried to help her find ease in their exchange, joking with her at her conversational transgressions and making his own on occasion.

He also eased her through things by taking the reins for the majority of their discussion.

For example, Ben brought up the topic of his employment. With Ben's explanation, Lily learned that one of her initial assumptions about Ben was actually true: his thick, cut body was, in fact, toned from working construction, landscaping, maintenance, and some other physical gigs. Ben did odd labor jobs to earn his keep.

More specifically, Ben described to Lily that his current "employment" was as a general groundskeeper and building worker for the landlord of the apartment building where he lived. In exchange for Ben's work, Ben was given a rent-free apartment in the building.

Lily thought that the barter arrangement was somewhat ingenious.

All said, with the exception of a few other interesting facts Ben disclosed about himself, their second night together progressed much like the first. They played video games for a while. Lily was triumphant in the matches. And the night ended with Lily walking Ben to the door and Ben asking for a hug, which Lily politely and innocently delivered.

Two days later, a third meeting took place. The only major discovery on that evening was Ben's discovery of Lily's two middle-aged pet Chihuahuas—Mimi and Mini—who he hadn't seen on his prior visits owing to their shared proclivity for sleeping in the pile of clothes at the bottom of Lily's bedroom closet.

When he did meet the dogs, he didn't meet them because he was in Lily's bedroom. He met them because Lily called them downstairs to feed them after Ben's arrival. Ben was so very excited to see the little barkers. He told Lily he loved dogs and asked if he could feed them—he said it'd been so long since he had fed a dog and he really missed it.

Lily found this odd request incredibly endearing.

Once the dogs were fed and Ben was done gawking at them, the pair returned to their regularly-scheduled program. The night played out like a rerun of the first two, with mild departures in the forms of different conversational topics and different video games. The goodnight hug, again, closed the evening.

On his next visit, Ben brought the dogs a gift of rawhide bones—an act Lily also found incredibly endearing, though it preceded another replay of their familiar evening.

Things went on like this for almost two months. Nothing spectacular, or even notable, took place between them, and nothing sexual ever happened. Nothing romantic or flirtatious ever happened. Nothing exciting.

The only thing that was at all noteworthy, and was in fact quite astonishing, was that Lily hadn't taken to the bars, or to anywhere for that matter, to hunt out sexual encounters. She saved her money, her liver, and the elasticity of her vagina by spending time with Ben.

Lily liked being with Ben, even if their time together wasn't wrought with excitement. Other than Irene, and other than Lily's grandmother, Ben was the first person who was recurrent in Lily's life. And she felt for him something she couldn't have ever felt for her grandmother or for Irene.

Lily wasn't sure if what she felt was love, but she knew it was a feeling specific to Ben's gender. She could feel for this man something she could not feel for the women who played significant roles in her life.

It could have been the security of a strong figure, or something coupling the pheromones he emitted. Perhaps the depth of his voice or size of his hands had something to do with it, or maybe his Adam's apple or long gait was the cause.

Lily couldn't put her finger on it. But there was something there. She saw it, felt it, and liked it. Ben was comforting and comfortable.

From time to time, Lily and Ben would go out for a meal. Ben was always the courteous gentleman—getting the door for her, pulling out her chair, picking up the check. They also went to bars sometimes.

The first few times they went to the bar, Lily slipped and made suggestive comments she hoped Ben would pick up on, which, of course, he didn't. Or, if he did pick up on them, he didn't act on them. After those first few drunken attempts, Lily gave up on dropping such comments.

Of all the places they went, however, they never went to Ben's apartment. He told her that it was a dismal place, without a television or any other furnishings but for a mattress and a lounge chair. Lily was fine with her home being their regular meeting place, since it was there that she was most contented.

Two months into their whatever-ship, Ben sat Lily down for what he referred to as a "very serious discussion."

"I really like you, Lily," he said. "So, there is something I should tell you.

Lily's mind raced. She started crunching facts in her head, afraid that he was going to tell her that he was married, was gay, or had some other secret that would validate their lack of sexual interaction as well as his having an apartment Lily never visited.

What Lily should have been crunching wasn't facts. It was numbers.

"I'm not 30, Lily. I'm 37. There, I told you. I'm so sorry I lied about my age. It's just, I knew you were like ten years younger than me, and Irene is around your age too. I didn't want you to think I was some old-timer or something."

Lily busted out laughing, both relieved to find out Ben hadn't been harboring some huge secret and vindicated to find out that Ben was older, as she had expected.

"Old-timer?" Lily asked. "Hell yeah, you're an old-timer! Let's see, ten years? You were in, what, fifth grade when I was born? You were starting high school when I was starting preschool, right?"

Lily's questions were jests, flaunts, to show Ben that she was okay with the age difference and okay with his lie.

Moving past his trepidation, and happy with the way she had handled the news, Ben added his own two cents, "Yeah and when I was learning to drive you were probably learning to read, huh?"

The issue of Ben's age didn't come up again until a few days later, when Lily shared with Ben what Irene had to say on the matter. What Irene had to say was, "Wow, that's good news. I didn't want to say it, but I thought that he looked really bad for 30, really worn, like he'd done a lot of drugs or seen a lot of hard times or something. But, hey, he looks great for 37!"

From then on, Lily liked to tease Ben about his age, like how she would poke jokes at him when convenience store or gas station attendants asked to check his ID before selling him chewing tobacco; or how she'd ask him if he had been classmates with a senior citizen they saw walking down the street.

It was all fun and games, until Ben sat Lily down for another "very serious discussion," which took place about a month or so after the discussion where Ben revealed his real age.

Lily's mind again raced. She wondered what he would reveal to her this time. What other secrets did he have? Was he lying about his name? His race? His gender? Did he have a kid somewhere? What?

And, again, she was concerned about his marital status or sexual preference, about how he might be hiding something that would explain their nonsexual relationship or his mysterious apartment.

Lily's racing mind had raced to the right conclusion, in part.

What Ben told her was about his apartment.

"I don't know what to do, Lily," he began. "Something really strange and really creepy happened the other night."

Lily was expecting to hear a ghost story, but what she heard was far more disturbing.

"I'm sleeping there in bed, on my mattress on the floor, when I hear something that wakes me up. There's a flash of light and a churning noise. So, I jump up out of bed, and I see someone there in my apartment… It was my landlord. He was in there taking pictures of me while I was sleeping."

"What?" Lily queried in disbelief.

"Right. My landlord was in there taking pictures of me in bed. I yelled at him and asked him what the fuck he was doing, and he started saying some shit about he was in there taking photos of my apartment for insurance reasons."

"At night? While you were sleeping?" Lily pressed.

"That's what I asked him. But he couldn't answer me. Instead, he turns and runs out of the apartment. I chase him into the hallway and I go to grab him, and he sprays me in the face with pepper spray."

Lily hadn't noticed the clusters of red dots around Ben's eyes until he said this. Ben always wore his baseball hats low on his forehead, so his eyes were often shadowed. Once Lily saw the dots and his enflamed eyelids, however, that was all she could see.

"Oh, Ben, that's just terrible," she said as she raked her hand across his shoulder. To her, this raking motion was a calming gesture, since anything softer was sexual in her opinion.

"I know. And the worst part is, it left me wondering if that's the first time he did that to me, or if he did it before. I sleep like a log, Lily. He could have been in there taking photos of me for months, and God only knows what he did with them. For all I know, they could be featured in a gay porn magazine or something."

"Oh, man," Lily said, because she couldn't think of anything better to say.

"One thing's for sure, I can't live there anymore. I need to find somewhere else to stay. Soon. Or else I'll have to leave Pittsburgh."

"Well, Ben, I guess you could stay here if you want—you know, until you find something better or permanent. No rent or anything, just help out around the house. Keep feeding the dogs like you do, take the garbage out, stuff like that."

"Oh, Lily! Are you for real?"

"Yeah, why not? You're here almost every day anyway. You'll save a lot of money on gas."

"Sweet, thank you so much, Lily."

"When are you gonna move in then?" Lily asked.

"I can do it tonight. I've got all my stuff out in my car," he replied.

Lily didn't ask him then, or ever, whether he had packed his car because he planned on leaving his apartment or because he planned on moving into her home, banking on her invitation.

In any event, he did move in that night, 28 years ago, and went on to live and die there.

~ 5 ~

"We've been dating for almost six months now, Lily. Don't you think we should celebrate? Maybe a trip or a vacation somewhere?"

Lily was absolutely floored when she heard Ben say those words, particularly the word "dating." Is that what they had been doing over the six months since they first met? Dating? Was this dating?

Was she dating this man who had lived in her house for the past three months, who slept in a separate bed in a separate room, who never had sex with her, who never kissed her, who never did anything more than hug her?

In the time during which Ben had lived with her, Lily did feel as though she was getting closer to him. She saw him more and more often and always made sure to say goodnight to him each night before bed. She looked forward to seeing him each morning.

She even started calling him "dear" or "Ben, dear" as a way of getting his attention when he was otherwise engaged, like when he was playing video games, or when she had a favor to ask.

"Ben, dear, can you pick up a box of tampons on your way home?" she once called to ask him while he was working at his legitimate job as an assistant house painter.

He seemed caught off guard by the question at first but nonetheless obliged her request, even though he failed to get her the exact brand and type of tampons she had ordered. In hindsight, wasn't that the type of question a woman would only ask a man she was dating? Or a task that a man would only perform for the woman he was dating?

Sometimes Ben would pluck flowers from the yards of the homes where he had been working, and he'd deliver to Lily, or to the kitchen table, a bouquet of non-bouquet flowers. He'd put them in a drinking glass filled with water, which would be muddied by the topsoil that still clung to the dangling roots of the flowers.

For all that Lily knew, these things added up to dating. She'd never dated before, and figured this was probably it, albeit in painstakingly slow motion. Ben surely knew more about dating than she did, so she figured he must have been right in his categorization.

Moreover, she didn't want to embarrass herself, or embarrass Ben, by challenging him.

So, instead of raising her questions, she answered his, "A trip would be nice. How about a weekend at the beach?"

A few days later, Lily and Ben wisped off to Ocean City, Maryland, where they arrived in the late afternoon and settled in at a swank hotel Lily paid for with money from her dwindling inheritance from her grandmother.

Their room was on the 12th floor of the hotel, with a beach-view balcony at its rear. The room was lush and extravagant. It had a stove, a dishwasher, a hot tub, a small round table and two chairs, and a king-sized bed.

That's right, the room had only one bed.

"I call the right side," Lily said as she jumped on the pillow-top mattress.

"Oh, Lily, I can sleep on the floor if you want me to," Ben offered.

"Don't be silly, Ben. It's a big bed, and, don't forget, we've been dating for six months."

Ben's smile was his reply.

But before they could go to sleep they had a few more

waking hours to fill. They freshened up and headed out to the boardwalk. They stopped and shopped along the boardwalk for over an hour before they decided to fill their bellies with food and libation.

Ben suggested that they stop in whatever restaurant looked the busiest, since that restaurant would probably have the best food. After walking only a bit farther down the boardwalk, Ben spotted a restaurant that had an outdoor patio buzzing with patrons.

He and Lily decided the place looked good enough, and they elected to dine there. Seated at a booth on the patio, they both ordered the same item, which often they did when dining out—crab cakes. When in Rome, Lily figured.

The crab cakes weren't heavy, but the shots of whiskey were, which balanced well against the creamy stout beer. The lager was a crisp refresher, as were the numerous shots of vodka accompanied by lemons and dashes of sugar. It was either the gimlet or the peppermint schnapps that was meant to calm both of their upset tummies, and the caffeine in the rum and cola was intended to keep them alert so that they could calculate the appropriate gratuity and be of sound enough mind to find their way back to the correct hotel.

The tequila shooters that closed out the night? Those were just for kicks.

Ben took care of the check and held Lily's hand as they stumbled out of the dining area and back on to the boardwalk. While they had been dining and drinking, Ben had noticed a train that continually rode the boardwalk, carrying passengers from one end of the commercial strip to the other. He'd hoped the train would still be running by the time they were done.

And it was. Ben pointed it out in the distance, several blocks up the boardwalk. They stood close to the entrance of the eatery they'd just exited and waited for the train to arrive.

Lily's feet were planted on the ground and her legs remained straight, but her entire upper body gave to swaying in circles. She was like a rotating cuff attached to a steady, permanent base, a never moving trunk.

Ben's behavior wasn't much different, though his feet and legs moved every now and then.

"I don't feel so good, Lily," he said as he leant back to sit against the wooden railing of the restaurant's bounds. He ended his comment with a burp, and gagged at the taste of the gas that came up into his mouth. It tasted like the day-old contents of a used chum bucket in which a molted crab or two had been encouraged to get drunk.

He burped again. This time, the nasty gas was joined by a small amount of regurgitated fluid. The fluid tasted mostly like the gas but slightly more acidic.

"Don't worry, Ben. We'll be back at the hotel soon."

With that, Lily uprooted her motionless trunk and moved to sit on the railing alongside Ben, rubbing his arm with her hand.

"What's the matter, old man? Can't handle your booze?" Lily teased, to buoy Ben.

Ben smiled, and, no sooner, Lily's words came back to haunt her, or rather, came up to haunt her. Like the hinge on a door that was just slammed shut, she abruptly bent over at the waist and upchucked on ground.

The vomit splashed to the ground and ricocheted onto her sling-back shoes and feet. Some hit Ben's boots as well. A few onlookers cringed; a few laughed.

"Oh, Lily, that's gross. Looks like you're the one who can't handle your booze," Ben said as he bent down to look at the still caved Lily.

The train arrived within less than a minute. The two sick drunkards boarded, paid their fares, and sat down. The motion of the train as it clopped over the boards in the boardwalk only made Lily's stomach feel worse, and the circus of light and sound created as the train moved past storefronts made Ben dizzy.

Lily and Ben derailed from the train when it arrived near their hotel. They stumbled through the lobby, to the elevators, and up to floor 12. After trying to enter the wrong room and getting pissed off when his key didn't work, Ben eventually found his way to the correct room and opened the door.

Once in the room, Lily jumped out of her shoes and ran straight to the bathroom to kneel down in front of the toilet and profusely puke. The sound, smell, and act of Lily puking made Ben sick enough to upheave himself. But he didn't, since the only proper receptacle was actively being used.

Ben stood by the door and watched Lily, not quite knowing exactly what to say. He asked her if she was okay a few times, asked if there was anything she needed or wanted, and asked her if she wanted to go to the hospital. Lily's response to each of these questions was the same: "No," followed by a stream of vomit.

Lily saw the colors of all her different beverages swirling together in the toilet bowl, with chunks of crab and green peppers swimming the rainbow river. Her head was pounding from the pressure of her digestive trauma.

Just when she felt like there was nothing more inside her to expel, she coughed up a few more tablespoons of sickness. She decided it was then time to clean up, lie down, and put this mess behind her.

When she emerged from the bathroom, she saw Ben sitting in a chair at the table, with his head buried in his hands as his elbows rested on the surface of the table. Ben looked up to see Lily and ask how she was feeling. His eyes were puffy, swollen, and red, much like they'd been the night his creepy landlord sprayed him in the face with pepper spray. Only this time they weren't this way because he had been sprayed. His eyes were this way because he had been crying.

His tears were out of concern for Lily. Ben didn't like seeing her sick and in pain. He had wished there was something he could have done to help her, and sobbed at his conclusion that he could do nothing.

Ben stood from his chair and approached Lily. He gave her a warm, tight hug and led her to the bed. He pulled down the covers, fluffed the pillows and signaled for her to lie down. She sunk into the spot Ben had prepared for her.

Walking over to the other side of the bed, Ben removed his shoes and then undressed his side of the bed the same way he'd undressed hers. He sat down on the bed and then very deliberately eased over to Lily. Lying down, he wrapped his arms around her and brought her close to his chest.

Ben kissed Lily on the forehead three or four times. Those kisses were the first he ever shared with Lily, the first time his lips ever touched her flesh, lightly brushing her sweaty brow. "It'll be okay, Lily," he said. "Just rest now. It'll all be better tomorrow."

She didn't respond to Ben immediately, opting instead to be comforted and lulled by his arms, soft kisses, and voice.

A few minutes later, she decided to speak, "Ben, dear, I don't think we should drink so much anymore."

"Me neither, Lily. Me neither," Ben replied, though Lily had begun already to fade into slumber. Ben too drifted off to sleep, his arms still wrapped around Lily.

And, though Lily had been with numerous men before,

this was for her the first time she'd ever actually slept with one.

Like many of the world's best laid plans, Lily's and Ben's plan to drink less was dismantled the very next day, when, as if the drunkenness and sickness had never happened, they again downed an excess of alcohol. While their drinking didn't cause either of them to toss either of their cookies, it did impair them and fuel them both to act lasciviously.

Lily and Ben found themselves on their room's balcony, having returned to the hotel after an evening of hopping from bar to bar along the boardwalk. They were joined on the balcony by two bottles of chardonnay Lily had ordered from room service.

The second bottle had been corked and was ready to pour. The first bottle was empty and Ben was using it as a spittoon, careful not to confuse it with the full one.

Each of them sat by different corners of the balcony, not because they wanted to be distanced from each other but because that was the way the furniture was laid out—one chair at each of the two ends of the balcony, with a small patio table by the chair in which Ben sat.

"Ben, can you come over here and pour me another glass of wine?" Lily asked.

Ben rose from his chair, picked up the correct bottle, and walked over to Lily. He parked at an angle beside her chair, to pour from the bottle into her glass. Lily closely watched every detail of his movement.

Before he was done pouring, Lily reached out and grabbed the top of his seasonally-inappropriate blue jeans. Ben pulled back a little but then moved forward again. Lily proceeded to rub her right hand up and down the flap of denim that covered Ben's pants' zipper and, more importantly, what was starting to take shape beneath.

Her left hand rose up to meet her right, to assist in undoing Ben's pants. As she pulled Ben's pants down, she leant forward to kiss his stomach near his bellybutton, the first kiss she ever gave him. Ben stood there, still holding the bottle of wine in one hand and Lily's full glass in the other, peering down to observe as Lily glided her tongue across the seam where the cloth of his boxers met with the flesh of his body.

Next, she pulled his boxers down, looking up at him with an intensely gratified smile. Ben's eyes met Lily's for a moment as she started to inch her face forward toward his expanded and engorged presence.

When he felt the warm, soft wetness of Lily's mouth against him, Ben sighed and glanced over his shoulder. The night sky was black with a new moon on the horizon, yet people still bustled on the boardwalk some twelve floors below. He could hear laughter and voices, the tides of the ocean, and Lily's slippery mouth.

While he was not at all self-conscious or worried, Ben wondered if anyone could see their public display. He knew that the balcony was probably too high up for boardwalk pedestrians to view them with any worthwhile detail, but he pondered whether there might be some lonely fisherman out on the ocean, standing at the helm of his vessel, taking delight at the spectacle visible through the eyeglass of his elongated scope.

Just as the tides lapped against the shore and wine lapped out of the bottle and glass Ben held, so too Lily's mouth lapped against him, back and forth, until his completion. Without words and still only half-robed, Ben moved to put the bottle and glass on the patio table and dug his finger into his mouth to remove a wad of chewing tobacco he'd been holding onto like a squirrel onto an acorn.

The tobacco that had been in his mouth was the reason

why Ben never interrupted Lily's advances for their first mouth-to-mouth kiss. And Lily never thought to start the episode off with a kiss since she'd become accustomed to not holding kissing out as a necessary element of sex, because she frequently liked to cut straight to the action and skip the chase.

So before Ben and Lily ever actually kissed, they'd shared an intimacy of an incredibly personal nature. And they were about to share yet a few more.

Ben walked back over to Lily and held out his hand to invite her to join him inside the hotel room. He slid the balcony door closed behind them, tossed off his hat, and began to peel the white T-shirt off of his body.

"Take your clothes off and get on the bed, Lily," he instructed.

Lily was pleased with his command of the situation and followed his directive. She slipped her shorts and undergarments down around her ankles and stepped out of them, next removing her own top and, finally, her bra. She jumped up onto the bed and positioned herself at its center, reclining against the pillows with her legs spread open and waiting.

Ben slowly made his way to the foot of the bed and crawled up to kneel between Lily's inviting legs. He grabbed her thighs to pull her closer to him, so that she was lying flat on the pillowy bed. His hands then traced the contours of her body, from her toes to her chest, until he was on top of her.

Lily's hands ran over Ben's shoulders and neck, to the back of his head, cupping it as he nestled his face and mouth against the side of her face. His breath was quick and hard against her, his tongue and mouth licking and sucking at her ear.

Though her body was somewhat numb from the large

amount of alcohol she'd consumed, she still felt him find her. She felt a slight sting when his finger touched against the most sensitive bud of her body. It was the same finger he'd used to remove the chewing tobacco from his mouth, and Lily assumed it was the residual nicotine that coldly burned her.

But what Lily felt was more pleasure than pain. Her body shuddered with his movements, which only made Ben's breathing and pulse quicken all the more. As her back arched, she let out a soulful cry that sent Ben over the edge. He pulled his hand away and lunged forward to dip inside her.

Their bodies worked together in conjugal conjunction. Pushing, pulling, clenching, and thrusting at all the right moments. Rocking, twisting, moaning—it was more than the physical act of sex they were enjoying.

For Lily, it was the first time she'd coupled with man with whom she was in any type of standing relationship. It was a new type of sex for her, a new virginity she was losing, an official stamp on a heretofore unofficial document.

Further yet, it was the first time she'd allowed tensions to build before reaching a climax. She'd never hung around with a guy before if she couldn't get what she wanted when she wanted it, never held off in regard or respect to another man's intentions. When Lily didn't get what Lily wanted from one man, Lily moved on to the next. But she hadn't done so with Ben. She'd stuck around. And now she was getting what she wanted in the first place. Only now it meant something different.

Lily imagined that the build-up, tension, and suspense leading up to this moment were what she missed out on in her youth. Not allowed to date, she had never experienced courtship and wooing. She had always considered sex a means to satisfy herself, rather than an end to any meaningful process.

Sex with Ben, however, was like finding a pot of gold at the end of a rainbow. It was something not automatically granted, something she could only work to discover in due time.

This mindset allowed Lily to elevate what was an otherwise ordinary, orthodox sexual encounter to a glorified level. What were square, imprecise movements, Lily saw as smooth, round perfection. The length of the romp, as well as of Ben, was magnified to exponential proportions to accommodate Lily's clouded perspective.

For Ben, too, the sex was meaningful. Though, its meaning to him was substantially different.

When their bodies collapsed together with a final haphazard heave, Lily lay awake in Ben's arms for several minutes, contemplating where their relationship would go from here, what the next day would hold for the couple.

This would be a tough act to follow, she thought.

But Ben delivered another noteworthy performance the next night. If their physical union had been some type of peak in their relationship, Ben brought it to plummet in no time.

The next night, which was the last of their trip to Ocean City, was the first time Ben hit Lily.

They'd been drinking throughout the day and evening. Drinking, again. Drunk, again. Although Ben had brought an ample amount of clothing with him on their vacation, he was wearing the same T-shirt he'd worn on the two days prior, for no reason other than convenience.

At a bar located along Coastal Highway, Lily made a joking comment to Ben that he'd over-worn the shirt. She said it smelled bad, like it'd been sitting in a few inches of dirty water at the bottom of a washing machine that someone forgot to add soap to or turn on.

Ben wouldn't have minded Lily's remarks so much had they not been overheard by some other drunkards at the adjacent table.

"Ew, that's gross!" said a young lady who was drinking from a long-neck bottle.

"What's gross?" asked her friend across the table.

The ladies' conversation flourished from there as expected, all the while overheard by both Ben and Lily.

On their walk back to the hotel, Ben repetitively asked Lily why she would say such a thing in a public place and told her how the response of the nearby eavesdroppers had very much embarrassed him. Lily kept telling him to lighten up and forget about it.

But he couldn't forget about it. As soon as they were safe and sound in their hotel room, Ben pushed Lily up against the wall and grabbed her by the chin to force her gaze upon him.

"What the hell is wrong with you, Lily?" he snarled at her, nailing her head hard into the soft swirls of wallpaper.

"I'm sorry, Ben," she muttered, trembling, shaking at his force. "I didn't know it would upset you. Really. I'm so sorry."

Lily was crying.

"Don't ever do anything like that again, or else!" Ben shouted.

He let go of Lily and turned away.

Lily tried to regain her composure: "I was just teasing you Ben, like I always do. You've gotta lighten up. I'd never say or do anything to intentionally hurt you."

Such a shame that Ben didn't feel the same way! He turned again to Lily and charged at her like a bull, his chin pressed downward toward his clavicle and his head angled forward, with thin-slit eyes straining upward. His motion was swift and unavoidable as he viciously butted his head against Lily's.

Lily's head and body slammed hard on the wall, while Ben stood by panting spit that splurted on his puffing cheeks. Before Lily could speak or move, Ben charged at her again, digging her even deeper into the unyielding wall behind her.

Finding her neck this time, Ben's hand scrunched and squeezed to further pin Lily to the wall and make it difficult for her to breath or to speak. Lily closed her eyes and prayed to God, perhaps to mother Lilith, as Ben spoke again.

His words were a firm whisper, a sickening moisture that warmed her face as he closed in on her, "Don't tell me to lighten up, Lily. Don't ever tell me what to do."

Because Lily's eyes were still closed, Ben reached his other hand up to her face to slap her cheek with several strong and speedy sure-fire successive slaps.

"Did you hear what I just said, Lily?" Ben asked with hushed deliberate articulation.

Lily did not respond. She couldn't.

"Look at me!" Ben shouted, as he resumed slapping. "Open your eyes and look at me!"

Reluctantly, Lily opened her eyes. Tears poured out and lubricated the cheek Ben was hurting.

"Good girl," Ben taunted. "Now, listen to me. Don't ever tell me what to do again, and don't ever make fun of me in public. You got that?"

Lily struggled to reply to Ben's question, but her efforts were stalemated by the way she was held in place against the wall. Ben could feel her stressed larynx and pharynx quiver as she attempted to speak. He could feel her neck muscles expand and contract as she tried to nod her head. He knew that she had received his message and that her response was in the affirmative.

Ben stepped back from Lily, releasing her from his hold. She folded down and fell to the floor with a cacophony of coughs and tears. Not knowing what else to do, she buried her head in her hands and continued to sob.

Perhaps she was waiting for Ben to apologize or to come over and scoop her up and carry her away to a place where they both could forget about what'd just happened. Or, maybe she was waiting to sprout wings so that she could fly away.

None of these things ever happened.

Instead, Lily found the answer to a question she'd asked many months ago: Could alcohol turn a little kitten into a lion?

Yes, she concluded, it could—not just into a lion, but into something much, much worse.

A beast.

An abuser.

And a coward.

After his assault on Lily, Ben retreated to the bathroom, where he locked himself away for over two hours as Lily tried to recuperate and pull herself back together.

The beastly abuser sat on his cowardly throne and reflected upon what he had just done. Some men lose interest in women after they have sex with them. Others lose respect. Ben lost neither but did something more than both.

Sex was a dirty, vile, and unnecessary thing in Ben's mind, even though an occasionally enjoyable and necessary practice for his body. His rigid upbringing had grounded in him certain beliefs he could not avoid. When his mother accidentally walked in on him masturbating at age 14, she scolded and reprimanded him and had his father remove the door from his bedroom. She called him a "sinner," cursed him to hell, and lectured him on how the pleasures of the body caused only the agony of the soul. After that, Ben didn't touch himself again for nearly three years, and it was just under a decade before he touched or was touched by another person.

Whenever Ben did allow himself to partake of sexual acts, he always felt guilty and depraved afterwards. Worse yet, he saw his partner as not only guilty and depraved as well, but also as the very cause of his physical and spiritual demise.

A woman who freely and willfully engaged in sex was a flawed and evil thing—scum, filth, slime, and sleaze. Only when sex resulted in a child was it worthwhile, and even then it was of limited use.

That was why Ben found himself single for most of his life. Any time he fornicated with a lady, he'd turn on her almost immediately after the fact. Physical, verbal, or mental violence and rage had become his most familiar afterglow.

Sure enough, violence and rage were the inevitable results of Ben's lack of sex. Testosterone, sperm, and hot air built up in his body and exploded inward to compensate for the fact that they were not often pleasurably released.

Upon such infrequent release, it was more than a tablespoon or two of semen that shot out of Ben's body. It was also gallons upon gallons of pent-up frustration, confusion, and mixed feelings about sex.

He'd turned on Lily the same way he'd turned on a half-dozen of women before. Maybe his exact words and actions hadn't matched up term for term, but his axis of rotation and point of no return were precisely the same.

He was sure he'd ruined things with Lily and that she would want nothing more to do with him—and perchance he wanted things this way. Or, perchance, he did not. He wasn't sure.

He knew that he cared deeply for her, since he'd held off for over six months when he could have had her on the first night they met. But he knew too that he thought little of her, since she'd given herself to him after only six months and would have done so much earlier had she had her way.

While Ben battled his conflicting thoughts in the bathroom, Lily remained on the floor for a while, weighed down by tears and verbal silence. She eventually found her way to the bed and curled up beneath the lush covers at the bed's end, to stare out past the balcony and swim in and out of sleep until morning.

Ben joined her in the bed at some point before dawn, laying on the other edge of the bed. His back facing hers, there was a great distance between them.

When they awoke the next morning, Lily and Ben packed up their things and left the hotel, only talking to each other in questions, sentence fragments, and single words. Their ride back to Pittsburgh was mostly the same slight conversation, and only at sporadic times.

Half way into their drive, Lily finally spoke up.

"Ben, dear, please don't hit me ever again. Ben. Dear. Please?"

"I won't, Lily. I promise. I'm so sorry."

A few moments of silence filled the air before Lily spoke again.

Grinning and giggling, she humored Ben, "Ben, dear.

Hmm, sounds like I called you 'Bender,' huh? That's kinda cute. Don't ya think?"

"Yeah, I like it," Ben smiled.

Lily nodded, "It's fitting, too."

"Yeah, I agree."

And so Ben was named "Bender" somewhere on the east end of the Pennsylvania Turnpike, even though he'd been born in Maryland the night before.

Lily's sense of humor filled the gap between them, allowing them to pick up and move on. It wasn't a remedy by any means, but it helped dull the pain.

Of course, Bender didn't stick to his promise. He did, in fact, hit Lily again. Several times, for each of which Lily used humor or some other human device as a hollow quick fix.

A permanent solution would come to Lily only in time, when she endured the one event that ultimately put a stop to her physical pain: *his* death.

~ 6 ~

Lily exits the bathroom and begins to make her way back to the sitting parlor, sidestepping bystanders standing in her way, looking past condoling faces and mouths ready to speak.

With each face Lily sees, she is reminded of how surreal this day has been. Blasts from her past have consistently caught her off guard and sent her mind reeling to memories she hadn't known she could still recall, as well as to those she always knew she'd never forget.

It is as if the entire day has been a jumbled recount of her life, a book with chapters alternating between her present and her past, the now opening her mind's doors to the then.

Just as she begins to wonder what other memories will unfold before this night's end, she is stopped from flipping to the next page.

When she nears the couch, Lily sees her purse sitting next to Leo and is reminded of the only other accessory she brought with her today, but for her engagement ring and wedding band.

Realizing that she left her precious paper on the sink in the bathroom, Lily is startled and terrified. She turns in place and sprints toward the seemingly distant bathroom.

And so a new chapter begins.

A much older lady is about to enter the restroom, but Lily tries to stop her by yelling, "No, Cookie, wait! I left something in there!"

Cookie does not appear to hear Lily, as she proceeds with her entry.

Lily runs faster and makes it to the bathroom door just as Cookie pivots to shut it. She slides through the narrowing passage in the nick of time.

"Dangernat, Cookie gotta piss real bad!" Cookie exclaims. "Cookie gone go piss pot now."

"But, Cookie, I just need to…," Lily begins before she is interrupted.

"Cookie gonna piss pot, piss pot. Cookie gonna piss pot, piss pot," Cookie sings.

Though the appropriate and politically correct term has changed over the decades, Cookie is what was once and is still sometimes referred to as "mentally retarded." Lily, however, always preferred more polite phrases to describe Cookie's condition, such as "developmentally disabled" and "intellectually challenged."

For as long as she has been alive, Lily has known Cookie. Once upon a time, Cookie was Lily's long-time neighbor. Now she resides in a convalescent home catering specifically to elderly individuals with mental impairments and/or other significant mental health issues.

"Cookie, I left my—… I left something in there. I have to get it," Lily explains.

"Cookie gonna piss pot, piss pot," Cookie continues to chant as she pulls down her purple polyester pants.

"Go ahead," Lily comments as Cookie exposes her rotund belly and unplumed bush of pubic hair.

Cookie sits down on the toilet, and Lily swiftly scoops up the piece of paper she had left on the sink counter. She is grateful that she was able to get to it before anyone else did and that it hadn't been destroyed or discarded.

The paper once again tightly fisted, Lily raises her right hand to her mouth and kisses the haunch of her thumb, welcoming back her belonging. She turns her back to Cookie to respect Cookie's privacy, despite the fact that her current predicament is anything but private.

Openly expelling gas as she goes piss pot, Cookie rocks back and forth in place and asks an uncomfortable question: "Why Benny's box all shut up?"

"It's called a 'closed casket,' Cookie," Lily clarifies. "The lid is closed so that people can remember him how they want to and not how bad he looked after what... after the accident."

If Cookie had still lived next door to Lily, she probably would have called the police to report a domestic disturbance at Lily's house the night Bender died. Cookie would have called the police that night, Lily knows, because Cookie had called the police to their neighborhood a few other times in the past.

It was Cookie who had called the police the second time Bender hit Lily, one month after their return from Ocean City.

That night, over a quarter of a century ago, Cookie heard the sound of glass breaking, followed by yelling and screaming. The breaking glass had sounded when Bender threw a wine goblet off of the porch, after Lily had firmly asked him to not use it as a spittoon. Next came the yelling and screaming, as Lily tried to run away from Bender, into the house, and Bender swiftly chased her, grabbing her by her hair and pushing her into the screen door.

When the police arrived, Lily didn't report the physical violence and the coppers gave the couple nothing more than a proviso, as Pennsylvania law prevented the police from taking action on a domestic disturbance call unless it also involved domestic violence or evidence thereof.

Cookie didn't have to call the police the next time Bender

hit Lily, three weeks later, when he slapped her across the face for taking a phone call from an ex sex partner. Lily's response was to implement a quick fix human device that prevented the episode from further escalating.

The device was marriage. After Bender bitch-slapped her, Lily blurted out, "Let's just get married!"

"Really?" Bender asked.

"Yeah, Bender," Lily said, tearing. "That way you'll know I'm yours forever and nobody else's."

"Okay, let's do it."

And that was that. Lily and Bender were married less than two months later. They had a small ceremony in the park located down the street from the home they shared. Irene and Jimmy Hayes were the only guests invited and in attendance, the only human ones at least. Mimi and Mini were there, along with a few random birds and grass mites.

For financial reasons, as Lily's inheritance was almost completely dwindled, their ceremony had to remain tiny and, from the bouquet to the cake, most everything had to homemade—except for the female officiant presiding over their union, who had been made a female by the acts of God and of her parents, and had been made an officiant by her successful completion of a 3-hour seminar held by a money-hungry judge in his home just outside of Philadelphia.

Lily's quick fix device seemed to have done the trick. From the time she proposed marriage to him to several months after their wedding, Bender didn't lay a hand on Lily other than to love her.

Too soon the honeymoon was over, notwithstanding that there hadn't actually been one.

Bender lashed out at Lily after she came upon him for sex late one night whilst he was playing a simulated war videogame. He'd taken to doing that quite often, staying up late in front of the living room television and game console. Of this, Lily had quickly grown tired.

She approached Bender as he sat sprawl-legged on the couch, sitting next to him and running her hand along his upper thigh. He wasn't at all moved and continued playing his game. So too did Lily. She leaned her chest up against his arm and brought her leg to his lap.

"Lily, stop that. I'm almost ready to beat my game. I have to at least get to the save point," Bender advised.

But Lily didn't stop. "You can finish playing your game later," she said. "It's time to play with me now."

Bender continued to press buttons and move knobs until Lily climbed on top of him to straddle him on the couch. She leant forward to kiss him. Instead of his lips meeting hers, his head turned away. Lily tried to refocus his face, but it was too late.

"Shit, Lily! Look what you did! My guy just died." Bender was starting to get mad.

"Forget about your game Bender. I swear you like that thing more than you like me."

Again, Lily tried to kiss Bender. This turn, instead of his lips meeting hers, his hands met her chest—but not to grope her. He pushed her off of his lap, causing her to fall back and hit the coffee table and then hit the floor. As she tried to get back up, he kicked at her chest to keep her down.

"My game didn't save, Lily," he said, looking down at her as he stomped his booted foot against her chest. "All my progress was ruined 'cause you wanted to fuck."

"You wanna play with something?" he asked. "Here... Play with this."

He took his boot off of her body, grabbed what appeared to be an empty water bottle he had tucked in between the cushions of the couch, and leaned over to pour its contents out on her chest and face.

The bottle hadn't been empty though. It contained a few ounces of fetid saliva and tobacco juice. He'd been using it as a spittoon. And now Lily had tiny puddles of his spit and chew on her cheeks, chin, neck, and shirt.

Lily's quick fix device, the fact that she and Bender were married, was no longer a solution to the abuse. She'd need to come up with something else to make things work. Thinking on her feet as she lay on her back, Lily came up with another quick fix human device she could use to remedy things.

The device was parenthood. She decided to justify her wanton approach in a way that might soften Bender.

"I just wanted to have sex so that maybe I could get pregnant," she said. "I think I may be ovulating, so it's a really good time."

She wasn't ovulating, and she knew it. But Bender didn't.

"Oh, really? Why didn't you just say so?" Bender asked as he bent down to get a closer look at his fallen wife.

"I didn't hurt you, did I?" he inquired with tremendous concern. "Here, let me help you up," he said, reaching out both of his arms as if he intended to use a hug to raise her body and spirit.

Like nothing had ever happened, like he hadn't just done what he'd just done, the husband winked at his wife, "So, let's go make that baby, baby."

They didn't conceive a child that night and wouldn't for a few more months.

"Poor Benny, all locked up in that box," Cookie says, shaking her head. "How do they even know he's in there? Poor Benny."

Lily wants to laugh at Cookie's grasp of the situation, but

knows it isn't wise. Laughing would mean she either didn't take the situation seriously or didn't take Cookie seriously—and she doesn't want to give either impression.

"Greta's box was open," Cookie says while her left hand scratches her ass. "Wanted to make dangernat sure she was in 'ere!"

The Greta Cookie is talking about was her twin sister, who passed away around 15 years ago and whose death brought about Cookie's move from a family home to a convalescent home. It was with Greta that Cookie lived in the house two doors down from Lily's, and it was Greta who had been Cookie's caregiver for most of her life.

Unlike her twin sister, Greta was developmentally abled, intellectually average, and mentally proficient. Greta dedicated her life to looking after Cookie, out of guilt that Cookie was the one who got the fragile X in their dizygotic conception.

"I miss 'em my Greta, oh I miss 'em… Good thing the twins got 'em each other still. Wish 'em I still had mine," Cookie opines.

Because Lily's and Bender's daughters, Tina and Robbie, looked so much alike and were only 16 months apart in age, Cookie had always thought they were "twins" because she could not comprehend that they were not. After all, Cookie was a twin, so it only made sense that those two very similar girlies had to be as well.

Both had bushy manes of blonde hair and bright blue eyes when each took her turn sliding out of Lily's vagina—at different times. Both grew into chubby toddler legs and thick toddler arms in due course—at different times.

Cookie saw both come home—at different times—and saw Tina walk while Robbie was still in the womb, but she managed to forget all of that by the time Robbie was 2 or 3.

Either that or she thought Robbie just took her time being born, trapped in Lily's belly until it was the right time to pop out. And maybe that had been the case.

No matter how erroneous her classification of the girls was, Cookie clearly understood that the children were special and beautiful, and she was an excellent playmate for short play periods throughout their toddlerhood. Cookie could relate to their fascination with the world, their unrealistic fears, and their mispronounced, broken words. A kid at heart, in mind too, she was happy to consider Tina and Robbie her best friends for some time.

And the girls felt the same way about her. To them, Cookie was the ideal and rare case of the playfulness of a child in the form of a grown adult. They saw her as their equal while also seeing her as a figure of some type of loose authority.

She was fun an entertaining, joyful and free. And, she'd proven to be a safe place for them on one very particular and unfortunate occasion when they needed her most.

When Lily was pregnant with the girls, and when she was raising them in their youngest years, Bender never hit her. They had a good run for a while.

Slowly but surely, however, things returned to their norm, and abruptly surpassed it.

It started with Bender grabbing Lily by the arm every now and then, to keep her in line. That led to pulling and pushing her by her arm, followed by twisting it behind her back, in no time. Next came the slapping, first on her upper arm, then along her side, against her ass, and, eventually, across her face. From there, things only got worse.

Bender's aggressions were extreme reactions to what he considered Lily's insubordinations, what he deemed an appropriate response to those instances when she challenged him, mocked him, tried to tell him what to do, or didn't listen to his instructions or live by his rules.

As commanding and cruel as Bender could be, he never acted on his impulses in front of, or on, his daughters. He'd follow Lily into another room and smack her, out of the girls' eyeshot, or wait until after the babies were fast asleep before coming at Lily. Sometimes, he'd hold his fists for so long before getting her alone that he forgot why he was hitting her in the first place.

How ever unlikely it was, Bender was actually a really great dad. He loved his daughters dearly and worked hard to meet their needs and entertain them. In many ways, Tina and Robbie favored their father. Bender was the fun one who made them laugh and smile, while Lily was the one who did everything else.

Lily didn't know how to interact with kids the way Bender did. She had spent so much of her time with her old grandma, and so much time with so many men, that she couldn't relate any of those skills to playing with juvenile girls. She was loving, nurturing, supportive, and encouraging, and she kept her babies healthy and clean, but she simply wasn't as good of a time.

The dirty work was Lily's job. She changed them, bathed them, fed them, and took care of them when they were sick. She taught them, fought them, and lulled them to sleep. As tiny tots, Tina and Robbie turned to Lily when they got booboos or needed help with drawing a straight line, and turned to Bender when they wanted to play and have fun.

When the girls misbehaved, it was Lily's job to scold or discipline them. And if she didn't do this the right way, if her efforts weren't effective at preventing future outbursts, it was Bender's job to scold or discipline Lily. After either or both of the girls acted out or threw a tantrum, Bender blamed Lily for not being able to control them and took things out on her.

He took other parenting frustrations out on her as well. Those times when one of the girls would jump up on their parents' big bed and wake them before dawn, those times were Lily's fault. When Tina spilled a sack of flour on the floor, and when Robbie colored her arm blue with a marker, those things were Lily's fault. Forks thrown in the garbage disposal, clogged drains, and overflowed toilets? Yep. Lily's fault too.

Slap. Smack. Hit. Punch. Kick. Push.

It was such a fight—over Lily's lack of parenting the way Bender saw fit—that landed Bender in jail one night, and Lily in the hospital for several hours.

It was much ado about a gate.

See, they had a few child-proof gates installed in doorways and halls, to stop the girls from running around as they pleased. At night, once the girls were asleep, Lily usually left the gates open so that she could maneuver the house with ease—since the gates had been there for a handful of years, they sagged a little from the walls, which made it necessary to lift them a little bit in order to open them.

Lily was always asking Bender to fix them, but Bender never found the time, until he found the time on one given night.

On that night, Robbie, who was around 3 years old at the time, snuck out of bed and found her way to the living room, where she climbed up on the back of a recliner and removed framed photos from the mantle while Lily was doing laundry in the basement and Bender was out on a tobacco run.

As a child-safety precaution, Bender and Lily had removed the glass from all of the frames. Robbie too decided to remove something. She tore the pictures out of their frames and ripped the pictures to shreds.

When Bender returned from the store, he saw Robbie perched on the chair in the nest of papers she'd torn.

"Look, daddy," she said, "I make paper."

"Yes you did!" Bender replied. "Where's mama?"

"Dunno, daddy. Think she downstair."

Bender picked up his daughter and held her to his chest, "Come on baby, it's time to go back to bed."

He took her upstairs, placed her in her tiny bed, told her a story, and walked out of the room as she dozed off with a smile so radiant, even in sleep.

On a mission, Bender walked downstairs to the basement and got his toolbox. He didn't say a word to Lily, who was still folding laundry a few feet away. Back up the steps he went, without halt, ignoring Lily's questions about what he was doing.

One by one, he went around to each gate in the house and tightened its screws and bolts.

Once Lily figured out what Bender was doing, she felt uplifted and honored that he was finally getting around to a chore he'd continually put off. She never suspected he was doing it for all the wrong reasons.

When he was done securing the gates, Bender returned to the living room and called for Lily. In she walked, ready to congratulate, thank, and commend Bender for a job well done. But before she could get her words out, she saw the mess of papers Robbie had made.

"What's all this?" she innocently asked.

"Your daughter did it," he said with a critical sneer. "You left the gate open again, Lily. Robbie came down here and ruined all these pictures."

He rose to his feet and slowly walked toward his wife,

"But it could've been worse… She could have opened the front door and gone outside… She could've been hit by a car or been kidnapped."

He stood in front of his wife now, looking her straight in the eyes, raising his eyebrows and squinting, talking in a sarcastically calm voice, "But I guess you don't care about that kinda shit, huh, Lily?"

Lily knew what was coming next, and she knew there was nothing she could do to stop it.

Bender grabbed Lily by the hair and pulled her over to the chair on which Robbie had made her mess. "Clean this up, Lily," he said as he pushed her to the ground. She landed hard on her knees and quickly commenced to collecting the ribbons of photographs that were scattered about.

Holding the photo paper to her body like Bender had earlier held Robbie to his, Lily worked fast, but was disrupted when Bender's booted foot met her backside, kicking her to a bent-over position on the floor.

What scraps she had collected fell from her grasp, and she collapsed flat on the floor.

"Get up, Lily! You got work to do," Bender demanded as he kicked at the side of her body, recycling his boot against her abdomen with tremendous force. Each time Lily tried to get up, she was knocked back down by another kick or stomp.

Once he could see that Lily was making no leeway on her task, Bender stopped his attack, turned away, and left the room without word. With plenty of work and recovery to accomplish, Lily jumped up as fast as she could and hurriedly started to clean the mess.

While she was at work, Bender had trekked down to the basement to find solace in song. He belted out the lyrics to a heavy metal tune he and his band had written and planned to debut at their next gig. They did mostly covers, but were able to sneak in an original every now and then.

On a glimmering stake of lustful piety you shall reign
As the god of my deviated warped domain.
With hallowed eyes and mocking breath
You'll be my savior until Death's death.
With broken glass and shattered dreams I reside.
And no one is eternally on my side.
Clothed nightmares are the medium for my aggressions
As I stroll through lapses and drown in digressions.
I'm forever the echo of your shadowed self's mind,
The null void nothing that you've left undefined.
I carry with me an inverted sense of self
With you as the soul basis for my moral health.
Trapped in your heart, I'm forever your slave.
I have no mentality, no soul to save.

Having thrown away every tattered and torn picture perfect memory, and tidied up the room in other noticeable ways, Lily headed to the kitchen and cracked open a bottle of dry red wine, which she carried with her to the porch. She sat down on a chair and started chugging the booze straight from the bottle, with Bender's voice and lyrics reverberating on the porch floor between them.

In no time at all, Lily finished the bottle of wine and went back into the kitchen to retrieve a second, stopping only to extract two prescription sedatives from the bottle she kept hidden in the spice rack on the kitchen counter.

She returned to the porch to treat the second bottle of wine much as she had treated the first—chugging, gulping, and not taking the time to enjoy its full body, sharp bite, and smooth undertones. But those things didn't matter to Lily, since she was drinking to get drunk not drinking to drink wine.

The desired click soon clacked in Lily's head—letting her know that the pills and alcohol had done their job and worked to relax and inebriate her body and mind.

Around the same time that her spirits were lifted by these chemical agents, Bender appeared on the porch, ready to bring her back down.

"You don't have any excuses left now, Lily. Those gates are nice and tight. So if the kids get out, it's your fault this time," Bender said to ground Lily's spirits' flight.

"Good, good," Lily said. "But it never would have happened in the first place if you'd fixed them long ago when I asked you to."

"Shut up, Lily. Don't try to blame this on me. You could've fixed them yourself, any time."

"Come on, Bender, that kinda shit's your job. You're the one that should've fixed them, or put them on right in the first place."

Installing gates, fixing gates, Lily was right. Those were Bender's jobs. Lily and Bender had always divided household labor according to somewhat archaic stereotypes: men worked with tools and equipment, lifting, screwing, and nailing, while women cleaned, cooked, and took care of the kids.

And, with Lily's criticism of him, Bender was about to give life to another archaic stereotype: the abusive husband.

Bender leapt across the porch to where Lily sat. He kicked the side of her chair, and it, and she, crashed to the floor with a bang. The bottle of wine she'd been holding spilled all over her and broke into chunks when it met the painted concrete of the porch.

As Bender kicked at Lily's fallen body, she scurried away toward the corner, where she found the strength to stand. Going to the corner probably wasn't such a wise idea, for, when Bender came at her again, he had her cornered with no means of escape.

His fist punched her face. When his knuckles contacted her nose, blood gushed out and Lily screamed in pain. Grabbing her by the arms and shaking her in place, Bender told her to be quiet, though his words were louder than hers had been.

Two doors down, Cookie woke up to the commotion and called the police, who were already familiar with Cookie's voice and the disturbing reason for which she called. A patrol car was in the area, the operator told Cookie, and would be there soon.

Soon turned out to be approximately three minutes. Without flashing lights or sirens, the patrol car pulled up in front of Lily's house to find Bender and Lily still in the corner of the porch.

"What's going on here tonight, buddy?" a well-built officer asked.

"Ah, looks like we finally caught you red-handed, huh?" inquired his loose-bodied partner.

These two officers had been here before, but could do nothing more than issue warnings since Bender's domestic disturbances usually showed no evidence of domestic violence. But this time, Bender had been caught red-handed—literally. The blood from Lily's nose was on his right fist.

In a futile effort to conceal her condition and protect Bender's fate, Lily tried to clean her face with the bottom of her shirt. But, as the blood had already started to congeal and crust on her skin, her efforts at removing it only made things worse, smearing the sticky clots into lines that painted even more of her face.

Stepping away from his victim, Bender transformed from

a ferocious beast into a timid, cowardly cat. Despite Lily's objections and comments that nothing had happened and that she didn't want to press charges or have Bender taken away, the loose-bodied officer strode onto the porch and handcuffed Bender's hands behind his back, leading him to the patrol car into which he was carelessly shoved.

Lily had no say in what happened to Bender at this point, the loose officer explained, since evidence of assault is evidence of assault, and assault is first and foremost a public criminal concern, not a private civil one.

The other officer, the well-built one, approached Lily and handed her a business card.

"I've been carrying this with me for a while," he said, "hoping that I'd never have to come back here and give it to you."

The card had on it information for domestic abuse outreach centers and information the officer had himself penned in regarding how to obtain a Protection From Abuse order from the county court.

"You can't keep letting him do this to you. This isn't love. Protect yourself," he told her as he walked away.

Lily stood sobbing on the porch and watched as the police car drove away with her husband in the backseat. This was not what Lily wanted. She did not want her husband to be arrested or taken to jail, to be without him for a night.

Since she didn't know what else to do, Lily decided to drink more wine. Still soaked in what wine had spilled on her on the porch, and still with dried blood on her face, Lily grabbed another bottle of wine and imbibed in the living room, regularly glancing at the now-undecorated mantle that had propped photos only a few hours earlier, and avoiding eye contact with the room's many things that reminded her of Bender.

Lily nursed the third bottle of wine more slowly. As she drained it of every drop, she worried about what discomforts Bender faced in police custody and wondered how or when he would be released and able to return to his family.

Once she finished the bottle, she sat in the living room for ten minutes that dragged on like ten hours. Surrounded by blaring silence, she was scared and lonely—she had never before spent a night without Bender since they started living together.

Terrified, tired, and in terrible pain, Lily decided to go upstairs to shower and try to find sleep. Sluggishly, she walked up the first flight of steps and turned to the small landing, where she was again reminded of her husband's absence when she saw the securely shut gate he had just repaired.

She ascended the small set of steps and attempted to open the gate. It was so tightly screwed, however, that she had great difficulty trying to open it. She pushed and pulled, trying to lift the metal toward her and then push it away as she jiggled it in place.

No matter how much strength she exerted, the gate seemed immovable and fixed. Fed up with things, she put her whole body into it and pulled upward and outward with all of her might.

It flung open.

And when it did, Lily fell backward, her foot kicking the gate shut again.

Tripping and skipping over the five steps behind her, Lily fell on her back onto the landing. The force of her fall propelled her body around the corner of the landing and down the first flight of stairs.

Her legs folded under her, and her arms were twisted in their sockets. Her head, which first hit the floor of the landing, dragged along the baseboards here and bounced off of the steps there, until it landed, with the rest of her body, at the bottom of the steps, near the arch that marked the entrance to the living room.

Lily was unconscious. Blood leaked out of slits and holes in her body.

The clanging of the gate and the sound of her mother's accidental descent down the stairs, along with the thump of her mother's body on the downstairs floor, woke 4-year-old Tina from her deep sleep.

Tina crawled out of bed and opened her bedroom door.

"Mama?" she asked.

There was no reply.

"Daddy? ... Robbie?" Tina followed.

Still no reply.

Tina crept over to Robbie's room, and, when she saw Robbie fast asleep, she next crept to her parents' room, where she found no one in bed. She returned to the gate and called out for her parents again. When she heard no reply, she went to her room, snatched the bench from her miniature toy piano, and used the bench to climb over the child-safety gate so that she could go downstairs.

Ah, how Tina quickly proved Bender's repairs moot! He'd fixed the gates to contain his children, one of whom was already spry and shrewd enough to escape in any event. Like a little problem-solving monkey, Tina could not be confined.

When she rounded the landing, Tina saw her mother sprawled out on the floor below. She hopped down the steps, calling for her mother's response. Lily lay lifeless as Tina knelt beside her and shook her body at her shoulder.

Luckily, Tina knew what to do in an emergency such as

this. She ran into the living room, grabbed the phone, and dialed 9-1-1.

"What's your emergency?" the operator asked.

"My mama is on the floor by the steps and won't wake up," Tina said with newfound purpose in her voice.

The operator stayed on the line with Tina until the first responders, the firefighters, were on the scene. At the operator's instruction, Tina opened the door to let the fire company medics into her home.

Two medics rushed over to tend to Lily, while a third went over to comfort young Tina. As he asked Tina for her name, age, mother's name, and what she knew about what had happened, the other two men tried to revive Lily to no avail. While she was living, she was not at all responsive and her vitals gave reason for concern.

The paramedics arrived at the door at the same time Cookie did. She'd been woken up by the sirens and wondered why emergency services had been called to Lily's house yet again, only a short while after the police's earlier appearance. Cookie knew that she hadn't dialed 9-1-1, and she wanted to know who had—and why.

Cookie walked in along with the responders, and found her way to Tina. When the fire medic asked her who she was, Cookie told him that she was a neighbor and informed him that there was another young child in the house, information that the crew of civil servants hadn't thought to ask Tina and that Tina hadn't thought to tell them.

The paramedics were going to take Tina to the hospital with them when they transported Lily. Had it not been for Cookie, Robbie, who was not yet as agile as her big sister, would have been left alone in the house, trapped upstairs by the gate Bender had so meticulously tightened. Robbie would have been thirsty, dirty, hungry, and frightened while her sister was placed in social services care on the children's floor of the hospital.

Thanks to Cookie, however, that didn't have to happen. Instead, one of the medics went upstairs to scoop up Robbie, who nestled into his chest and sucked her thumb as he carried her to a second ambulance, which had been called to the house to haul the children.

Cookie tried to convince the paramedics to let the girls to stay with her, but they wouldn't have it since Lily was not alert to assent, since Cookie was an unknown stranger to them, and since Cookie was mentally substandard.

As the men in blue loaded Lily and her children onto the ambulances, Cookie ran back to her house. Greta was watching things unfold from her screen door. Cookie begged her to follow the wagons to the hospital so that they could be with the girls during the ordeal. Though Greta was tired and somewhat disinterested, she agreed, grabbed her keys, and walked with Cookie to her car.

Greta tailgated the second ambulance all the way to the hospital, even running red lights in her turn.

At the hospital, the twin women tried to follow the paramedics and children through the emergency doors, but were stopped by security, and would have been prevented from further accompanying the girls had it not been for Tina's and Robbie's frantic insistence.

The four of them were taken to the children's floor, where Tina and Robbie were allowed to play in a waiting room full of toys and Cookie and Greta were allowed to join them. While Greta mostly sat by and watched, Cookie played with the girls, distracting them from where they were and why they were there. She rocked Robbie to sleep when she grew tired and attempted to braid Tina's curly hair.

For over four hours, she playfully interacted with them

and made them feel safe in an unfamiliar place. And during that time, while Bender was stewing in lockup at Allegheny County Jail, Lily remained unconscious as doctors, nurses, and technicians put her through a battery of medical tests and treatments, including x-rays, a CAT scan, blood tests, and IVs.

The first thing that she saw when she awoke up from her trauma-induced slumber was a gothicly made-up nurse tapping a button on the screen monitoring her vitals.

"Where am I?" Lily asked in a haze.

"Shit, you're awake," the nurse replied. "You're in the hospital, babe. Let me go get your doctor."

As Lily examined the exam room she was in, she tried to move her limbs and was very nervous when she couldn't lift her right arm, which was bound up because it had been broken.

With terror, she cringed at the heaviness of her legs, at their swollen size and sliced flesh.

"Mrs. Frysk," said a man in a white coat by the door, calling Lily by her last name.

"I'm Dr. Homer. First, let me say that you're basically fine. Your right arm is broken, and you have numerous scrapes and bruises. You're dehydrated, and your vitals aren't quite yet where we want them to be. But, all these things are just superficial and won't result in any permanent, significant damage.

"It pains me to tell you one other thing," Dr. Homer said, after a brief pause. "I'm sorry, but you lost the baby."

"Lost the what?!?!" Lily shouted. "What are you—..."

Before she could finish her question, the doctor cut her off, "Oh, dear God, you didn't know! ... Well, that explains a lot."

What it explained to the doctor was why a pregnant woman would willingly drink until her blood alcohol level more than twice surpassed the legal limit used to regulate criminal driving offenses, regardless of whether or not she was driving; why a pregnant woman would willingly take a schedule C drug known to cross the placenta and believed to cause congenital abnormalities in babies; and why a pregnant woman would not seek treatment for the physical indications of past and present abdominal trauma that bruised and scarred her body.

What the doctor then explained to Lily was that she had been approximately 11 weeks pregnant and miscarried her fetus. He could point to none of her physical impairments as the sole causal or definitive agent that brought about her miscarriage. Was it the fall? The alcohol? The sedatives? The abuse she didn't report? Only God and Lily's dead fetus knew for sure, and neither one of them was willing or able to talk at the moment.

The fact that she had miscarried, let alone that she had been pregnant, was very staggering to Lily. She didn't even think that pregnancy was possible because she received a hormonal birth control shot every three months to prevent ovulation. But the fact that she had become pregnant, despite the reliable method of birth control she had selected, only proved that Lily was very much one in a million, or, rather, one of .03% in 100.

The anguish that Lily felt upon receiving this alarming and unnerving news was far greater than the physical pain she felt, far greater than her forgotten thoughts of Bender's predicament, and comparable to only one other fear, which now overwhelmed her.

Having just suffered through the death of one baby, Lily's mind went immediately to thoughts of her two daughters.

"Where are my girls? My daughters—where are they?"

"They're here at the hospital, upstairs on the children's floor. Your neighbors are here with them," the doctor informed her. "If they're awake, I'll have them sent down to see you if you like."

"I want to see them," Lily said, meaning it more than she'd meant anything she'd ever said before.

In less than an hour, Tina and Robbie ran into the room to greet their mother. They both positioned themselves on the bed on either side of her, dodging cables, tubes, and cords. Greta and Cookie had come up to the room too, and hung around for a bit, until they all were told that Lily would be released from the hospital soon, upon which notification Greta and Cookie left so that Greta could drop off Cookie, pick up the girls' car seats, and return to jitney the Frysk ladies back to their home.

Naturally, Lily didn't tell her children about their dead, unborn sibling, nor did she tell her neighbors. She kept it from them, and argued back and forth with herself as to whether or not she should tell Bender.

Bender, ah yes, Bender! What about Bender?

By the time Lily and her daughters got home, it was late morning. Once inside, she discovered that there were more than a dozen messages on the answering machine. A few were the tail ends of unanswered collect calls, presumably from Bender. The remainder was from various bond brokers, who had obtained Lily's phone number from the jail and were calling to negotiate bond arrangements.

After getting the girls something to eat and meandering around the house for a while in search of something to do, Lily sat down beside the phone and waited for it to ring. When it did ring, it was a collect call, and it was from Bender.

In an uncharacteristically mollified voice, Bender

requested that Lily come downtown, bail him out of jail, and bring him home. Lily, of course, agreed to do as he asked.

Lily's broken arm did not allow her to drive, so she dropped her daughters off at Greta's and Cookie's and called for a cab. Her first stop was at the bank, to withdraw $250, to cover Bender's $150 bail and money to handle the cab fares and other essentials.

Her next stop was at a convenience store, to pick up a tin of chewing tobacco, which she knew her husband would be craving. Next she hit the courthouse, to pay the bond. And, finally, she went to the jail to sit outside on a bench and await Bender's release.

His release took longer than she had expected, as it involved a drawn out quasi-judicial process. He didn't emerge from the jailhouse until late afternoon, at which time Lily was incredibly happy to see him. She ran to him and wrapped her unbroken arm around him.

"What the hell happened to you, Lily?" he inquired as she hugged him.

"It's a long story, Bender," she said, "a very long story."

Lily called the cab company from a phone booth. Waiting for the cab to arrive, Lily described to Bender the basic elements of what had happened the night before, leaving out, for now, the information about her miscarriage. Bender appeared sincerely concerned about Lily's condition, though he also appeared substantially distracted and unwilling to commit to the conversation as fully as he committed to a fingerful of chew.

Their cab ride home was pretty much without incident, mostly silence spiked with brief dialog about the welfare of their daughters.

Upon their arrival home, Bender picked his girls up from their neighbors' house and played with them for a while, telling them he'd been away for the night on work. He scarfed down a pair of hearty sandwiches that Tina helped Lily make for him.

Evening came soon, and Bender got the babies ready for bed since Lily was temporarily incapacitated.

All the while that Bender had been back at home, neither he nor Lily spoke to each other or to their children about what had happened to either or both of them the night before. But once Tina and Robbie were in bed, the topic was fair game.

As Lily was picking up toys and crayons from the living room floor, Bender came down the steps, the very steps Lily had fallen down not 24 hours earlier, and walked toward his wife. Their eyes met, and Lily saw in Bender's face an all too familiar look: he was about to come at her.

To stop his progress before he advanced, Lily decided to implement yet another quick fix human device. She didn't have to think hard to settle on this one.

The device was bereavement.

Without hesitation, Lily's truth burst out: "I was pregnant, Bender. I lost the baby... I had a miscarriage!"

Bender's look of rage instantly turned to a look of compassion, and his hands, once intent on delivering harm, changed to hands intent on delivering comfort. He hugged his wife. It was a circuitry like nothing she'd felt from him in ages, possibly hadn't felt from him ever before, a near venerable embrace to condole her.

"I'm sorry," he whispered as he began to cry.

Lily didn't know whether Bender was apologizing for her miscarriage, his actions, or the role his actions might have, and probably, played in her miscarriage. But for whatever reason he offered his apology, Lily graciously accepted it.

"Let's go upstairs and hold each other, Lily."

They went upstairs together to their bedroom, and Bender tackled the troublesome gate at the top of the steps. In their bed, they burrowed together and took turns crying, discussing the loss of a child neither had known existed.

"It would have been a boy," Bender asserted for no supported reason. "I lost my son."

Lily, too, concluded that the deceased fetus was likely male, and she decided to name him.

She named him Fox. Fox Juniper Frysk.

Though both parents were completely heartbroken, Lily was considerably more affected. In addition to the fact that the baby had died inside her body, and in addition to other considerations, Lily's outlook on life and death was relatively conservative and preservative.

Because she herself was the product of an unplanned pregnancy, as was her mother and, likely, her grandmother, she was pro-life and believed in the sanctity of the spirit from the initial moment of conception to the final moment of death.

She was fundamentally opposed to abortion, euthanasia, suicide, capital punishment, and murder, and anything else that caused the intentional cessation of life and living. For one with such fundamental oppositions, the loss of a fetus, even if only 11 weeks prenatally-old and undiscovered, was the loss of a living person—a loss that Lily would mourn for the rest of her life.

Bender's views were notably more liberal. He was a proponent of most, if not all, of those death acts Lily opposed. Nonetheless, he was hurt by her miscarriage, as it was a reality he faced rather than an abstract ideal he harbored.

Though Lily fell asleep in his arms, too exhausted to fight

sleep as she normally would, Bender remained awake for a few more hours. Sadness and accountability kept rolling over in his head. He knew that he was at least partially to blame for the death of their son.

So, for whatever role his actions might have, and probably, played in Lily's miscarriage, Bender made an important decision: It was no longer prudent to slap, punch, kick, or hit his wife.

He was determined to never hurt her again.

But, unfortunately, he did.

~ 7 ~

"What's that in your hand, Lily?"

Lily is sitting in the corner of the couch, alone. Her legs are crossed, and her right hand rests, closed, on her right knee, flicking up and down in an irregular motion. She does not hear his question as he walks toward her.

"Lily? Can you hear me? Hello? What's that in your hand?"

Lily senses his presence more than his words and looks up at him as he approaches the couch. He has just come out of the bathroom, and the smell of shit, hand soap, and chewing tobacco is fresh on his body.

She smiles as he sits down beside her.

"What's that in your hand, Lily?"

"Oh, this?" she asks him, raising her fist. "It's nothing."

"If it's nothing, why are you holding onto it so tightly?" he inquires as he reaches his own right hand toward hers.

"Really, it's nothing," she follows. "Nothing important."

His right hand is now on top of hers. He lifts it.

"Let me see, Lily. Show me what you've got there."

Lily's grasp limps, and she rotates her wrist so that her palm is facing upward. She unfolds her fingers to expose the folded-up strip of crinkled paper she is holding.

He pinches the paper from her hand and unfolds it.

It is a receipt. A grocery store receipt.

"You went grocery shopping? Is that where you were earlier this morning?" he asks her.

"Yeah," she replies. "I had some things to get at the store, so I woke up super early and went shopping."

"What's the big deal then?" he presses. "You're sitting here lost in a daze, holding on to a grocery receipt like it's something important."

"No big deal. I just don't want to lose it. I need to return some stuff I didn't mean to buy."

"Okay, well, here you go," he says, handing the receipt back to Lily.

He stands up and walks away, but stops to ask her another question: "Want a cup of coffee? I'm gonna go get one."

"No thanks," she says in a somber voice.

"Man, lighten up, Lily! You're acting like somebody died or something," he jokes.

"Right," she affirms. "Sorry, Bender, I just have a lot on my mind right now."

That was the first time Lily ever saw Bender after she cheated on him with Leo.

She was 37 years old at the time.

Bender found Lily on the couch, where she'd sat for over an hour after she got home from her adulterous visit with Leo, an extramarital lover of whom Bender certainly would not have approved.

Though it wasn't until much, much later in the day that he would be able to put two and two together, and though Lily later admitted and acknowledged it, Lily's trip to the store was an alibi.

And it was a damn good one—before she blew it, that is.

But before she blew it, she blew Leo. And after she did that, she needed an excuse for her late-night absence, should Bender be awake when she got home.

When she left Leo's brother's house that night, Lily was simultaneously overjoyed and overwhelmed. She had felt a sexual gratification and achievement she hadn't felt in years, as well as a guilt she'd never felt before.

Her body still tingled from Leo's touch as she drove away. His spit was still moist on her body, his salty aftertaste still flavored her throat. She kept replaying the sex in her head, aroused by thoughts of all that she and Leo had shared.

She thought too of Bender, how he didn't deserve to be betrayed, and how mad he would be if he found out.

Lily wondered if she had done what she'd done because she wanted the sex with Leo or because she wanted to hurt Bender.

Did she do what she did because she wanted to show herself or Bender that she could still get another man who could make her feel good? Had she acted so that Bender would be reminded of her desirability, so that he might want her more or regret all the bad things he'd ever done to her? Did she do it because she wanted Bender to hate someone other than her?

If she did it for any of these reasons, Bender would have to know about the affair in order for the desired effect to play out. Lily wasn't sure whether she wanted Bender to know, though.

So, possibly, she was just fulfilling a prophecy in doing what she did—either the one Jill had set out for her by selecting her name, or the one Bender had set out by regularly calling her nicknames like slut and whore.

Maybe, at the bottom line, Lily was nothing more than a slut or a whore. That could be why she did it—to get off; to scream and squeal; to have her type of man take her hard and dirty against the steps; to feel sexy, desired, wanted, and appreciated.

For whatever reasons she'd done what she'd done, Lily had done what she'd done. And she didn't know if she could live with herself after the fact. What she did know was that she had to do her best to conceal her whereabouts until she figured things out.

It didn't take long for Lily to think of a viable excuse. As a mother of two young daughters, she often went on household shopping trips late at night, to stores that were open 24 hours, so that she could shop without the her children in tow, while they were sleeping so that Bender didn't have to tend to them much during her absence.

Lily sped off to a 24-hour box store, where she ran through the first few aisles and filled her cart with whatever foods and household items she recognized as commonly consumed in her home. She didn't pay much attention to what she tossed in her cart, for the purchase of the products was more important than the nature or purpose of the products themselves.

After a 15-minute shopping spree, Lily went to the check-out lane and unloaded her items onto the small conveyor belt. Though she noticed some things she knew she didn't need or want, she went about her transaction without second thought, deciding to later return any unnecessary or unfamiliar purchases.

As quickly as Lily sped to the store, she sped away from it, exceeding the speed limit, running stale yellow lights, and not coming to full stops at stop signs. It was still very early in the morning, and Lily hoped that her infractions, all of her infractions, would go unnoticed.

She pulled into her driveway, sliding the gear shift into park while the car was still in motion, jolting it forward and back in a very grounding way. When she turned the car off, everything seemed to slow down significantly. The birds were chirping and singing, and the sound of other cars and children filled the streets around her.

From the trunk of her car, she unloaded her set of several shopping bags. Upon entering her home, she realized that her family was still sleeping, so she took her time and carefully unpacked the bags to examine what she had bought in her great hurry.

She sorted through the items, making the determinations one would usually make in the store in her kitchen. She decided to keep all fresh perishables, since it would be awkward to return them, even though she knew her husband and children would not eat the honey wheat bread and turnips she had purchased. Other things, such as canned yams, canned asparagus, and 13-gallon garbage bags, she piled on one side of the counter, to rebag and return at some later time.

Once everything was put away or set aside, Lily glided mindlessly into the living room, clinging to the sales receipt, and parked herself on the couch, where she sat for upwards of an hour until Bender woke up, took a shit, came downstairs, and saw her.

After their brief conversation, Lily was even more nervous than she had been before. She feared that Bender would see the number of items she had to return and question her about her shopping, that she had made some veiled comment Bender would later question, or that he'd smell sex or happiness on her.

But these things never happened. Bender went about his day like any other, never suspecting a thing and never approaching Lily with any questions or concerns.

It was Lily who approached Bender on the matter.

She'd spent the entire day as a cluster of clichés. Like a zombie, she walked on eggshells, with a cloud of guilt hanging above her. She was in another place—her mind was somewhere else. It vacillated between hot thoughts of sexing Leo and self-condemning thoughts of betraying Bender.

It all poured out after the girls were in bed for the night, when Bender made an offhand remark about how Lily had forgotten to drain the ground beef before adding the sauce to make sloppy joes for dinner.

"It was disgusting, Lily! How could you feed that garbage to your family? What good are you if you can't even feed us right!"

"Stop talking to me like that Bender," she hollered.

"I'll stop talking to you like that when you stop messing things up, you good-for-nothing idiot. You're a failure as a wife, and a failure as a mother," Bender countered.

Lily was hurt by his words. Though she was accustomed to his insults, she still took great offense at those times he criticized her execution of her role as mother. She prided herself on being a good mom who took excellent care of her children and made sacrifices for them daily. Motherhood was very important to Lily. It was the only job to which she had ever fully committed herself and in which she took the most pride. She allowed motherhood to define her. So when Bender criticized her parenting in any way, he was attacking the core of who she was.

"You're right, Bender, I am a failure as a wife... I cheated on you... last night... with Leo."

Immediately after saying this, Lily drew her hands up to guard her face. She expected, knew, that Bender would punch her in the face or beat her.

But he didn't.

In fact, he didn't do anything.

He just stood there and studied his wife, his face burning.

Lily lowered her hands from her face and, remaining on

guard, looked at Bender.

"Did you hear what I just said, Bender?" she asked.

Looking down at the floor, unwilling to let his eyes meet hers, he replied: "Yeah, I heard you, Lily. I heard you."

"Well?" she followed. "Don't you have anything to say?"

"What do you want me to say, Lily?"

"I don't know," she responded. "Something. Anything."

Her tone was quieter now, as she realized that she didn't know what she wanted him to say. She didn't know how she wanted him to respond at all.

"Come on, Lily," he began sarcastically. "I knew what kind of girl you were when I met you, but I married you anyway... I always knew you were gonna cheat on me, and I always knew it would be with him. It was just a matter of time."

Lily was stunned by Bender's words. Whatever response she wanted, this was not it.

"Honestly, I have to admit I'm a little surprised, though... I would've thought you guys had something going on for years... I'm not blind, Lily. I saw the way you guys carried on around each other back in the day. I'm shocked to find out you weren't fucking then."

Irrespective of what Bender may have thought now or then, Lily and Leo weren't fucking back in the day, which was a sad reality that Lily had to come to terms with over and over again from the first time she met him.

Bender had joined forces with Leo during Lily's second pregnancy, after Tina was born but before Robbie was, and long before Fox died. He'd seen a sign posted in a bar he frequented for a few beers after each and every long work day.

The sign read:

Heavy metal band looking for KICK ASS singer.
We got an axe shredder, a drum tapper, a reverend
of reverb, and a key master. All we need is a hard
core dude who can rip some vocals. Call Leo London
for your audition.

Bender tore a strip of paper off of the posting and called
the number on it. He talked to Leo and learnt more about the
band, which he auditioned for a few days later. Bender made
the cut and was inducted into the nameless band shortly
thereafter.

The five fellows got together twice a week for jam
sessions and creative meetings. They worked on some cover
tunes and started writing their own original songs. Early on,
they hit open stage nights at local bars, to play for free and
gather a following.

Within a few months of being together, the band
marshaled a considerable number of fans who religiously
showed up at their performances. Consequently, they
decided to search for paying gigs, so that they could bank on
their growing local celebrity. But, before they could do that,
they had one little thing to take care of: They needed to come
up with a name for their band.

They toyed around with several different names, like
Sinner's Banquet, Misfit Circus, and The Bloody BoyScouts,
before they finally decided on Bender's Bender, a name
which won by a narrow majority in a vote. Three were for
the name, and two were against.

But a vote of three was all that was needed to name the
band. And the name had been set, much to Bender's
pleasure.

Bender's success with the band, and his triumph in
naming it, put him in a most kind and loving disposition,
which was warmly received and reciprocated by Lily in her

pregnant condition. Because of her pregnancy, however, she was unable to make it out to any of her husband's shows, and didn't care to tag along to any of his practices or meetings.

She was happy just to support him behind the scenes, and she asked very little of him since things were going so well between them. Even when Bender had to cancel a bar gig on the evening Lily went into labor, he wasn't upset. The birth of Robbie was a good reason, the only reason, to cancel his artistic performance.

With a new baby in the house, as well as a toddler, it was some time before Lily ever got around to seeing Bender's Bender perform, or to meet the other members of the band. It wasn't until Robbie was almost 1 that she finally got the chance to do these things.

Lily had weaned Robbie from breast milk and was aching for some booze and some adult company. She asked Irene to sit with the girls one evening, so that she could join Bender for a night out on the town and sit in VIP audience to his creative expression.

She dug out a shirt that she used to sport in her single days, a vestige of her former self, and stretched it over her recently-weaned, engorged breasts. The shirt was olive green with distressed-yellow writing that read, "I'm with the band!"

She finished getting ready, dolling herself up, and climbed into the shabby white utility van Bender used for work and musical play, a van he'd bought for $500 from a retired house painter for whom he once worked.

The band was scheduled to hit the stage at 9:30 that night, but Bender and his boys planned to arrive much earlier, to set up their equipment and run sound. Bender pulled into the bar's parking lot around 7:30, and Lily went to sit at the bar while he unloaded his equipment.

Around 8:00, Bender joined Lily at the bar. Together, they did two shots, each, of tequila, before Bender told Lily that some of the other guys in the band had arrived and that he'd like to introduce her.

She walked with him to the upstairs bar, where the stage was located. The first of Bender's bandmates she met was Bob Cargon, the drummer. He was a man of mixed race, though Lily couldn't decipher of which races he was composed. His skin was dark and smooth, with coarse, tight hair growing out of the follicles on his arms, chin, and scalp. It was a dark brown, almost black, similar in color to his eyes, eyes that were quick and ever-moving, buggy and jittery.

He spoke as quickly as his eyes moved, stuttering and repeating words and ideas that spilled out of his thin lips. Lily assumed that he was this way because of some type of drug addiction, probably meth. And Lily was correct in her assumption.

Lily next met Corey Renner, the bassist, and Shannon Mitchell, the keyboardist, who were seated together at a small round high-top table against the back wall of the room. Based on the way they were interacting with each other, and how neither one of them really paid her much attention or gave her a second glance, Lilly assumed something about them. She assumed that they were homosexual lovers.

But, if you asked either Renner or Mitchell, they both would tell you that Lily was incorrect in her assumption. Renner was a married man, after all, with a 5-year-old son. And Mitchell was a single guy who liked to play the field.

How very wrong Lily was in her assumption! Quite wrong, indeed. These men were nothing more than very close friends who liked to do a list of fun things together— like play music, watch sports broadcasts, masturbate, and shoot darts.

The final member of the band, a Mr. Leo London, hadn't shown up at the bar yet. Leo was usually a last minute arrival, Bender told Lily.

Lily was standing beside the table where Renner and Mitchell sat, hovering next to Bender and Bob, when she felt an arm wrap around her shoulder.

"You must be our Bender's wife, love," said a strong man with a weak British accent. "I'm Leo, and I'm ever glad to finally meet you."

Lily turned to see the man who had just greeted her. He looked familiar, though Lily was certain she'd never met him before.

He was a tall, lean man with long waves of messy dirty-blonde hair and grey-blue eyes—at least Lily thought they were grey in the dimly lit bar. He had a square chin that jutted out to bend upward and make a hard dimple at the point where his jaw ended.

The clothing he wore was worn snug to his body. From the high cut of his short-sleeved V-neck shirt's short sleeves, and from the low cut of his skin-tight velvet pants, Lily surmised that his clothes were probably women's clothes. But that didn't matter to Lily, or to him, or to anyone else, because he looked damn good in those clothes—though, Lily thought, he probably would look even better without them.

Peeking out from beneath the V of his shirt was a pair of hissing snake tattoos mirrored on each of his pronounced collarbones. Lily wondered where else he might have tattoos, if he had any others that were hiding. She imagined herself searching for them, and licking them when she found them.

Suffice to say, he was definitely Lily's type. If it hadn't been for the fact that she was married to Bender, Lily would have gone home with him at the drop of a hat. Actually, she would have gone anywhere with him—his house, her house, the parking lot, the back alley, the women's restroom. Anywhere.

Yes, Lily had met him before. Seventy-five times. She'd seen and been with 75 men just like him. Seventy-five men who looked largely the same, sharing a common set of physical features and attributes. Seventy-five men, tall and thin, with long hair and some form of ink or metal disrupting their skin.

Since she had gathered those 75 men during what she now considered a closed chapter in her life, their images fused together in her mind. Each of them was but one of 75 parts of the only man she'd ever known before Bender, 75 anonymous male appendages dangling from a singular male machine like utters from a cow.

And now, meeting Leo was like coming face to face with that machine after years apart from it, like giving a discrete identity to a general form, sharpening something that was all too blurry. She was reminded of something she could no longer have, as the man before her represented the only thing she'd ever had before.

Lily caught herself before her mind wandered too far. She was married, she told herself, even if not entirely happily so, and should not think such thoughts about Bender's bandmate, a man she'd only just met, a man who wasn't her husband.

"Lily, this is Leo," Bender said as a form of introduction. "Leo, Lily."

"Hmm, Lily, like the flower," Leo grinned.

"Oh, no way, man," Bender laughed. "Don't say that! She hates that... Now she's gonna go on some rant about a demon goddess or a painting or some shit like that. You're really in for it, Leo!"

"No, really, it's okay," Lily interjected. "I like it."

And Lily did like it. She liked the way he said "flower," the way his front teeth fell down below his lower lip, causing a puff of air to sweep across his jawline as he effortlessly articulated the "f" sound at the lead of his utterance.

"Then 'Flower' it is," Leo said, as his grin turned from innocent to loaded.

At that moment, something sparked between Lily and Leo, and they both felt it. It would have been visible, too, to everyone else, had anyone taken the time to notice.

Lily was confronted and confused by the chemistry between them. She knew that she could not act on it, because such action would be morally unacceptable. But what of the chemistry itself?

Surely, just because one was married, she thought, that didn't mean that his or her attractions to others came to an end. The human condition, Darwinism, and the course of history, showed, if not dictated, that men and women were not monogamous creatures by nature. Marriage was a social construct, with moral guidelines. Refraining from acting upon a sexual impulse was a psychological decision, not a biological imperative.

So, even if the action could be prevented, it seemed to Lily that the feelings could not. At best, those feelings would have to be addressed in some other way, resolved or dealt with in time.

She tried to think about how other married persons might handle this type of situation. But she couldn't reach any type of conclusion, since she didn't have many friends, let alone friends who were married, and never had any understanding or example of the dynamics of married life when she was growing up.

She'd have to face this challenge on her own. Should

she tell Bender? Confront Leo? Should she walk away from the bar tonight and vow to never set eyes on Leo again or to never be in his company?

No. These things would be actions. And they would be pointless. None of these actions would make the feelings go away, just as how preventing sexual action wouldn't prevent sexual feelings.

Worse yet, these actions would have unfavorable outcomes. Telling Bender would only make him mad and jealous. Confronting Leo would be embarrassing, and could lead to even more trouble if he decided to further pursue Lily's affirmed interest. And walking away from Leo, or vowing to never be around him, simply was not something Lily was willing to do.

She wanted to be around him. She wanted to feel the feelings that he roused in her, and she wanted to know that she was rousing something in him.

While she couldn't have sex with him, she could have this. This, an intense burning that reminded her how alive she was, and how alive she had once been; something that eroded her tough skin to make it soft again, to make her feel good when most everything else made her feel bad.

Instead of staying away from Leo, Lily ended up spending more time with him. On the night they met, the greatest extent of conversation had been between the two of them, and it was pretty much the same on most of the nights that followed.

Lily started going out to more and more of the band's shows, arriving early and leaving late with Bender. She became well acquainted with the band, its music, and its members. Each of the fellows, especially Leo, became more than her husband's bandmates to Lily. They also became her friends.

And the guys liked hanging out with Lily. She was a guys' gal, but in a different way than she'd been before. They thought she was cool to hang out with. She was funny, loud, and had a very dirty sense of humor.

Every once in a while, when an attractive lady would pass their table in the bar and she'd see one or more of the fellows gawk, Lily would make a comment, such as, "Yeah, that one had some nice boobs, huh?" or "Her ass looks ready for a grabbin'!"

Such comments could have been an expression of the otherwise dormant homosexuality gene she inherited from her lesbian mother, but, really, they were probably nothing more than her vulgarly voiced appreciations of beauty.

Lily's candid style was only one of the things that Bender's bandmates enjoyed about Bender's wife. They also liked that she was down-to-earth, approachable, and not at all stuck up. Plus, it didn't hurt that she was nice to look at.

More than any of the other guys, even more so than Bender, Leo appreciated all of these things, and more, about Lily. He developed a terribly sincere fondness for her, which made his physical attraction to her swell and fester.

Their flirtations were mild and harmless, for the most part. One would welcomingly encroach the other's personal space or press physical contact during conversation. Suggestive comments were made. Big smiles and full cheeks, batting eyelashes and proud postures.

Leo would sit beside Lily in crammed booths, putting his arm on the back of the seat behind them or allowing the knee of his crossed leg to twitch near her body. Lily would do the same, angling her body to suggest invitation, throwing her hand on his knee or thigh at fitting moments in common discussions.

When standing, they'd let little space between them,

often having to whisper to each other in loud bar or club settings, warm breath against warm ears, noses nudging necks, cheeks brushing together.

Bender never acknowledged or addressed any of these behaviors as offensive or as violations of Lily's marital vows. He let Lily and Leo go about their interactions without any interference.

Arguably, Bender may have even encouraged it at a few points over the course of Leo's involvement in their lives, whether he knew it or not.

Bender was the one to place them in a very comfortable position one night sometime in the middle of the band's career.

After about three years of extensive flirtation and limited closeness, Lily was tossed onto Leo's lap, literally, as a necessary solution at the end of an eventful evening in the band's development.

Bender's Bender had been booked for its first out-of-town gig, at a college bar outside of Altoona, Pennsylvania. Lily joined Bender for the 2-hour trip, as the passenger in his loaded utility van. Renner and Mitchell drove to the venue together, and Leo hitched a ride with Bob.

A huge crowd came out to the small bar, and the band rocked the place like no other band had ever rocked it before. It was a great show by all measures. The bar made a ton of money from cover charges and drink sales, and ended up paying the band a good deal more than their agreed-upon percentage of cover fees.

It was an uncommonly good night for Bob, who ended up leaving the bar with a female meth-head college student who'd caught his eye. They went back to her dorm to get high and screw while her roommate hid beneath her blankets and hoped that their presence was just another whiskey-induced nightmare.

Spending most of what they'd earned that night, the rest of the guys from Bender's Bender stuck around, with Lily, and drank to their success until the bar closed, at which point Leo came to an unnerving realization: He didn't have a ride home.

Bob had driven his car to the college campus to score a fix and some sex, and Leo was stranded at the bar—in Altoona, two hours away from Pittsburgh. Mitchell didn't have room for Leo in his car. Renner was his passenger, and the backseat and trunk of the car were already loaded with instruments, equipment, and other rubbish.

Even if there had been room in Mitchell's car, neither he nor Renner would have wanted Leo along for the ride, as they had plans to finish off the night as they finished themselves off during the drive home, with a quick stop along the highway to jerk off together.

Riding home with Bender and Lily was Leo's only viable option. But Bender's van was packed tightly—with his sound system, musical equipment, and random implements of his landscaping and maintenance business— and would be even more loaded with Leo's guitar and amp. Thus, there remained only two seats in the car, but three people to fill them.

Bender suggested that Lily sit on Leo's lap during the drive home. There was no other room for him in the van, and any other combination of shared seating seemed ridiculous to Bender. He sure as hell wasn't going to share a seat with Leo, and he didn't want Leo driving his precious beat-up van—holding his precious beat-up wife, however, was perfectly fine.

"Don't get any ideas, buddy," Bender quipped as Lily solicitously mounted herself on Leo's lap. "I'll kill you!"

Lily was uncertain as to whether Bender was talking to Leo, or to her.

But Lily wasn't so much interested in that fact as she was in the fact that she was about to go on one hell of a joyride.

The feeling of Lily's body against and on top of his was something that Leo found very satisfying and unbelievably tempting. The chemistry he felt for her was enhanced by chemicals—alcohol and pheromones, each of which had more palpable import by reason of their practical physical proximity.

Leo could smell Lily's perspiration and body odor, mixed with shampoo and perfume and precipitated by humidity and smoke. By her, he was made drunker than he had already been, though he'd already been pretty damn drunk, something which made him all the more excitable in the first place.

Before Bender even turned the van on, Leo was already turned on—and even more so when Bender revved the engine. Because the van was in very poor condition, the whole automobile shook with slight vibrations upon ignition, slight vibrations which spread through Leo's and Lily's bodies, rattling their bones and jittering their clothed flesh together.

At the first jarring bounce, Leo closed his eyes and bit his lip. He knew that there was no escaping his body's forthcoming involuntary reaction.

Leo couldn't mute the messages his brain sent throughout his nervous system. He couldn't prevent them from reaching the spongy tissues of his corpus cavernosa, the blood vessels of which were relaxed by his excitement. It was too late to stop those vessels from yawning ever wider and swallowing more blood, filling his corpus cavernosa and stiffening their smooth muscle walls. Taut, engorged, enflamed, the pressure caused by these rigid walls had already shut off the flow of fleeing blood to the rest of his body.

In other words, Leo was producing an inevitable erection.

And Lily was delighted to feel him grow beneath her.

The fabric of her skirt was thin and wispy, providing a minimal barrier between her body and his. Though Leo's pants were made of bulky faux leather, his swelling still reached Lily and sent bolts of pleasure upward through the core of her wanting body.

She was grateful for Bender's erratic, drunken driving, for his swerving, short stops, and slapdash maneuvers, the things that caused her and Leo's bodies to rub and thrust against each other. Little bumps on the road lifted her bottom up an inch or two off of Leo's lap and caused her to fall hard back onto him. Loosely driven curves swayed their bodies in opposite directions, providing both friction and resistance for their enjoyment.

These things titillated Leo too, enlivening others of his organs. His heart raced and skipped beats each time Lily's hind quarters clapped against his pelvis. His respiratory system contracted at every instance where her body twisted counter to his erect direction. It was becoming unbearable.

He was so aroused on the ride that he barely spoke, out of fear that he might unknowingly let slip something he was thinking or that his rapid breathing or glazed-over speech would unquestionably indicate his arousal.

What little conversation he did engage in was vacant and superficial. He was unable to submit to anything other than his attraction to, and contact with, Lily. The only discourse he initiated was in reference to the tattoo of angel wings Lily had on the back of her neck, which he'd never before noticed.

"Show him your other tattoo, Lily," Bender instructed.

Lily was not at all troubled to follow Bender's direct order. She leaned forward and reached both of her hands behind her, to lower the waistband of her skirt and reveal a cursive tattoo that read: "Property of Bender."

"Oh, man, that's awesome," Leo whimpered. But he wasn't talking about Lily's tattoo. He was talking about the way her body dug into his when she leant forward, how her rear-end grinded into his front-end and exerted just the right amount of pressure on his pulsing virility.

He put his hands on her hips, under the guise of further inspecting her tattoo but with the actual intendment of steering her body to curry deeper into the crook of him.

"You like that, huh?" Bender asked Leo. "I got one too."

This time, it was Leo who was uncertain about Bender's comment. Was he talking about a tattoo or a hard-on?

Lily didn't have to wonder, because she knew. Bender had a tattoo similar to Lily's, in the same location with a different owner named. His read: "Property of Lily."

"We got them a couple days after we were married," Bender disclosed. "They're a little more permanent than your average wedding ring, right babe?"

"Yeah," Lily riposted. She too was too flustered to speak at any great length.

Leo's nether nerves were peaked with critical excitement, sending messages to his spinal cord and brain. His vas deferens were contracting and squeezing his differentiated cells toward the back of his urethra, where they were met by the secretions discharged from his seminal vesicles.

Before Leo's posterior urethra apperceived his build-up of fluids, before it sent signals to his spinal cord, before his spinal cord could command a series of rapid and vigorous contractions, Leo acted suddenly to pull Lily's back against his chest, so that she would no longer press against his manhood.

In other words, Leo was preventing an inevitable ejaculation.

And Lily was disappointed to have him stop it.

"Good grief," he murmured. "That's too much, my Flower."

Yes, Lily was a flower, and Leo was her stem—the thick, hard protrusion that held her firmly in place.

She was plucked, uprooted, when Bender's driving stopped in the alleyway behind Leo's apartment, at which point Leo exited the van, collected his gear, and ran up the back steps to duck into his cave-like dwelling.

As soon as he saw that Leo was safely inside, Bender got ready to drive away. But Lily stopped him.

"Hold on a second, Bender. I have an idea," she said coyly.

She reached over and removed the key from the ignition, and then reached up under her skirt to peel down her underthings and throw them on the vehicle's floor. She slithered over towards her husband and clambered on top of him, unzipping his pants and working him to attention.

On any other night, Bender probably would have pushed Lily aside without hesitation and drove away. Sex between the couple had become sparse, and Bender was typically irresponsive to even the most direct of Lily's advances.

But this night was different. Every cell in Bender's body was awake and anxious, stimulated by, and teeming from, the high of his outstanding musical performance earlier in the evening. For this reason, and for this reason alone, he allowed Lily to progress in her seduction, and willingly let her guide him into her body.

Their sex was clumsy and rough, but Lily enjoyed it, especially because it had been more than two months since last they were together. All the while they were congressing, Lily kept hoping that Leo would look out of his window or elsewise see what they were doing. She wanted Leo to know that he had spurred her to action, and she wanted him to see her looking for him, so that he could know it was of him, not Bender, she was thinking.

To the best of Lily's knowledge and inspection, Leo never saw what happened, and the sex ended as hastily as it had begun. Physically satisfied, at least, Lily derailed from her husband and returned to the passenger seat, where she sat for the duration of the ride home.

She felt guilty for having come upon Bender with another man in mind, a feeling that was only made worse by Bender's remarks at how remarkable the sex had been. They were the types of comments to which Lily had grown accustomed over the years, but hadn't heard in what felt like forever. From Bender's mouth, they sounded cheap and irrelevant—the way that Lily also felt, no doubt. Cheap for wanting one man, and irrelevant as the wife of another.

Detached from the man with whom she'd just had intercourse, she felt like a hooker being returned to her corner when she reached her home. But her john was ready for a second helping.

Upon entering the house, Bender decided to enter Lily again. He led her to the kitchen, past Irene, who was sleeping on the couch underneath a blanket of coloring book pages. He bent her over the kitchen table, and held her down as he let down his pants and pulled her skirt up. He pushed himself hard inside her.

The sex was slower, longer, harder and more genial than before. Bender seemed to be on a mission, like an artist determined to make his career-breaking impression, unceasingly dabbing his wet brush across a freshly weaved canvas until finally dousing it with a warm spurt of his richest color, the signature on his masterpiece.

It was less than three months later that Lily and Bender had the fight which landed her in the hospital and contributed to her miscarriage. But it wasn't until a few days after her miscarriage that Lily would do the math. According to her calculations, it must have been on that particular evening that her lost, unborn baby was conceived. She and Bender hadn't had sex for over two months prior to that night, and hadn't engaged in it for the following three months.

That night, that particular night, had to be the night that she became pregnant.

And like Jill, her ersatz lesbian parent before her, Lily fancied the pregnancy not as the result of the physical act which caused insemination but of the intense passion which preceded it. The baby she lost was not hers and Bender's—it had been hers and Leo's, notwithstanding that his sperm and her ovum never yoked.

Obviously, Lily knew better than to tell either Bender or Leo about the paternity she envisaged, and she never told Leo about the pregnancy or miscarriage at all. But the loss of her unborn baby was something that Lily would always recognize as not just the loss of a life but also the loss of something else she never had.

She was reminded of what she never had with Leo for the rest of his stint with Bender's Bender, which ended some two years later. During those two years, Lily saw him regularly and their chemistry persisted. But something other than sexual chemistry transpired between them, and what it was, was something that bordered on romantic enchantment.

Both Leo and Lily looked forward to things other than brushing up against each other, sharing space, or exchanging evocative words or glances. Each also looked forward to spending time with, and learning more about, the other, to smiling and laughing together.

The attachment they were developing was uncharacteristic of a clean-handed extramarital friendship, and it came to threaten the institution of Lily's and Bender's marriage, if only for the fact that it was sure to eventually raise suspicion.

Leo came to know Lily better than Bender knew her, an intimacy Lily couldn't have ever fathomed. For her 34th birthday, Leo purchased her a vintage coin binder in which she could store her collection of rare and valuable coins. She was touched more by this gift than by the pair of black and pink sneakers gifted to her by her husband, who was unaware that Lily collected coins, and that she'd been doing so for the greater part of her life.

Leo was able to complete some of Lily's sentences and to anticipate her thoughts, words, and movements before she was able to articulate them. Inside jokes, lengthy phone conversations. Happiness and life lived in concert.

There were those who, at the time, speculated as to the true nature of Lily's and Leo's affiliation, even some who questioned Lily or Leo directly or publicly mocked them. But Bender was never one of those persons. He appeared ignorant and unconcerned.

When Bender addressed Lily after her admission of her adultery, however, when he said to her, "I saw the way you guys carried on around each other back in the day," Lily reassessed her previous outlook on Bender's take on the situation.

Looking back on things, Lily concluded that Bender hadn't been oblivious, but, rather, had been complicit. He'd thought he knew what was going on and did nothing to try to stop it.

But Bender didn't know what was really going on.

"I'm shocked to find out you weren't fucking then," is what he'd said to Lily when she broke the news.

No, Bender, Lily and Leo weren't fucking back then.

They were doing much more than that.

~ 8 ~

"We are gathered here today to mourn the loss of a dear friend, a kind and loving creature, who left this earth too soon," said Jimmy Hayes, as part of the eulogy he was delivering.

"As we commit these ashes to the ground," he continued, "let's not let sadness and grief overcome us. Let us remember the good times, not the bad; the health, not the sickness; the fun, not the fatigue; the bark, not the bite.

"Let us celebrate life and living in the form of a fiesta— it's the way that adorable little bitch would have wanted it."

The afternoon of Mimi's funeral was a dark day in the lives of Lily, Bender, their kids, and their friends. Mimi had to be put to sleep because she had suffered from the same ailment of which her sibling, Mini, died a month earlier— canine congestive heart failure.

Neither Lily nor Bender had thought anything of the dogs' coughing and lack of interest in play. The Chihuahuas were each 13 years old, so it wasn't a surprise that they tired easily or couldn't handle a lot of activity. But when Lily woke up one morning to find Mimi licking the caked blood and vomit off of her dead dog-sister's mouth, Lily realized that, perhaps, it was more than old age that plagued her pets.

There was nothing she could do for Mini, other than pay $200 to have her cremated at an animal mortuary outside of Allegheny County. Two days after Mini's memorial service was held, and her ashes were interred into the ground of Lily's and Bender's backyard, Lily took Mimi to the vet to get her checked.

The diagnosis was late-stage congestive heart failure, and

the prognosis was grim. Mimi's resting cough and pot belly
were indications that both the left and right ventricles of her
heart were already failing. The veterinarian told Lily that it
was just a matter of time, and that nothing could be done to
save Mimi as extensive, irremediable damage to her heart
had already occurred.

Lily's only recourse was to await Mimi's death. She was
told she could help alleviate some of Mimi's symptoms by
giving her diuretics and vitamin B supplements. But there
was nothing that could be done to lessen the pain the dog
likely felt, since narcotics would only relax her already weak
heart muscles and pollute her liver, which was surely
compromised as well.

For a month, Lily tried to cure Mimi through
medications, diet foods, and prayer. Nothing worked,
however—just like the vet told her nothing would. But Lily
had to try.

With each of Lily's efforts, Mimi's condition seemed
to only get worse—not because Lily was making it worse,
but because it was simply getting worse. The old gal started
fainting and vomiting blood. Her neck would heave as she
gasped for air.

Though Lily couldn't stand to see Mimi this way, she
took issue with the vet's suggestion that she might want to
think about putting the dog to sleep. Putting a dog down,
euthanizing a life, after all, was something to which Lily was
fundamentally opposed.

Bender fought with Lily, not with violence but with pleas,
to put an end to the poor dog's pain. Tina and Robbie were
sickened by Mimi, since her sounds, appearance, and odor
were as vile as the rotten juices that seeped out of her mouth.
Soon, the girls started begging their mother to make the
scary dog go away, asking what happened to the old Mimi,

afraid that their friendly dog had contracted rabies or been bitten by a werewolf.

Begrudgingly, Lily agreed to put Mimi to sleep, although it was against everything in which she believed. In the end, withal, she knew it was the right thing to do. She just didn't like that she had to do it. It was the first time she'd ever had to consider giving up on a life rather than trying to save it. But it wouldn't be the last.

Unlike Mini's demise, Mimi's was predictable, so Lily and her family were able to plan for it. Lily scheduled Mimi's appointment with death for a Friday afternoon, with her remains to be charred and delivered home in a tiny metal box the next day. A proper funeral and wake for the dog was to follow that afternoon.

More people were invited to Mimi's funeral and wake than had been invited to Lily's and Bender's wedding. Twenty people, give or take, showed up for the event, including Jimmy Hayes, Irene, Cookie and Greta, and Leo and the other guys from Bender's Bender.

Bender presided over the burial, as Lily was too upset by the part she'd played in the death of her dog. Irene delivered an eulogy before Jimmy Hayes did, with the latter orating the words that closed out the funeral portion of the day.

In referring to Mimi's wake as a fiesta, Jimmy Hayes was spot on. Lily and Bender had decided to center the wake on a fiesta theme, in observance of the fact that Mimi was a Chihuahua, a famed Mexican breed.

After taking Mimi to the vet on Friday, Lily had gone shopping to purchase a wide variety of Mexican foods and drinks. She stayed away from those foods that were already prepared or were easily made because they were microwaveable, bakeable, or could be poured out of a jar, can, or bag.

She'd spent the rest of Friday night and Saturday morning getting ready for the fiesta, decorating, making party trays ready, and cooking whatever foods would refrigerate well. Staying busy was Lily's approach to dealing with tough times. She had to occupy her body to keep her mind at bay.

Unable to sleep or find rest in tough times, Lily usually ended up cooking elaborate meals, meticulously cleaning, or doing some other superfluous chore. On the very night her grandmother passed away, Lily drove to the store, bought an entire round of Pecorino Romano cheese and a dozen cheese shakers, and grated cheese for three or four hours, jarring it to give to grief-stricken visitors who called on her over the next few days.

When Mimi was put to death, Lily stayed up the entire night and made, among other things, homemade corn tortillas. She even stone-ground the corn herself!

So, needless to say, Lily had prepared quite the fiesta for Mimi's wake, replete with Mexican beverages as well, such as imported beers, tequila, and margaritas. Papaya nectar was available for the girls.

The fiesta proved to be a very successful function, so successful that most of the guests conveniently forgot the reason they had convened. The food was delicious, the booze abundant, and music and talk boomed—it was more of a happy party than a somber reception.

Not for Lily though. For Lily, it was still a very mournful occasion, in spite of the fun going on around her. True, she wanted her guests to celebrate life and live it up, but their disregard of Mimi's death, their dismissal of the loss of life, disturbed Lily in a most lugubrious way.

To circumvent the cheer, Lily fled the party and went to her safe place, a part of her home that she regularly visited to get away from her troubles, from Bender, from her young children, from anyone or anything that bothered her in any way.

Lily's safe place was on a flat square of slate located on the roof of her house, a small patio-like space, not intended for domestic use, that sat outside the attic's only window, flushing to the recessed brick wall that tapered up to the triangular apex of her home. It was a tiny lot, approximately six feet long from side to side and four feet deep from edge to window.

Small, but big enough for Lily to sit and relax, with a snack, a drink, or, once in a blue moon, a thin joint of reefer to smoke—or with nothing at all, other than her thoughts, which was usually the case.

The space had always been a part of the house, but Lily only uncovered it in the early part of her third decade living there, slightly more than a year before the fiesta, a few months after Fox would have been, but was not, born.

She'd never had any reason to look for it or know it was there. She just happened to find it at a point in her life when she needed it.

A little more than a year ago, after Bender had reminded her once again how useless she was, and had given her the third degree about not removing outdated and outgrown clothes from their daughters' closets, Lily condensed a few drawers of garments into two storage bins and set off to move them to the attic.

Attempting to carry both large bins at the same time, Lily was overburdened and had to drop the plastic boxes down at the top of the attic steps before she could wade through the items that scattered the floor. When the boxes fell down, the top one swayed back and fell against the cloth dressing of what Lily thought was the wall. But the sound it made wasn't the sound of plastic on brick or drywall. The pitch of the pop was too sharp and high, even though muffled by thick fabric.

Lily moved in to draw back the dressing and discovered that it was the window treatment of a medium-sized rectangular window that sat on vertical hinges, to be opened inward like a barn door. What's more, the window was a fairly artful one, divided into four tall panels separated by lead lines, alternating between stained-glass and clear-glass, the former of which depicted intricate dashes of birds nipping at blossoms.

Opening the window and peering out, Lily saw for the first time her future place of refuge, a landing pad at the end of the 3-foot descent from the window's outer sill. She visualized the layout of the house, trying to plot over where that little lot sat. She ascertained that it sat somewhere above the wall between Tina's and Robbie's bedrooms, and, in all likelihood, topped off some type of insulation or crawlspace hovering the chambers below, another feature of her home she had never before discerned.

For no reason other than exploration, Lily aped down to land on the pad. Once outside, she met feelings of power, pride, and, most of all, peace. The roof's outstanding view reached far beyond her backyard, to the city neighborhoods that cascaded down the hill on which Lily's home resided.

Lily felt small and anonymous as compared to the expanse of the view, a feeling which pacified her, because that smallness, that anonymity, meant that she was but one part of a larger unit, but one element in a larger design. Smallness, a smallness so different from the smallness Bender used to define her—not small is in worthless, but small as in an integral part, a necessary screw.

When Lily would visit this spot again and again, that

smallness also helped her keep her perspective in check.
With each siren or argument she heard, with each glimpse
of a cripple in a wheelchair or of a disobedient brat getting
spanked, Lily was reminded that she was not the only person
in the world who suffered at times, and that there were others
out there who braved even worse fates than she.

Similarly, every loving couple who walked hand-in-hand,
every chipper child on a cycle, every bird that sang, and
every car that blasted pop music reminded Lily of something
as well—that there was beauty and bliss to be found in this
world and that not even her own agony or grief, not even
Bender, or his fists or his words, could eradicate the
happiness that pocked the rest of the world.

Retreat—that little spot also provided Lily a campground
for her retreat, where retreat is employed here as a military
noun, a term referring to the strategic withdrawal of force
from enemy lines. Those times Bender gave Lily guff, Lily
employed a common military tactic: She took to higher
ground. But not for its better vantage point or advantageous
sniping range, instead for its seclusion as a combat-free zone.

As it turns out, Bender, the beast, the abuser, the coward,
was deathly afraid of heights.

He would not follow Lily to her safe place. Acrophobia
kept him from stepping out onto Lily's pad, and
allodoxaphobia stopped him from shouting at her from inside
the window. Whenever Lily headed up the steps toward the
attic door, Bender declined to trail her.

The attic door had an eye-hole lock on it at its top, so
that the kids couldn't scurry up there to unbury treasures and
secrets or crawl out of Lily's escape hatch. Once, Bender
had locked the door from the outside, to trap Lily inside as
punishment for her finding sanctuary. But he only did that
once—only once because he had to care for their daughters

during the time she was locked up, only once because he wanted to make sure his daughters' mother could execute her duties.

But Lily's flight to her heighted hideaway was not noticed by Bender on the day of Mimi's funeral and fiesta. It appeared that no one was privy to her leave as she glided up the stairs.

Once seated on her slate slab of solace, Lily endeavored to recover perspective. Bereft, she reflected on the lost life of her pet, focusing on the word pet. Relative to other things, the loss of a pet was not so egregious. She thought of the baby she'd lost approximately two years earlier, of the grandmother she lost nearly eight years prior, and of the mother she could barely remember but for the fact that that mother abandoned her. Each of these things Lily deemed worse than the loss of her pet.

Lily thought not only of her losses but also of her gains, of the two incredible children who continued to amaze her each day, of the way she loved that pair of little troublemakers more than she loved herself. She thought too of her friendships, the two most important of which were with Irene and with Leo.

Leo, loverly Leo, she was thankful for Leo, for whatever it was she had, as well as what she didn't have, with him. Thoughts of Leo turned to thoughts of Bender, whom she labeled another gain, for whom she was also grateful. Things with Bender were not perfect, not perfect at all, but he had been the one to give her Tina and her Robbie.

Grateful, thankful, appreciative, Lily acknowledged that she had less than some and recognized that she had more than many. What losses of life she had witnessed were slight in light of others, minimal reductions to her holiday shopping lists as compared to catastrophic devastations. Hurricanes, earthquakes, Charles Manson, Jim Jones, genocide, terrorist attacks, serial killers, and drive-by shootings—when it came to tragedy, Lily was no trendsetter.

At last, after a day of woe, Lily felt again grounded, and her mind was free to roam to more benign, mundane topics. She thought of more inviting things, like Robbie's upcoming enrollment in preschool ballet classes, like her recent trip to an ink shop with Irene, where Irene received her first tattoo, a Rod of Asclepius, not a caduceus, to commemorate her admission to medical school.

A series of noises startled Lily: the turning of the attic doorknob, the sound of feet shuffling, and the creaking of hardwood. She was fearful that one or both of her daughters had come looking for her and would uncover her safe spot, only to have her secret become their obsession, to have them demand their own access to her site, something which would probably cause Bender to board up the window, forever closing off her hallowed highplace.

She hopped up just in time to see Leo's face framed in the window. His right leg was the next thing she saw, as it straddled over the sill to lead the rest of his body out from the window.

Leo touched down on the roof with a thud and brushed his hands across the ass pockets of his pants, as if to dislodge any dirt or dust resulting from his plummet, a motion more reflexive than purposeful.

"Hi," he said, with a rebounding beam.

And, "Hi," Lily said in her turn.

"I hope I'm not bothering you," Leo remarked. "I just had to talk to you about something."

"No, no, you're not bothering me, not at all. I just came up here to think about things, to weigh some stuff out... I come up here a lot to do that."

"I know," Leo breathed. "You told me."

It didn't register with Lily right away when Leo fell onto her rooftop, but she had mentioned her haven to him before, twice or thrice. She was elated, or further elevated, that he remembered what she had considered an insignificant, off-hand aside on her part. Though it wasn't unexpected for Leo to recall such a thing, as it wasn't unexpected for him to recall anything Lily chose to tell him.

When he'd seen Lily exit the downstairs some while ago and hadn't seen her return, he knew this was where her journey ended. He waited an appropriate amount of time before discharging himself to join her. With all the merriment down below, no one had detected his leave, just as no one, but he, had detected Lily's leave afore.

"I came up here to tell you…," Leo started, leaning forward and collapsing his forehead to the brick and mortar of Lily's home, "to tell you that I'm leaving."

"Oh," Lily reacted. "Well, thanks for coming. It means a lot to me that you were here today, and I'm sure Mimi would have—…"

"No!" Leo shouted, grinding his dome against the wall.

He winced as he pulled his head back to gape at Lily. His forehead was dirty, with specks of gritty concrete flecking his brow, a tiny cut across the bridge of his nose.

"I'm *leaving*, Flower. I'm leaving Pittsburgh," he clarified.

Lily felt something break inside her, but she wasn't foolish enough to believe it was her heart. It was something much deeper, something that had turned over inward to split and splinter farther down her body, splattering somewhere between her bellybutton and her sternum.

A brutal discomfort infected whatever part of her body had ruptured at her center, causing her to think she would keel over and retch.

Only moments ago Lily had counted Leo as one of her blessings, one of the things that helped her put her loss and life into perspective. And now that saving grace would save no more. Without Leo, Lily would have one less source of sustenance.

She felt the urge to transcend time and place, to find herself in a tropical ecosystem or standing on a fault line, to dine at Tate manor or drink the punch in Guyana, to be on Hitler's hit list or employed atop either of the Twin Towers, to help Ted Bundy to his car or take up residency in a ghetto. Lily wanted to die, to be snuffed out swiftly, so that she would not have to endure the agony of her remaining lifetime without Leo.

But Leo had something else in mind.

"I want you to come with me."

It would be cliché to say that Lily was at a loss for words. It would also be incorrect, for Lily was flooded with words. She just couldn't select which ones to use, or in which order to express them.

Calling on her maternal instinct, she chose the least fitting thing to say. She drew her right thumb to her mouth and wet it with her tongue. "Your face is all dirty," she said, bringing her thumb to Leo's forehead and coasting it across. The loose grains of mortar were transferred to her thumb, but the residual dust was smudged against his skin, giving him the look of a parishioner who'd just been blessed on Ash Wednesday.

Lily wiped her hand clean against her black-wash denim slacks and raised it to her mouth to prepare herself for a second swipe. Before she could lick her digit, however, Leo latched on to Lily, pressing his palm to her pulse and forming a circlet around her wrist with his own thumb and middle finger. He stopped her hand from further moving.

"I don't care about my face, damn it," Leo said without reservation. "Did you hear what I just said? … I'm leaving, and I want you to come with me."

Leo was yelling, but it wasn't an angry yell. It was an urgent one.

"Don't be silly," Lily laughed as she pulled his grip away from her wrist and went about freshening him up as she had intended, again calling on her maternal instinct, acting like a mother and treating him like a child who had made a big mess, trying to distract him from his goals and clean him into compliance.

"I'm not being silly, Flower… I'm being totally serious."

The way he shrugged off her laughter and tried to push her hands away as she blotted his face, the way he rolled his eyes at her words, echoed the things her own children would do in this type of situation.

But changing the topic with Leo was not so simple. She could not overpower his efforts at communication.

"Stop! Listen to me," Leo shouted.

Abruptly, rudely, and loudly, Lily finally responded: "I heard what you said, Leo. I heard. And it's preposterous. It's ridiculous and insane… Is that why you came up here? To try and get a married woman to run away with you? Did you even think about what you were asking before you put it out there?"

"Of course I did… I've been thinking about it for months. It's not preposterous or ridiculous. It's not insane… I can't take it here anymore, Flower. I'm tired of being second-best in every fucking thing I do. I thought you'd be tired too."

"Tired? Tired of what?"

Their discussion had taken on a new form, a form that was new not only to this solemn afternoon but to their relationship in general. Their words to each other were rough and sharp, their sentences delivered bluntly and in a cold, hard matter-of-fact way.

Perhaps this was their form of fighting.

"Are you serious?" Leo scoffed. "Tired... Aren't you tired of the way he treats you? Do you think no one else knows what's going on? ... Get real. I see the way he treats you, how he pushes you around, grabs you, drags you, how he yells at you and calls you cruel, demeaning names, criticizes you and tells you what to do. Shit, Flower, if he does that stuff to you in front of other people, I don't even want to think about what he does to you behind locked doors when nobody else is around... And you're telling me you're not tired of that? You're telling me that you don't want to get away from him? You don't wanna stop living under his thumb? ... Maybe you're not the person I thought you were after all."

"Maybe I'm not... I'm a wife and a mother. That's who I am... You can't come here and ask a wife and a mother to leave her family just because you're tired of being second-best. You can't put your career above my family, Leo. That's not how it works."

"You think I'm talking about my career? ... That's not at all what I'm talking about... Yeah, I'm tired of being in a band that's named after a lead singer who was the last to sign up. And I'm tired of always having to play lists in his order and have him book all the gigs... But that's not what gets to me most... What gets to me most? ... I'm tired of being second-best when it comes to you. I'm tired of being your friend, or whatever I am, while he gets a woman he doesn't deserve. And I'm tired of watching him treat you the way he does while I sit back and do nothing. Don't you want things to change? Don't you want to leave him and be with me instead?"

Over the years, Lily had entertained fantasies of being with Leo. But that's all they were to her—fantasies, fodder for a lonely housewife. She never expected that life with him could ever become a reality. But now that Leo was presenting her with an option, she had the chance to realize her fantasies. She was reluctant to do it. She couldn't do it.

In all her fantasizing, Lily had imagined life with Leo without ever dealing with practical concerns. Her daydreams were of snuggling, sex, and socializing in a world where her husband and children simply did not exist, not because she didn't want them to exist, but because their absence was more convenient for the storylines of her fiction.

In a few make-believe worlds of Lily's creation, Lily had never met Bender, or Ben, and Tina and Robbie had never been born. It was too complicated for her to author their placement in her fantasies, so she opted not to include them and implicitly pen their exclusion. To confront their existences, she would have had to dispose of them in some way, to write them off in some manner. Not only did she not know how to do this, she didn't want to.

Certainly, she couldn't, and wouldn't, kill them off in her fabrications. And she felt guilty envisioning any other disposition. Having Bender play the role of husband in her story meant that her relations with Leo would be adulterous, and an adulterer was something she did not want to be, at least not yet. If she storied the breakup of her marriage, that'd mean she was a failure, and she'd still have to disenfranchise herself from her children to find paradise with Leo, something that'd make her a deadbeat mom who abandoned her children. Lily knew what it felt like to be the child of a deadbeat mom who abandoned her, and she didn't want to do that to her children—not even in a pipedream.

"Even if I could leave Bender, which I don't want to do, I still have kids. I'm a mother, Leo. I can't leave my kids."

"I'm not asking you to leave them," Leo assured her. "You can bring them with you… We'll all leave together."

"Are you kidding me? … You've got to be kidding! Do you even understand what you're proposing? … You're willing to raise another man's kids and change your life?"

"Yes, I am," Leo asserted.

"I have a hard time buying that… I don't think you've thought this through."

Leo had, however, thought things through. He'd been thinking about leaving Pittsburgh for months now, and had been thinking about asking Lily and her daughters to join him. He too had his fantasies, ones which included Bender, Tina, and Robbie, ones where Lily chose him over her husband and chose him as her children's father. Those choices were key to Leo's design, forming the very foundation that supported his high hopes.

He'd thought the decision-making through, but neglected other parts of the situation. He never contemplated the practical considerations, how he'd support his artificial step-family, how he'd take care of them when he couldn't even take care of himself, and how he'd ease Lily's children through the transition.

In five years, Leo had lived in eight different apartments, three of which he was evicted from for nonpayment of rent. The other five were places he left because he didn't like his random roommate or was somehow displeased with the digs. He crashed on his brother's living room couch between domiciles and sometimes had one night stands that lasted a few days longer than he wanted, just so he could rest his head and take a shower.

Unlike Bender, Leo did not have a day job of any type. His money came only from playing gigs with Bender's Bender, which only happened once or twice a month and pulled in a few hundred dollars that had to be divided five ways. What money he brought in was not a very pretty penny.

How could this man, who couldn't support himself financially or domestically, be a solid support for a pair of young children? Lily asked herself this question and came up with only one answer: He couldn't.

"You're not their father, Leo. You don't know how to raise kids. How could you? … The girls already have a father. They love him. And… And I do, too… He's made a nice life for us and takes good care of us… I can't take them away from all of that, from their dad… Plus, he'd never let it happen."

"Then we won't tell him," Leo said. "We'll just run away and won't tell anyone where we're going."

"Oh my god, Leo, listen to what you're saying! That's horrible… I couldn't do that to my girls… I couldn't take them away from their dad and have them never see him again… And, shit, I couldn't do that to Bender! I couldn't rob him of what he loves most in this world. None of them deserve something like that… I'd be the worst person in the world! … I can't believe you're even asking me this! You're being so thoughtless and greedy."

"Thoughtless? Greedy? You should listen to what **you're** saying… You're going on and on like you have some beautiful life, like you have some wonderful thing that you can't leave behind… But your life isn't beautiful, Flower. It's a mess. And I want to help you change that."

"I don't need your help… I never said my life was perfect… But it's fine—just fine. I like things the way they are and don't need anything to change."

Lily meant what she said. She was fine with things the way they were and didn't need or want anything to change.

She'd gotten used to imperfection and disorder in her life. In fact, she relied on it. Perfection and order seemed impossible and impractical, ideals that only hindered the operation of reality.

While some people reached for the stars or set lofty ambitions, Lily was content to hang low and stay steady. Bender and Leo, Bob, Renner and Mitchell—they pushed the envelope, to their own varying lengths, Irene too. They always wanted more, to get to the greener grass on the other side, to reframe defeat as cause for triumph and reason to move on. Not Lily, though. She was fine with what she had. She didn't look for silver linings on dark clouds. She looked for aluminum ones, because aluminum was a far more practical alloy.

"I'm giving you a chance, Flower," Leo claimed, "a chance to get away from all of this and start over with someone who will treat you right and love you like there is no tomorrow... Maybe you should think about it before you automatically dismiss it... I know you want this as much as me—you have to."

"I don't need time to think about it. I've already made up my mind, and there's nothing you can say to change it... You're the one who needs to think about this more. And when you realize how stupid you're being, I'll gladly accept your apology."

Leo's head jerked back as he sniveled a clap of sarcastic laughter, "I'll never apologize for asking you to leave with me... In fact, if you don't come with me, you'll be the one who's sorry someday."

"Is that some kind of threat?"

"Not at all, not at all. It's just my prediction."

Lily felt her blood boil beneath her skin. She was genuinely pissed off at Leo, and the acerbic delivery of his last comments pushed her to the edge. She narrowed her eyes and raised her eyebrows, shaking her head slowly from side to side. "Your prediction is a piece of shit, Leo. And so are you," she hissed.

"I know you don't mean that, Lily."

Lily. He never called her that, not since the first day he met her when he said it once, and only once, as a repetition of Bender's introduction. He called her it now, and it sickened her to hear it. It sounded unnatural and unpleasant, more callous than the nasty names Bender had only recently begun to call her.

She didn't like the way he said "Lily," the way his tongue pressed up against the roof of his mouth and backs of his front teeth, causing his lips to widen and spread across his jawline as he strenuously articulated the "l" sound at the lead of his utterance.

Lily lowered her body to sit down on the slate roof. She looked up at Leo and offered what she was feeling: "I want you to leave, Leo."

Was she talking about Leo leaving the roof or Leo leaving Pittsburgh? Leo wasn't sure, and neither was Lily.

Leo reached into his back pocket and extracted a folded up wad of paper. He handed it to her with verbal instructions.

"Take this," he said. "Think about it... And if you make the right decision, I'll see you then."

With that, Leo hopped up and raised his leg to climb into the attic window. Once inside, he looked down at Lily, watching as she unfolded what he'd given her.

Three tickets. Three Greyhound bus tickets, each marked with Las Vegas as a destination and a date four days from this day as their shared departure. Midnight. A midnight bus to Vegas.

Lily listened as Leo clomped down the attic stairs and shut the door behind him. She leaned her head back against the brick and mortar of her home, drawing her knees to her chest and slapping the tickets against her right shin.

Three tickets, yes, Leo had considered Lily's children. Three tickets, to Vegas, leaving on the midnight between a Tuesday and a Wednesday. Three tickets, Lily decided then and there, that she'd never use but would keep forever.

Lily would never use the tickets because she could never leave her husband. Even if he was vicious, rancorous, and abusive at times, he was still her husband and the father of her children. No matter what, she loved him. She had chosen a life with him and was committed to living it.

And when he wasn't being Bender the abuser, Bender was a good man. There was beautiful stuff between the ugly moments, beautiful comfort and companionship, the beautiful passing of time.

Beautiful memories, of seeing Bender's face the first time he held Tina, Tina still covered in globs of placental sap, the huge pupils of her tiny eyes struggling against the light of the outside world, the whining cackle of her infant's voice, Bender glancing down at her, his eyes flooding with tears at the beauty of his baby, his body shaking even more than his voice as he cradled tiny Tina in his strong arms.

Beautiful memories, of seeing Bender's face when he brought Tina to the hospital the day after Robbie was born, the way his eyes widened when sister met sister, the way his laughter bred with sobbing when Robbie wrapped her hand around Tina's index and middle fingers, how he crawled into the small hospital bed with Lily and their babies, his head on Lily's breast, and stared across at his little Robbie, who was nestled in his wife's arm next to a his cozy Tina.

Beautiful memories. Too beautiful. And too many. She

could never leave the man with whom she'd made and shared those memories. Never. Not now. Not ever.

So the three tickets would go unused, at least in the intended, most traditional sense. Lily and her daughters would never hand them in, or redeem them, for their passage on a bus bound for Vegas. But the tickets would find another use for Lily—as keepsake. Not a *keepsake*, just keepsake, which is here used more as an adjective than as a noun, something to qualify, describe, and frame the persons, places, and things in Lily's life, to give her perspective similar to how her rooftop gave her perspective, but to give her a perspective different than the perspective her rooftop gave her.

Lily would keep the tickets forever so that she could be reminded of the choices she made, both when and before they were presented to her. When it seemed like life with Bender was too much, when he hurt her with his words, she could turn to those tickets to remind herself that she had made the decision to stay with him. Moreover, she could remind herself of why she chose to stay with him. She could put whatever moment of displeasure that caused her to look at them into overall perspective, weighing a minute instance of hardship against the larger instances of joy and tipping the scales back in Bender's favor.

So too she could turn to the tickets as a cue to recollect Leo's choices, remembering how he chose to spend his scant money on tickets he could never know for certain she'd use, and remembering how Leo had wanted her and her children. Those times that Lily felt worthless at Bender's confrontations, the tickets would remind her of her worth— she was at least worth the few hundred dollars Leo wasted on the unused vouchers, worth even more given what Leo was willing to sacrifice and change for a life with her.

Wasted, no, the few hundred dollars Leo spent on the

tickets was not wasted per se. It was spent to give Lily years upon years of perspective. The tickets were there when she needed them, even after they expired. For the unique perspective they gave her, and for the substitute perspective they gave her when her roof haven was unavailable due to things such as inclement weather, the tickets were a priceless gift.

Less than an hour after Leo left Lily listless on her gable, Lily decided to rejoin the festivities that flourished in her home. She tucked the tickets into her freshman year high school yearbook, which sat on the shelf cattycorner to the attic window. She figured it was a safe and accessible place to lodge them, since Bender would not foreseeably have the inclination to look through a book with nostalgic meaning only to Lily. Plus, it was only natural that her two gateways to salvation lie adjacent to each other, giving her the option to carry her thoughts outside through one and inside through the other.

Lily passed Robbie's room, where she saw her two daughters soundly sleeping, snuggled together in Robbie's small bed. She smiled at the simple splendor of her children and thought, for a brief moment, of joining them in their slumber. She knew better though. T'was wisest to let sleeping babies, much like sleeping dogs, lie.

Sleeping dogs! Lily's mind harked back to Mimi's death, the reason for the day's gathering, which she too had forgotten in all that had happened since she slipped away some time ago. She blamed Leo for the lull in her grieving. It made her feel better to hold someone else accountable.

Lily made her way downstairs, where she discovered that the party was still raging, even though the headcount had noticeably fallen.

It was the type of party that would have made the ancients proud. Four or five people were in the kitchen, throwing back drinks and dipping their dirty fingers into bowls and plates of curdled, discarded foodstuffs. The garbage can had become a makeshift vomitorium, as at least two persons had spit up there.

Bender and Jimmy Hayes were battling each other in a cybernetic arena, playing a videogame where seamlessly pixelated warriors struck each other with fists, weapons, and mystical powers. Then there was Irene, who sat on the loveseat tonguing Mitchell's open mouth as Renner sat pressed up, hard, behind her. Renner's left arm was wrapped around Irene's waist, stroking beneath her blouse, and his eyes were in fixed alternation between Mitchell's mouth and the stiffmost part of Mitchell's excited body.

Looking at the three bodies tangled together on her loveseat, Lily first thought how fortunate it was for Renner that his wife was unable to attend the party. She then pondered the peculiarity of Irene's propensity to hook up with clandestine homosexuals.

Lily felt like an outsider to all that was going on around her. Collections of people were going about their business in ways upon which she could not intrude. Her husband and his friend were playing a two-player game, Irene was engaging in an awkward threesome, and the folks in the kitchen were drunk beyond Lily's interest. There was no place for her in her own home.

She chose to find a place with the aid of a bottle. As she grabbed a fifth of gin and a two-liter of lemon-lime soda, she decided to drink herself silly, to the point that, perhaps, one of the goings-on would appeal to her, or to the point that, perhaps, she'd lose consciousness if not conscience. When in Rome, Lily figured.

Sitting on the bottom step of the lower-level staircase, Lily chugged gulps of gin straight from the fifth and chased them with sips of lemon-lime soda straight from the two-liter. She watched Bender and Jimmy Hayes play round after round of their videogame. Bender was repeatedly triumphant, not necessarily because of his skill but because he was not as distracted as Jimmy Hayes.

It was impossible for Jimmy Hayes to keep his eyes off of the love triangle on the loveseat for any length of time. He could not remain as unaware as Bender, who appeared oblivious to the way Mitchell, Renner, and Irene were going at each other so insistently.

Irene had come to straddle Mitchell, with Renner sitting on his knees beside them. Renner's right hand had trekked to the inside of Irene's undergarments, and he played with her womanhood with unbearable yearning. As Irene rode herself against Renner's occupied digits, his hand pressed against Mitchell's swollen sex, grinding up against it to the rhythm of Irene's movements like a flexible fleshy barrier between two very different worlds, enjoying the best of both.

Jimmy Hayes liked what he was watching. His mouth watered at the spectacle before him. This was the type of thing he usually paid good money to see. He didn't have enough charisma to pick up women, or to keep them, but he had a credit card that allowed him to pay for their mass-marketed video reproductions. He couldn't pass on the chance to see a live, real-life rendition of the sex life he wished he had.

As pleased as Jimmy Hayes was with the free show, Lily was equally displeased. She wasn't used to seeing Irene this way. Irene generally had her wits about her. She was anything but easy, and this type of behavior was disturbingly uncharacteristic of her.

Lily used the faint, lingering odors of sweet jane and bong water as clues to solve the mystery of what had caused Irene's libidinous conduct. For Irene, booze was one thing, and weed was another. Their combination, however, usually made her a ball of hormones, a ball ready for a roll in the hay. Lily concluded that the musty stench of reefer, in part, must have come from Irene's partaking.

Irene was being the self that she was only when she used substances in combination, acting in a way Lily knew for sure Irene would regret later. How embarrassed Irene would feel when she recollected how she'd acted!

It wasn't just Irene's looming disgrace that distressed Lily. She was also upset to see Mitchell and Renner use Irene the way they were using her, not as a subject or object of sex, which would have been okay with Lily, but as the obligatory meat in the sandwich of their otherwise homosexual activity. They were using her so that they could be with each other, and that didn't sit well with Lily.

When she noticed Renner unbuckling his buckle out of the corner of her eye, it was the final straw for Lily. She could not allow things to go any further, to watch Irene go all the way, in any way, with either of these fellows, as a public display of intoxicated attraction.

Still sitting on the steps, Lily spoke to intervene: "Okay, everybody, that's it for today… Time for you all to get the hell out of my house."

It was as if Lily hadn't spoken at all. The voices in the kitchen continued to speak loudly; Bender and Jimmy Hayes played their videogame with no interruption more than the latter's preoccupation with the sex show across the room; and Irene went about kissing Renner as he undid the rest of the bells and whistles holding up his trousers, with Mitchell eying his every movement.

"Party's over!" Lily shouted, rising to her feet. "All of you, out!"

This time, Lily's words reached their intended audience. Irene pulled her mouth away from Mitchell with an astonished look on her face, most likely because she only just then realized where she was and what she was actually doing.

"Get home to your wife, Renner," Lily said snidely.

Again, Irene's look was one of astonishment. Like most people who knew Renner, she often overlooked the fact that he was married since he was always seen in the company of only Mitchell, his wife never in the picture.

With eyes meant to entice, Irene gazed at Mitchell. "Wanna give me a ride home?" she asked.

"Ah, I can't," he responded, breaking eye contact with her, casting his eyes downward, as if to stare at his own arousal.

At Mitchell's words, Renner was intrigued, for he knew that it was he, not Irene, who would get a ride home with Mitchell. He craved the fogged up windows, the shaking of the car in concert with their aggressive stroking.

"I'll give you a ride, Irene."

It was Jimmy Hayes who said this. And he said it in hopes that Irene would be horny and desperate enough to have him by the time they reached her home. And, lucky for him, she was.

Getting rid of the people in the kitchen was far easier than Lily had expected. Lenny, who was a work buddy of Bender's, was perfectly polite upon hearing Lily's instructions. He and his wife, Natalie, split the scene with jolly drunken pleasantries.

The checkout girl from the gas station where Lily regularly and reluctantly purchased Bender's chewing tobacco had been in the kitchen too. Her name was Brenda, and she was accompanied by some guy with whom neither Lily nor Bender were acquainted. She didn't give Lily any lip when Lily decided to abruptly call an end to the evening.

But she deliberately took her time in leaving, sticking around for a few extra minutes to shop the kitchen and salvage some unopened or unemptied beer cans and a plate or two of food.

Bender remained seated on the couch, in front of the television and game console, as the last of their guests exited. He switched the videogame from the two-player battle to his favorite football game, where he could hit the field against a preloaded player profile.

Once the house was cleared, Lily began to clean up the mess Mimi's wake had left behind.

"Geez, Lily, I never realized what a dirty little tramp Irene was," Bender chuckled to, or at, Lily.

"What?" Lily demanded defensively.

"She's a dirty little tramp, that Irene. The way she was messing around with Mitchell and Renner right here in the middle of a party, right where everyone could see her—only a tramp would do that... Know what I mean?"

"Yeah, Bender, I get what you're saying... But it's not true. Irene isn't a tramp."

"Coulda fooled me, honey. I saw the way she was acting."

"She was drunk and high—that's not how she usually acts."

"Come on, Lily! She doesn't act like that? I saw her acting like that right in front of me, in front of anyone who could see. Her actions speak louder than your words."

Bender was laughing, and his laughter infuriated Lily.

"Well, you don't know her like I do... You never took the time to get to know her."

"Shit, maybe I should've taken the time to get to know her! Looks like she would have been a blast to get to know...

Would've been a good time getting to know that dirty little tramp."

"Shut up, Bender."

"Oh, I'm sorry… I forgot. You used to be like that too, huh? Is that the kind of stuff you used to do when the two of you went out together? Drunken threesomes and orgies… I bet you're jealous of her, that she still gets to be a slut while you're stuck married to me. Poor Lily, doesn't get to be a slut anymore… You're nothing but a joke that isn't funny."

"That's right, Bender. I'm jealous of Irene, that's why I'm defending her… I'm jealous that I can't be a whore because I'm married… But at least I remember that I'm married, which is more than I can say about that punk-ass Renner who just cheated on his wife… Yeah, you're friends are sooo much better than mine."

"Renner's an idiot… That's not news to me, or to anyone. It wasn't really cheating anyway. He was drunk and Irene was all over him… What was he supposed to do? They were just messing around. It's not like they had sex or anything."

"Are you serious? You don't consider what he did cheating? He was with a woman who wasn't his wife, Bender. That's the definition of cheating… I suppose you do that kinda shit too then, maybe more."

"No, I don't. Sex and foreplay aren't that important to me. When I want something, I get it from you. There's no need to go elsewhere."

The reality was that Bender didn't really want anything all that often. Their couplings and intimacies had grown fewer and farther between over the course of their marriage, such that Lily could count months rather than days or weeks since they'd last been together. In her single life, Lily had seen more sex in one month than she came to see in the most recent year of marriage with Bender.

"Oh, it's so nice that your fidelity is for such noble reasons, Bender. Really, I'm touched."

"Stop, Lily, before this gets ugly," Bender warned.

And Lily obeyed her husband. She returned to her cleaning, her psyche burning with a red-hot rawness. As she picked up empty cans and bottles, as she amassed dirty plates and filmed eating utensils, as her husband sat by lazing, Lily thought of Leo and his offer. She questioned whether she'd made the right decision. It was a question she'd ask herself frequently from this day forward.

~ 9 ~

When Leo left for Las Vegas, he left without a lot of things and left a lot of things without. He left without most of his belongings, and without the object of his longings. He was devastated when Lily and her children didn't show up at the Greyhound station. Like a lovesick protagonist in a trite chick flick, he stared out of the bus window as it drove away, hoping to see his Flower running toward him with her arms outstretched, howling his name. But he never saw her. She never came.

He blew town without telling any others he was leaving, not his bandmates, not his roommate, not even his own brother. He left without proper exit, without proper excuse, leaving his roommate without his due portion of the rent, his band without a guitarist, and Lily without a best friend.

Only Lily had known he was leaving, and only Lily knew where he was when those others starting asking. She kept quiet, however, so that she wouldn't have to explain how she became privy to such classified information.

It wasn't until nearly a week after Leo fled that those-he-left-without discovered his whereabouts. Leo had mailed each of his bandmates, his former roommate, and his brother a postcard from Las Vegas. The postcards were very similar in what attractions they depicted and identical in their messages, but for the different addressees and addresses. Lily was not surprised to not receive one.

If Bender had been there when the mail was delivered, he probably would have killed the postman. He was livid when he read Leo's message:

Hey Bender,

Here's a postcard from Vegas, my new
home! I decided to come here to go chase
my dreams. Sorry I didn't tell you I was
leaving, but I left spur of the moment.
Good luck with everything. Hope to see
you when I come back to visit.

Leo

Bender read the postcard to Lily three times, each time
louder than the time before. Its script became the refrain of a
song that vilified Leo, the chorus he returned to after singing
select words and phrases of his own creation. Foul names,
coarse language, and condescending conclusions, Bender
made express his newfound hatred of Leo.

More than she paid attention to Bender's words, Lily
paid attention to Leo's. "Spur of the moment" was not an
accurate term to describe Leo's exodus, not bearing in mind
the things he'd told her or the tickets he'd given her. It was a
premeditated and predetermined act, not a "spur of the
moment" decision. Lily knew that Leo was a liar.

But she understood his motives for lying. They'd had to
have been analogous to her own, why she kept her mouth
shut when asked if she'd heard from Leo or knew where he
was. Her saying "no" or "I don't know" was the same as Leo
writing "spur of the moment." They were falsities of
convenience, equally proffered to sidestep accountability.

And just as Bender had believed Lily when she feigned
ignorance, he believed Leo's spurious "spur of the moment"
statement. Indeed, it was easy to believe that Leo left spur of
the moment, as Bender, Bob, Mitchell, and Renner all agreed
that any responsible musician would undoubtedly provide
his brethren with advance notice of his envisioned plans to
abscond. The average day job dictated two weeks' notice,

and artistry warranted even more.

Day in and day out, Bender droned on and on about how irresponsible it was for Leo to move without letting the members of Bender's Bender know ahead of time.

"He should have told us and helped us find his replacement."

"Why didn't he let us know? We had gigs on the books already! Now we'll have to cancel."

"We can't find anybody on short notice like this. Do you have any idea how long it'll take a new guy to learn our music?"

"Blah, blah, blah... Leo is a loser."

Leo's sudden disappearance caused a remarkable thing. It shifted Bender's critical focus off of Lily. Leo was public enemy number one now, not Lily. For the first time in a long time, Lily was not the object of Bender's disaffections. Leo was.

By no means did this make Lily happy, but it made her a little safer, more protected and less endangered, than she would have been had Leo still been in the equation. Though she winced every time Bender spoke damningly of Leo, Lily realized that this was the second priceless gift Leo had given her.

On top of his own self-interests, Leo had asked Lily to go with him so that she could get away from an abusive husband and find something better. Both of these things were accomplished when Leo left, even if not in the precise manner he'd hoped for or expected.

Lily no longer had the need to leave her abusive husband because the abusiveness had left her husband, giving way to a better Bender. For how ever long it would last, and how ever unintentional, how ever relative, it really was a priceless gift, and it really came from Leo.

Bender had a new target to exploit. He cut Leo down as a musician, tagging Leo a no-talent hack who cared more about his stage presence than about his musical performance. Harsh words, but every time Bender mentioned Leo as a failed musician was one less time he mentioned Lily as a failed wife or mother.

Leo's talent, or perceived lack thereof, wasn't the only of Leo's faults at which Bender picked. He dredged through everything he knew about Leo to find any and all things that could give way to contemptuous catcalling.

For Leo's status as a ladies' man, Bender coined him a "man-whore." It was an absurd term, but it diverted the name-calling away from Lily. Leo was a "fag" for wearing women's clothing, which obviously clashed with some of Bender's other conclusions but nonetheless did its job of directing unwanted attention to someone other than Lily.

Bender made fun of Leo's hair and hygiene, his living arrangements and employment status, his phony accent and candid personality, and his name.

"Leo London... What the hell kind of name is *that*?"

It was as if Bender had been programmed with a preset amount of hatred he had to vent daily. If he got the requisite amount out of his system within the set period of time, he was fine and, dare say, friendly. If, however, he didn't get it all out, he was a confrontation waiting to happen.

To whom, where, or what his anger was delivered was not as important as the fact that it was delivered. It had long been Lily on the receiving end, but now Leo took Lily's customary place in the process.

Having another repository for Bender's rage made Lily's predicament both more comfortable and uncomfortable at the same time. It was nice to be out of the sour limelight, but heartbreaking to hear Bender say such awful things about Leo.

Time and again, Bender's rambling insults about Leo turned into insinuations or retellings of gossip and speculation. Some of the very things for which Bender criticized Leo gave way to apparently conflicting conclusions.

For example, Bender ridiculed Leo for having a fake accent and made-up last name. But to support his inference that Leo was homosexual, Bender took Leo's last name and British accent as true features. Since Leo did not share these true features with his "brother," in whose home he intermittingly resided, that had to mean that Leo's brother was not at all his brother but rather his lover.

And that was something patently incongruous with some of Bender's other conclusions, such as the tall tale he related about Leo being a daddy. He deducted that Leo was the father of a toddler named Clover, whose mother, Maria, used to be a groupie in Leo's league of ladies. Maria never made such allegations, but her stalking of Leo was implied paternity for Bender's purposes.

Lily had done enough Punnet squares to know Leo wasn't Clover's father. She knew there was no way Clover's rich brown eyes could have resulted from a cross of Leo's grey eyes and Maria's blue eyes. But it was too bothersome to explain this to Bender. Why give him reason to react against her?

According to Bender, Leo was a bogus, cross-dressing homosexual ladies' man who had a bastard son and screwed his brother. He didn't bathe, had no talent, and couldn't hold a job. So on and so forth.

While the things Bender said about Leo were pretty extreme, Bender did, in fact, have good reason to be riled at Leo. Even Lily couldn't deny that what Leo had done was incredibly unprofessional and ill-mannered. He left a struggling band struggling even harder. A band without a guitarist isn't really much of a band, after all.

They had to cancel shows, and some of the cancellations resulted in lost money. The booking fees they'd paid in advance were nonrefundable, and all the money spent on signs, fliers, and other promotions was completely wasted.

Professional courtesy dictated a standard Leo had not met. If he had told the other members of Bender's Bender about his plans, they could have worked together to find and acclimate his replacement. The band could have trained the fledgling and given him time to learn the music while they continued to play out with Leo up until his departure.

But Leo never gave them this courtesy. Instead he left them hanging. It was two months before the remainder of Bender's Bender found a suitable guitarist, and when they found him it took two more months to make him stage-ready. And he only hit the stage three times with the band before finding a new calling.

That new guitarist, Adam, was much younger than his new bandmates, somewhere in his very early-20s, and wasn't really into heavy rock music. He took his place in Bender's Bender as a temporary position, a chance to build his musical curriculum vitae and network with other musicians. When he was approached by the percussionist of a folk band who'd been in the audience of his second and third official performances with Bender and his crew, Adam dropped out of Bender's Bender. He'd left as quickly as he came.

Bender didn't abhor Adam for moving on. He abhorred Leo. The whole mess had been Leo's fault from the beginning. So it was Leo's fault that Adam left, since Adam wouldn't have been there at all if it hadn't been for Leo's neglect.

After Adam removed himself, Bender's Bender was once again tasked to find a replacement guitarist. The guys auditioned player after player, inviting one here and one there to join the band, but ultimately losing each because of some creative difference, objection, or inability. It was a montage of unsuitable replacements with varying degrees of talent, personality, and long hair.

This one was too inexperienced. That one was too demanding. This one was too young. That one was too old. This one wasn't outgoing enough. And that one wanted only to take center stage. Bender's Bender was a Goldilocks unable to find Baby Bear's guitarist. No one was "just right."

It went on like this for nearly two years, a drawn-out trial unaccompanied by tribulation. Bender grew more and more frustrated with the situation as time passed. Though he still hated Leo, his expression of that hate changed from criticism of Leo to his wonted verbal abuse of Lily, perchance because he didn't want to acknowledge that Leo had been some type of glue, an adhesive rockstar polymer, that had held the band together for so long.

If he'd had his way, Bender would have never given up on the search for someone to fill Leo's slot. He would have kept going until he found someone who could spur the band's meteoric rise to stardom. But something else happened to thwart the progress of Bender's Bender.

A damning fate came in the form of Bob Cargon's incapacitation. Bob, the shifty-eyed meth-head drummer, had insufflated one too many lines of his favored drug, causing him to suffer an infirmity far worse than the minimal deterioration of his nasal cavity and noticeable yellowing of his teeth. While tweaked out on a high-grade score one afternoon, he had a brain attack, or, in other words, a stroke.

Years of meth use had finally caught up with Bob. A hefty lineup of snorts, snuffles, and sniffs had weakened the blood vessels in his brain, to the point where one little vessel could take it no more. That little vessel broke and burst, causing blood to leak into Bob's brain.

Flying high, Bob wasn't able to notice anything wrong with his body for a while. He went about his daily doped-up activities. He was rollerblading in the park when his body caved in because of what had happened in his brain. He lost his footing on the concrete path and fell over. Like tumbleweed, he trundled down the hill at his side, landing at its bottom between a rock and a hard place. He laid there for just under an hour before a group of eight young Girl Scouts found him during a nature walk with their troop leaders. The girls had been on a search for butterflies when they discovered his mangled, bleeding body.

As one troop leader led the startled girls away from the site and went to call for help, the second leader stayed behind to look after the body. She urgently poked at Bob with the toe of her shoe several times, both in an attempt to rouse him and to satiate her imp of the perverse. She thought he was dead and wanted to know what it'd feel like to kick a dead body.

But Bob wasn't dead, just irreparably disabled. He was rushed off to a nearby hospital where a less-than-famous neurosurgeon did his best to repair the damage.

It turned out that the rebellious vessel that burst had been a resident of the anterior region of Bob's brain, in the neighborhood of his left posterior interior frontal gyrus. When it burst, it flooded its 'hood, which those in the know knew as Broca's area.

The result? Broca's aphasia, a neurological disorder that left Bob unable to produce spoken or written language with any amount of ease or accuracy. What words he said were usually said in isolation and always disjointed from one another. He could no longer speak in sentences. He was like a prisoner in his own broken body, incapable of expressing the words that filled him. So too he had difficulty understanding the communications of others, often transposing the subjects and objects of even the simplest of sentences.

Since Bob's family and friends had long ago disowned him because of his drug use and refusal to seek help or rehabilitation, Bob became a ward of the state upon his impairment. And any hopes for the future of Bender's Bender became nothing short of a castle in the sky.

Replacing a guitarist was one thing, but replacing a guitarist **and** a drummer was another. If the band had once been a human body, Bender had been its head, Mitchell and Renner had been its arms, and Bob and Leo had been its legs. One of it legs was chopped off when Leo left, and Bob's handicap removed the other. The band had no legs to stand on, a condition from which full recovery was impossible.

And so ended Bender's Bender.

The initial response from the three other members of the band was concern for their fallen brother. They each visited him in the hospital and showed compassion and grief in their own unique ways. But soon enough their outreaches faded and shifted focus. Both Mitchell and Renner gave up on the band, and on Bob and on Bender, and on the performance of music in general.

Bender, however, wasn't ready to give up on Bob or on music. He realized that Bob's days of being a drummer were over, but his days of being a friend were not. As it happened, although few people ever realized it, Bender immediately began a tradition of visiting Bob once a week, a tradition he would observe for the rest of his life.

Visiting Bob was not an eventful activity but, rather, something mild. Bender would stop by the institutional home in which Bob had been placed and spend time with him in his room for a while, maybe go for a walk on the grounds or mess around in the recreations room.

Bob could no longer read well, so Bender would often read to him—newspapers, music magazines, comic books, things of that ilk. Sometimes Bender would vent to Bob about things that were troubling him in his daily life or share the male equivalent of gossip with him. Other times, Bender would just lean back in his chair and let silence prevail, being Bob's company for the sake of company alone.

Bob was Bender's rooftop, his set of hidden Vegas-bound bus tickets. He was where Bender went to take a break from the world and find his own perspective about things. No matter how bad things seemed in Bender's life, Bender needed only to look at Bob to be reminded that things could be much, much worse.

Because Bob could barely communicate in any meaningful way, Bender was never quite sure whether Bob actually comprehended the things he told him. But the fact of the matter was Bob did. He just wasn't able to convey it.

If Bob had been able to carry on a conversation, he might have told Bender about another person who'd visited him— Leo.

A short while after Leo's brother informed him of Bob's unfortunate circumstances, Leo flew back to Pittsburgh to check in on his one-time friend. He phoned Lily a few weeks prior to his trip, to ask if she and Bender would like to get together for drinks or a meal. When Lily told Bender about Leo's call, he laughed in her face. There was no way in hell he was going to meet up with that de facto defector.

For days, Bender ranted and raved about the absurdity of Leo's request. He went on and on about how Leo had betrayed him and now had no place in their lives. Leo was a traitor, and he cursed his wife for even taking his call.

What happened after that was, as they say, one for the books—a story already told. One of passion, adultery, and oral sex.

After Lily told Bender what she had done, Bender went and told Bob later that very same day. He turned to Bob to profess his woes. Unloading burdens on Bob had the same effect of going to a priest or a prostitute. It was a confidential transaction, the subject matter of which was expected to never be explicitly shared with anyone else.

Bender's recount of Lily's confession was detailed and blunt. About twenty minutes after Bender spilled the beans, Bob tried to speak.

"Here... ... he... Leo... ... Bender... ... ... told... ... Lily... about... ... me... was... ... today."

Those two handfuls of words took Bob approximately three minutes to articulate. Bender couldn't make any sense of them though—he took them as a jumbled sentiment of sympathy on Bob's part, or at least a reiteration of some of the key words he'd just said.

What Bob was in fact trying to say was something quite different. Bob's scrambled code was meant to be deciphered as such: "Leo was here today, Bender. He told me about Lily."

But Bender didn't know how to solve Bob's puzzle, and he never understood what Bob had said in his mind before the words came out wrong from his mouth. Nor did he understand that Bob wasn't imbued with the trustworthiness of a holy man or holey woman.

So Bender would never learn that Leo had gone to see Bob that same day or that seeing Bob had been the reason for Leo's brief visit to his hometown.

Lily had known the purpose of Leo's momentary return, but she never told Bender, not because she wanted to withhold information, but because she didn't consider it relevant or necessary information. And, in any event, it came to be trivial in light of the other things she had to tell Bender about Leo's visit.

And while Lily knew about Leo's meeting with Bob, she didn't know about Bender's. She had no idea that he had a standing practice of dropping in on Bob weekly. True, she was aware that Bender had gone to see Bob when he was in the hospital, and that he made his way to the institutional facility where Bob had been placed. But it never occurred to her that Bender gave his time to Bob with a dedicated rate of recurrence.

Whenever Bender would leave the house to go see Bob, Lily assumed he was embarking on some other ordinary endeavor. Namely, she presumed that he was heading out to hit a bar for karaoke or an open stage night, which was the primary way he maintained his relationship with music after the complete dismemberment of Bender's Bender.

It was on these inferior stages that Bender was forced to pursue his rockstar ambitions. He was hard-pressed to find anyone who wanted to pick up and start a band with a lead singer already in his early late-40s. The type of music he longed to perform was no longer popular, his vocal style was archaic and banal, and his lyrics were throwbacks to a different era.

But what wasn't good enough for the generation of a new group was good enough to entertain small collections of singers who found vicarious stardom by singing the altered karaoke tracks of well-known artists. Bender's performances of Anthrax, Suicidal Tendencies, and Pantera songs always stirred bar-going listeners. Little did Bender know, however, that what he thought were cheers were actually jeers, ill-intended merriment and applause at his heartfelt renditions. It was Bender who was no longer popular and was archaic and banal. Bender was the throwback. And he was none the wiser.

Part of the pretentious praise Bender received for his secondhand performances came in the form of free drinks from drunkards at the bars. High fives and taps on his shoulder were the precursors to discussions that always ended in phrases like "Let me buy you a drink, buddy." Bender received these actions and phrases as accolades, rather than as the consolations and condolences they were meant to be when submitted.

Without fail, one drink would lead to another, and Bender was usually trashed by the time he got home. Thankfully, Lily was smart. She'd already seen how alcohol made Bender's hairline trigger even thinner. So she restrained from interacting with him when he came home sloshed.

She would sit tight in their bedroom while he was out playing and simulate sleep when she heard him stumble up the steps, because anything else, even a benign action, had the potential to set him off on a rampage

Something as simple as telling him "goodnight" could get him started. At least it did one night. On that night, he'd come home to find her watching television on the couch. He went to the kitchen to toss down some leftovers. She came in while he was eating and told him she was going to go to bed.

"Goodnight," she said.

"What the hell is that supposed to mean, Lily?" he asked her, with spaghetti sauce dripping from his lips.

"Nothing, Bender," she defended. "I'm going to bed."

"Don't tell me what to do, Lily!" he screamed at her. "Just because you're going to bed, that doesn't mean I have to too. I'm not tired, and I don't want to lie next to your pig body."

"No, no. I didn't mean that you should go to bed. I was just saying…"

"You were just saying what?" Bender butted in.

He didn't give her time to answer.

"Here's some slop, pig!" he said, picking up his plate of microwaved spaghetti and hurling it in her direction, not aiming at her but at the floor beneath her, which was where the plate landed. Chunks of broken ceramic and jets of sauce shot outward and upward from the point of impact.

"Clean up this mess," Bender demanded as he stood up and charged out of the kitchen.

And Lily did as she had been instructed.

Episodes like this were the reason Lily decided it was better to entirely avoid her husband on nights when he'd been drinking. Since she couldn't know for sure on which nights he would imbibe, she treated every night that he went out like a potentially threatening darkness.

As it was, Bender got belligerently drunk once or twice a week, if that. Even though the odds were in Lily's favor, she wasn't willing to take the gamble. It was a very smart decision on her part.

But it wasn't always drunkenness that embroidered Bender. It was often the mundane elements of his daily existence. And while it was possible for Lily to avoid Bender at night by faking sleep, there was little she could feign to avoid him by day. So it simply became a matter of sidestepping him. She would busy herself in another part of the house, or take a rooftop retreat.

When she couldn't avoid Bender, Lily tried to placate him. At some point over the years, she'd realized the futility of defending or explaining herself against his verbal affronts. He never listened to what she had to say, and her words only added fuel to his fire. Letting him carry on, agreeing with whatever he said, no matter how insulting, was the only way to survive.

In order to do this, Lily herself had to stop listening to what Bender said. But unlike her words to him, his words to her did not add fuel to any fire. They were far too cold and raw to do that.

On good days, when she was otherwise content or preoccupied with something else, Lily was able to deflect his invectives, like pellets of hail ricocheting off of a windshield. Not all days, however, were good days—and not all hail rained down in pellets. Some orbs of hail were the size of golf balls, the kind that doesn't bounce off of a windshield but, instead, cracks it. And just like those sleeted golf balls, sometimes Bender's comments hit Lily hard and gave way to an intricate web of damage.

Whether by dusk or dawn, be they deflected or damaging, most of Bender's insults were criticisms of Lily's household management or parenting skills, and though Lily was proficient in both respects, Bender still found reason to denigrate her daily.

But why? Why spit slander and slurs? Why look for something, anything, to pick apart?

The answer is quite simple, really: Misery loves company.

Bender felt like a failure. He was unfulfilled without the steady presence of music in his life, and working his day job wasn't at all filling. Nothing could appease his hunger for recognition as a musician—nothing but that very recognition, which he surely wasn't getting. Neither the bustle at bars nor how he misconstrued it satisfied him. It wasn't substantial or strong enough to make him happy.

His time was running out, the spotlight was fading, and he knew it.

The only thing he could do to make himself feel better was to make someone else feel worse. And Lily was the perfect target. So he habitually turned against her, to bring her down, to make damningly sure that he was not alone in his misery.

But it wasn't all Bender's fault. Lily was at least partially to blame. She just held steady and let it happen. She let him bring her down with him—perhaps one time too many.

~ 10 ~

Lily turns to look at Cookie once the trickle of her tinkle no longer sounds. She raises her eyebrow, as if to ask by gesture alone, "Aren't you forgetting something?"

Though Cookie is already standing, she sits back down on the toilet.

"Cookie done piss pot and almost forgot to wipe," Cookie says with a whistle. She moves her hand toward the roll of toilet paper posted on the wall beside her and gathers a handful of tissue in her palm.

"Oh, dangernat! … This is the good stuff!" Cookie shouts. "Not like that hard stuff they give 'em Cookie at the home place… Nice 'n soft!"

Cookie proceeds to wipe herself with the superior toilet tissue. When she is done, she wipes herself again. And then again. She collects a few more handfuls of the tissue, balls it up into a few separate bundles, and shoves the wads into her pants pockets and both cups of her bra.

She rises from the commode and redresses her pants, turning to leave the restroom.

Lily again raises her eyebrow.

Ah, maternal instinct! A mother is always a mother, even after her children are grown. Her instinct to rear may not emerge until she bears child, but, once emerged, it never leaves. Lily was forever a mother, to her own children and to the rest of the world.

Cookie clunks over to the sink and washes her hands carelessly while Lily stands by to make sure the chore is done to conclusion.

Cookie grabs two disposable hand towel napkins and dries her hands before turning to leave.

Satisfied with Cookie's display of bathroom etiquette, Lily follows Cookie out the door. In her hand, she once again holds her sacred scrap of paper, the lost and recovered treasure that had brought her to join Cookie in the bathroom in the first place.

When Lily and Cookie emerge from the bathroom together, no one looks at them in judgment. Lily figures it's because most of the people here today are aware of Cookie's state, and of her longtime relationship with Lily—why would anyone be surprised to discover that they had been together in the lavatory?

Though she loves Cookie and is comforted to have her in attendance, Lily does not want to spend what's left of the evening with her. Less than half an hour remains before the funeral home closes for the night, and Lily would rather spend that time in quiet calmness than in dealing with Cookie's excessive verbiage. Lily has enough on her mind and doesn't need to add looking after Cookie to the list of things that plague her.

There is no polite way for Lily to tell Cookie this. So, instead, she accompanies Cookie on a search for the personal care assistant who had brought her to the funeral home this evening.

Together, Lily and Cookie paddle through clusters of people. Lily hopes that she will find Cookie's aid in the hallway or smaller room, since she does not, under any circumstances, want to enter the main receiving area of the funeral home.

Entering the smaller room which Lily has called home for the whole day, Lily spots an obese young woman, whom she does not recognize, dressed in scrubs, standing by the door to the smokers' patio where she expects Celia is still situated.

"Oh there's my Judy!" says Cookie, taking notice of the girl as well.

Lily escorts Cookie to Judy. As Cookie begins telling Judy about the soft toilet paper she encountered in the bathroom, Lily turns and walks away.

Walking back to the couch, which still holds her heat and body's impression, Lily notices that Leo is standing there by himself. His conversation with Jimmy Hayes must have concluded, and he now stands there alone, as if waiting for something or someone. Lily wants to believe that he is waiting for her.

She wonders if this was how he looked awaiting her arrival at the bus terminal nearly twenty years ago— standing tall, his body rigid over his firmly planted legs, his arms across his chest, his hands clasped beneath his lowered chin. Years ago, his hands might have been clasped to pray for Lily's appearance, but now they are clasped out of something else—maybe convenience, maybe circumstance.

His head turns, and his eyes open wide, every time someone walks past him, and he bows again when he registers the face of each person. Years ago, his head might have turned, his eyes might have opened wide, to search for Lily's visage. Is it for this reason that they do so today?

Lily watches as Leo's lips form a tiny, kindhearted smile. Lily smiles too, though she works carefully to hide it. Years ago, their smiles might have marked the start of a new life together, but now they mark nothing. His smile isn't even meant for her. It is meant for Jimmy Hayes, who is again at Leo's side, with two Styrofoam cups of coffee in his hands.

He hands one to Leo, and Leo takes a sip as they pick up their conversation where they left off.

A little let down, Lily walks over to the couch and sits. She lets the men go about their conversation without remark on her part.

Back on her couch, she thinks of then, of now, and of the years that elapsed between them. How different things would have been, she ruminates, had she gone to Vegas with Leo.

This isn't, of course, the first time she has thought about this. She pondered it hundreds of times over the years. In her mind, she had lived an assortment of lives with Leo.

They all started exactly the same and ended somewhat alike, opening with delight and progressing to despair. This was something of Lily's inadvertent design—a way of allowing her to confront her desires while also justifying her decision. Beautiful beginnings to her lives with Leo made her long for an alternative. Troublesome conclusions reminded her that, at best, any life with Leo would have been only the lesser of two evils, if that.

She could not picture a life with Leo that was not wrought with complication—there could be no life lived happily ever after. Something always popped up to prevent their fairytale ending, which said a lot about Lily's outlook on life and living. Since it was impossible for her to imagine an idyllic existence, Lily had no goal to motivate her, no line that had to be met, no line that shouldn't, or couldn't, be crossed.

She put up with things that happened to and around her because she believed she had to. Change was futile. Something bad was bound to transpire at some point, whether now or later, here or there, with Bender or with Leo.

But before each of Lily's fabled sagas reached their unique, unhappy open-ends, they all began the same, in a way different than Leo had intended. A vital fact remained true, however: She never went to meet Leo at the bus terminal on the night he left. Leo still left without her and her children. It was later that they ventured west to join him.

Another fact that was accurately represented in Lily's make-believe world was that the tickets Leo had given her were nonrefundable, but could be traded in within 45 days of their face date for a 50% discount toward the purchase price of future tickets.

Lily always dreamt herself trading the tickets in for a new set at the eleventh hour, for a last-minute later departure to the same destination. By luck, chance, or whatever, she envisioned herself able to quickly and easily find Leo upon their touchdown in Sin City.

Granted, this was a weak part of her storyline, a deus ex machina to solve her plot problems. But it served its purpose and satisfied Lily, who was, in the end, her stories' only critic.

As the common thread of her unrealities continued, she found Leo performing an acoustic set during the off-time at a dinner theater that wasn't very popular. She and the girls entered inconspicuously, against the hazy light of the moderately populated venue. As they made their way to a small, round table, Leo took notice of them. His voice cracked and his fingers stumbled when he saw them. He lost his place in the song he was performing.

Leo struggled to get back on track, and, when he did, he rushed through the rest of the song. When he was done playing the tune, he chucked his guitar to his side and jumped off of the stage to run to Lily and her children. He burst into tears as he wrapped his arms around them.

What followed after that was pretty predictable. It played out as a rapidly progressing timeline of compelling moments. Smiles. Laughter. Hugs. Kisses. Settling into Leo's small apartment. Eating dinner together. And sex.

Ground-breaking, earth-quaking sex. Lily devoted a great deal of time and thought to the sex she conceived. It was the headlining act of her fantasies, and it varied from time to time, depending on Lily's particular cravings.

But it wasn't the variations in sex that contrasted Lily's lives with Leo. What distinguished them was what happened later in the story, at some point further down the rapidly progressing timeline, in the chronicles of her cast of characters.

From the broad base of one story, a sundry of other stories branched out and gave way to divergent destinies for Lily, Leo, Tina and Robbie, and Bender. Of this kindling, Lily had her pet twigs, a few specific scenarios she revisited on frequent occasion.

While these scenarios were more a part of Lily's thought process in the years immediately following Leo's leave, they were something that she never let go of, not even after she let go of Leo after their illicit coupling.

Ah, now is so much later than then, but the scenarios are still fresh in her mind. She is able to revive them at the drop of hat. And although no hat has dropped, at least not to Lily's knowledge, she decides to revive them at present.

Scenario #1: Lily and Leo, on the Lam. *A few days after Lily and her girls settle into their new home with Leo, after the tingle of sex with Leo dulls a little, Lily's heart starts to pound. There's a ringing in her ears. A sixth sense is awakened. She knows that something is afoot. But what, she does not know.*

She feels as though all eyes are upon her. She is being watched. She rushes around corners, always checks her back. Those people who are whispering, are they whispering about her?

She's sitting at home with Tina and Robbie, kneeled down

in front of the coffee table, playing a memory-match card game while Leo is at work. Unexpectedly, Leo bursts through the door.

"We have to leave!" he shouts.

Lily springs to her feet and runs over to Leo.

"Why? What's going on?"

Leo whispers, and, yes, he is whispering about her, and to her as well, "He's here, Flower. He found us."

"Who?"

"Who do you think? ... Bender!"

"Oh shit," Lily whines.

Slightly less serendipitously than Lily had found Leo, Bender had found him too. Bender's timing was off though— he strolled into Leo's dinner theater venue during a time when Leo was not there.

Leo learned about Bender's visit when he went into work that night. The hostess greeted him with unwelcomed news. She told him that a thick, angry fellow had been in earlier that day, toting around photographs of his estranged bandmate, wife, and kids. The hostess told Leo she hadn't been forthright with the man, but that she couldn't say whether anyone else at the restaurant had. Leo knew that it was only a matter of time before Bender found out that he worked there.

"I knew this would happen, Leo... I knew he'd never let me and the girls go... I don't know what he'll do if he finds us."

"Let's not stick round to find out then... Get the girls ready. Just throw some stuff together... We'll leave tonight... I just need to take care of a few things first."

Only hours after she'd finished unpacking the last of their sparse belongings, Lily finds herself packing them again.

She tosses clothes into their bags without folding them, and leaves what will not fit behind.

As she's shoving nonperishable foodstuffs into a bag, Leo again bursts through the door.

"Let's go," he says, as he grabs the bags she had placed by the door.

Lily stops packing the food bag. She lifts Robbie into her arms and leads Tina by the hand. Swiftly, they run down the steps of the apartment building in which they'd only momentarily resided. Leo is loading Lily's bags into the trunk of a worn Chevy Cavalier that's probably only a decade younger than Lily.

"Where did this car come from?" Lily inquires as she pushes her daughters into the backseat.

"I sold my Les Paul," Leo offers offhandedly.

Lily stops what she is doing with a start, "You did WHAT?"

"I sold my guitar, Flower," Leo shrugs. "It doesn't matter to me anymore. All that matters is getting the hell out of here as quickly as we can."

He slams the trunk shut and walks over to Lily, pulling her close to his chest. He shoves his hand toward the back of her neck, scooping her long hair in his hand and cupping it to the back of her head, as he draws her face to his for a violent, hard, beautiful kiss.

"Get in," he instructs, opening the passenger side door, before running over to the other side of the car and diving into the driver's seat.

Leo slams his foot onto the gas pedal and they speed away. They pass through the neon of the Vegas night toward a blanket of black, a sprawling panorama of shadowed tumbleweed and buried bull skulls.

Their destination is California, but not any well-known spot. They'll find a territory without a lot of life—somewhere with the least amount of stores and bars, somewhere that isn't too hip or fun, somewhere Bender would never expect them to go.

When they land in Somewhere, California, they feel safe. Leo finds a job as a gas station attendant at a truck stop in propinquity to the sleazy motel they now call home. Things are going smoothly until Leo gets word that someone's looking for him.

It's time for them to again run away. This time, they head to Somewhere, Washington. What happens next is no surprise: They are hunted, again.

Next stop, Somewhere, Montana, followed by Somewhere Wyoming. Just in case Bender had figured out the pattern behind Leo's travel route, Leo mixes things up and heads next to Somewhere, Idaho. He thought he'd throw Bender for a real loop when their next destination was Somewhere, Nevada.

They can't fool him, though. Bender is always one step behind. He always finds their location, no matter what, without finding them.

As a precaution, Lily changes her appearance, and the appearances of her young daughters, several times. That way, Bender will not recognize them should he be in the same place at the same time—and they could elude any vigilante who wanted to prove his worth by uniting a concerned father with his absconded wife and children.

They pass the Canadian border, the Mexican border, back and forth and back again. They can't stay in any one place for too long. Three or four months, at max, pass in each and any place before the questions and suspicions are raised once more.

Lily's daughters are no longer young children, and they

don't understand why they are always on the run. Tina and Robbie barely remember their father anymore, and remember ordinary life even less.

Lily feels guilty for having put her children in a situation like this, and for bringing about the end of Leo's career. She even feels guilty for putting Bender on the hunt, though she's not willing to surrender to him.

This story has no definite end. It plays out like this until the end of time.

The only conclusion it reaches is this: It was a mistake to leave a man like Bender, a strong-willed titan who would do anything to have life lived his way.

No, Lily should not have left him.

"Excuse me," a man's voice calls. "Excuse me?"

Lily's head jerks to the side to see the man standing to her left, near Leo and Jimmy Hayes. She accepts that she's finally been caught, finally been found. Her secret will be a secret no more.

"Yes?" she asks, relieved to see that the man beside her is the funeral home director. Leo and Jimmy Hayes direct their attention to him as well.

"We'll be closing for the evening in approximately fifteen minutes," he says. "We've already asked guests to clear out of the main room, and now we're asking the same of those in here. Tina and Robbie have requested a private viewing before we shut down for the night."

Lily is glad that the funeral director did not ask her if she would like to join her daughters for the private viewing. Because, if he'd asked her that, she would have told him that she most certainly did not. She is relieved that she did not have to exercise shrewdness in the face of an opportunity that begged her to hastily speak.

She's been shrewd throughout this whole ordeal, despite how strange it has been. If she'd had her way, she wouldn't have made such a big deal out of Bender's death, maybe just held a funeral and nothing more, to extend a nicety to their closest friends, to give them a chance to pay their respects before Bender was put to the ground. To Lily, the idea of a "viewing" was pointless since it would be a closed casket affair.

But she hadn't done the planning for this event. She let her daughters do that, so that they could go about their father's farewell as they saw fit. And her daughters would not settle for a funeral alone. They wanted more. So she sat back and let them handle the details while she got lost in other things.

Having a viewing would accomplish something else as well. It would be a distraction. The closer Lily adhered to tradition, the less suspicious she would appear. If there'd just been a funeral without any public display, people probably would have asked questions. And Lily definitely didn't want to answer any of those.

She'd decided to hold herself out as the archetypical grieving widow, lest anyone suspect the executive role she'd played in her husband's death. Killing Bender was, after all, something for which Lily did not want to be widely accredited.

And that's why she continues to carry herself as she's carried herself all day—why she sticks mostly to the corner, alone on the couch, minding her own business, listening in on conversations with little or no remark, avoiding touching or being touched at every chance, and forefending her eyes from locking into even the shortest eye-to-eye gaze.

"I am fine staying here," Lily maintains, though she was not asked.

Even if the funeral home director hadn't told her that Tina and Robbie wanted a private viewing, Lily would have expected as much. She has always been able to anticipate her children's needs and wishes, and the present situation is no exception to this rule.

For most of Tina's and Robbie's lives, she had her finger right on their pulses. When they were children, she flawlessly predicted when they'd be scared and what they wanted to find under the Christmas tree. She knew when they were lying to her or hiding something as teens, and she was gifted at relating well to them as adults.

Lily was a good mother. Lily is a good mother. Always had been, and always would be. Always has been, and always will be. Syntax versus semantics—wording is not important here, it's the meaning that is. From the moment Lily discovered the presence of an embryo in her womb, Lily was no longer number one in Lily's life.

Being a good mom, however, was not something that Lily would have ever claimed to be. Humbleness may prevent some mothers from boasting, but what prevented Lily was good old-fashioned self-doubt. She questioned every move she made when raising her kids and was terribly disappointed in herself when she, like any mother, made the wrong choices at times.

Taking her daughters to live in Vegas was one wrong choice Lily was glad she'd never made. She couldn't imagine that life there could have ever brought them to true joy or success.

Scenario #2: A Lewd Lifestyle for Lily's Little Ones. *Bender does not chase after Lily and the girls. He is happy to let well enough alone—either that or he doesn't notice that they're gone. Lily's new life with Leo is running smoothly. Everyone is having a great time.*

But the great time is more about being together than about anything else. Once the novelty of the living situation and personal relationships wears off, Lily finds herself and her daughters in a foreign place.

They are folks from east of the Midwest transplanted to just north of perdition. Lily had been wild in her own right and way in her younger days, but even her sexual lifestyle was nothing compared to what goes on in Las Vegas on a daily basis.

There are scantily-clad showgirls on billboards that mark practically every mile. Drunk gamblers traverse streets where there are strippers on one corner and hookers on the next.

Lily does the best she can to shield and shelter her little ones from the blatant sex of this town. But she can only do so much. Sex is everywhere around them. It's even in their home.

Though Lily and Leo mute their moans and cries during intercourse, Tina and Robbie are nonetheless lulled to sleep each night by the steady thumping of the headboard against the thin wall that separates their bedroom from that of their mother and her mate. The occasional rattling of handcuffs, the gentle hum of sex toys, and the crack of a whip are some of the last things they hear before they fall asleep.

Leo and Lily are having a hard time making ends meet. Leo's career is not bringing home enough money to support two adults and two kids in a city where the cost of living is excruciatingly high. So Lily is compelled to enter the workforce. She turns to the bustling Vegas strip, where she has a hard time finding a suitable job and is forced to take on employ at a cocktail lounge where partially-nude exotic dancers grace the stage.

Her job is not as a dancer, but as a cocktail waitress. It's not that she is too proud to dance in her skibbies. It's that she is too old. She's pushing 40 now, and no club or lounge would hire a woman that ancient when there are countless starry-eyed prospects out there who are half her age and twice as eager to please.

Lily is required to dress provocatively for work. Tight and tiny is the dress code. High heels and low-cut tops. Whatever highlights Lily's assets. She tries her damnedest to not let her daughters see her in her work garb. Rather than leaving or returning to the apartment in her sexy getups, she carries them with her to work, where she changes before beginning her shift and changes again at her shift's end.

Tina and Robbie may not see the clothes on their mother, but they see them in laundry baskets, on hangers, and in drawers. They see Lily purchase them at stores. The fact that such clothes are hidden away does not negate the fact that they exist. If anything, it makes them more appealing to Lily's explorative young children.

As Lily gets older, her tips at the lounge get smaller. She takes on extra shifts to make extra cash. With both Lily and Leo working more and more hours just to pay the bills, the girls are left home alone quite often once they reach middle school. They have small parties almost every day, inviting other kids over to play. Some bring beer. Some bring pot. And some bring even harder things.

By the time Tina is in her early-teen years, she starts dressing in ways that emphasize her developing form. Like her mother, Tina carries a change of clothes with her when she leaves the apartment. She changes into slutty outfits once she reaches her destination, and changes again before returning home.

Tina is not sexually active—not yet. She does, however, use her supple body to get whatever she wants. She smiles, bats her eyelashes, and sticks her chest out to put teenage boys and grown men alike under her spell. It's a skill that proves very useful as she progresses through high school.

Robbie develops an eating disorder at age 15. She is not fat but she thinks she is because all the women around her are so thin. At least the women who matter most are—the models, the showgirls, the actresses, and Tina. A victim of low self-esteem, Robbie becomes sexually active, something that Lily discovers for the first time when Robbie has a pregnancy scare.

At 17, Tina starts dating a much older man who doesn't mind spoiling her in order to have her on his arm. She starts skipping school two or three times a week. There is no need for her to better her mind when she can use her body to get ahead.

Tina drops out of school in the middle of her senior year, which is around the time Robbie has her second pregnancy scare. Only this time it isn't a scare. It's the real deal. Robbie is pregnant, and Tina is the only one who knows. Tina helps Robbie find a doctor who will perform an abortion. And just like that, bam! Lily's grandchild is killed and vacuumed out of Robbie's body.

Lily is not oblivious as to what's going on with her daughters. While she is unaware of some things, she is painfully aware of others. But she does nothing to reprimand, repair, or prevent the misadventures in their lives. She is too exhausted and jaded to try.

And, besides, this is all of her doing. Tina and Robbie are just living the life she gave them. It was her selfish act that brought them to Vegas, her desire to be with Leo that took them away from a simpler place and deposited them in a city replete with sin. Why chastise them for her wrongdoing?

This story has no definite end. It plays out like this until Lily doesn't want to think about what else could go wrong.

The only conclusion it reaches is this: It was a mistake to leave a man like Bender, a virtual puritan who would never have allowed so much secondhand sex to reach his daughters, who would have worked his ass off to provide for them and ensure their safety and success.

No, Lily should not have left him.

The funeral home director's voice emanates from several

strategically placed speakers affixed to the height of each room's walls: "Attention, guests, we kindly ask that you gather your belongings and say your final farewells to each other at this time. We will be closing for the night in ten minutes, and will reopen tomorrow at 9 a.m. for a brief viewing prior to the funeral service, which will begin at 9:30 sharp."

"Hmm, 9:30 a.m. sharp," Leo repeats. "Hopefully the jetlag will wear off by then."

"You're coming tomorrow?" Jimmy Hayes probes.

"Of course."

Lily gives her right hand and its wrinkled paper stuffing a few quick pumps.

Leo walks over to throw his empty coffee cup into a garbage can cleverly concealed behind a potted plant. "I probably won't bring Celia with me though," he says upon his return. "She's so immature. She's like excess baggage when it comes to these types of things."

"Baggage?" Lily asks, incensed by what Leo'd just said. "You're talking about your wife, Leo. Why would you say something so rude?"

Jimmy Hayes chortles.

"It's the truth… She doesn't know how to handle herself. She's more or less socially dumb. She gets by on her looks, and that's all… She couldn't carry on a meaningful conversation if her life depended on it… I guess that's what I get for marrying one of my models."

Leo's statements confirm one thing, and suggest a few others, to Lily.

His words reveal key elements of the couple's backstory. Celia is one of Leo's models, though Lily hadn't known that fact until now. Regardless, Lily would have never been able to recognize Celia as such, since it wasn't her face that was put on exhibit.

Leo is the founder, owner, and operator—the president, CEO, CFO, and other titles—of a very successful company that manufactures and sells high-end designer belts and belt buckles. His company is called Young Buck Belts & Buckles.

This is the fame that Leo's move to Las Vegas allowed him to find.

He had tried to make it in music, but he never did. Part of Leo London's stage presence was to dress in fabulous hardcore rock n' roll attire, most of which he tailored to reflect his own style. He got more compliments on his appearance and attire than on the way he performed.

To craft his own look, he'd buy tight leather pants and then rip, scuff, and stain them according to his artistic insights. He'd treat tiny T-shirts and button-downs the same way.

But his most impressive creations were his belts. Plain black leather belts were the medium for his art. From coins and rhinestones to bottle caps and cigarette butts, Leo decked out his belts with various bedazzlements that added undeniable flare. His belt buckles were just as impressive, and often vulgar.

He started off by attaching various trinkets and bobbles to his belts' existing buckles. But he soon went on to more ambitious buckle projects, affixing interactive things like light switches or tiny pinwheels. His body of work came to include buckles adorning 3-square-inch squares of stretched canvas featuring various suggestive illustrations, such as and arrow that pointed downward to his crotch and a graffiti rendition of a set of glistening female lips.

People, including other, more successful musicians,

began contacting Leo to commission his belt and buckle work. What was intended to be a gag to promote his reputation as a musician garnered a reputation of its own. His belts, not him, were in popular demand. And so he decided to legitimize his craft and take it into the commercial mainstream.

Finding financial backing was not at all as difficult as Leo presumed it would be. All he had to do was ask around. It turned out that one of the clients for whom he'd made two or three specialty belts knew a guy who knew a guy whose cousin was a hedger with some extra scratch to spare. He invested in Leo and got an exponential return.

It's been twelve years since Young Buck Belts & Buckles was legally born. In that time, more carefully-crafted, mass-marketed versions of Leo's designs came to at least thrice circle the globe. Young bucks, and old stags, on every continent sport belts and buckles from Leo's line. And Leo is a millionaire several times over.

The genius of Leo's selling strategy had always been in the dripping sensuality of his advertisements. Though his products were intended for male consumption, his publicities never contained a male. They contained only females, and only in the most unseemly ways.

Young Buck's stable of women were featured on billboards and on full-page ads in the pages of men's health and leisure magazines. Never in porno magazines though—it was beneath Leo to promote his products that way.

His controversial campaigns raised a lot of criticism for the demeaning ways they portrayed women. A young lady wearing a collar to which one of Young Buck's most popular belts was attached as a leash. A pair of naked girls facing each other, about to kiss, full breasts mashing against full breasts, bound together by one belt girdling both of their thin waists.

And then there was Celia's spread, in which she was nude and strapped to a chain-link fence by two Young Buck belts applied at prime spots on her body. The first belt ran across her chest, hugging so hard against her bulbous bosom that her flesh noticeably bulged out above and below it. The second belt sprawled her stomach an inch above her navel. The belts didn't loop around her but rather were laid out across her with their ends clasped on the fence, mounting her to the fence in a way reminiscent of how a patient with a neck or spinal cord trauma would be tied down on a body board for immediate transport to a medical facility.

Celia's face did not appear in the picture, and it was never meant to. Just her body. Her body, the fence, two belts, and Leo's business' name and its trademarked catchphrase:

> Young Buck Belts & Buckles
> For All Your Wrangling Needs

Leo knew what men wanted to see, and it made his business venture very successful. It was that success that seduced his young wife. He liked her tight young body and beautiful face, and the fact that she reminded him a little bit of his Flower. Celia liked his money and fame, and the fact that he reminded her a little bit of her father, who was eight years May of Leo's December.

"Sometimes I ask myself why I even married her," Leo starts, out of the blue. "But then I look at her and I'm reminded why, and I ask myself 'Why the hell not?' I'm not getting any younger here. I decided I'd better marry someone before I got too old... And she was the best thing I could find. I'll enjoy her while I still can... Hopefully she'll stick around to take care of me and make me look good when I'm a senile old man... She'll have to if she wants to keep spending my money. If she ever leaves me, she won't get a penny... The prenup made damn sure of that."

Lily feels her blood pressure rise as she pumps her fistful of secrets several quick times. She is staggered to hear Leo so unabashedly objectify and depersonalize his wife. It makes her contemplate why Leo would speak this way. Was it that his fame and fortune had gone to his head? Or, had he always been this brash?

She considers a question she's considered many times before: How would Leo have ended up treating her had she gone to Las Vegas to live life with him?

Scenario #3: Leo Leaves Lily Listless. *Lily and her daughters make it to Vegas, and Bender never follows. They join Leo in his dingy apartment, where they reside for only a brief time before the four of them search for housing in an area that is better fitted for raising children.*

In a suburb on the outskirts of Las Vegas proper, where the bright lights of the city are but tiny pockmarks on the horizon, Lily, Leo, Tina, and Robbie start their life together anew. All that sex is still out there, but Lily's little girls are considerably removed. They aren't fed it as part of their daily routines.

They aren't, but Leo is. While Lily can safeguard her children from the excessive sex culture of Vegas, there is no way she can safeguard Leo. He works on the main drag. Traveling to and from work each day, he treks streets flooded with sex, sex, and more sex. Strippers hailing cabs, prostitutes licking their lips, drunken bachelorettes and bridesmaids looking for a good time.

The waitresses at the venue where Leo works are young and fresh, dressed in tight garments and back-arching heels. And some of the female patrons hit on Leo from time to time, touching his arms, pressing up against him, offering him anonymous no-strings-attached fun.

None of this means anything to Leo at first. Naturally, he observes what's going on around him, but he does not react. In other words, he looks but does not touch. He doesn't even stare. The sex around him is meaningless since he's found love.

But this isn't something that lasts very long.

Leo wakes up one morning, alone in bed. After pulling himself together, he walks into the living room, where he has an epiphany of sorts. Tina and Robbie are fighting over a doll, while Lily is folding laundry on the couch. She's dressed in sweatpants and a worn-out T-shirt. Her hair is pulled up into a messy bun at the top of her head, and she doesn't have a drop of make-up on her face.

All of a sudden, Leo is hit hard with a feeling that overwhelms his body and mind. This is the moment when the novelty of his living situation and personal relationships completely wears off. He is dumbfounded by his station in life.

It seems like only yesterday he was a carefree unattached man living by his own rules. Now, he is part of a family unit, committed to three other people, to a woman and to another man's children. What a leap! From singular to plural in a matter of months, he has reached a final destination without ever having taken the journey to get there.

There was no transition from his wild lifestyle to his domestic one. He was not weaned. He gave up his freedoms cold turkey, and what comes next are his symptoms of withdrawal.

He realizes that he never had the chance to partake of Vegas' pleasures before Lily and her girls hit town. So when he travels to and from work now, he gets caught up in the undertow of the sex that floods the streets. He cannot avert his eyes or obviate his obscene thoughts. He wants to hop in the back of cabs with strippers, have hookers lick his lips, and show those bachelorettes and bridesmaids a good time. He stares at the waitresses he works with and finds it hard to ignore the female customers who want to give him more than a tip.

More than anything, Leo wants to react, or, better yet, act.

But he doesn't. He won't. He can't do that to Lily. He was the reason she came to Las Vegas and left everything but her kids behind. He can't betray a woman who betrayed another to be with him.

But this too isn't something that lasts very long.

As Tina and Robbie get older, and as the cost of living increases and the economy gets shittier, it becomes ever more difficult to support a family of four with a musician's meager wages. Lily gets a part-time job at a local grocery store and works a few daytime hours each day while the girls are at school. But it still isn't enough to break even, let alone get ahead. So Leo decides to pick up another job in addition to his regular music gigs at the same old dinner theater he's been playing for years.

The job he picks up is as a bartender at a gentlemen's club. Call it what they may, it's a fancy strip joint. He works there daily, during the same short daytime shift that Lily works at the grocery store. Since the club isn't too busy during the day, he gets an amazing view of the girls on stage.

The girls who dance there are of the corn-fed type, more like surgically enhanced college students than strippers. They're young and pretty and full of life—and nude, but for the miniscule sheer panties they are required to wear. He carries out his bartending duties with his eyes fixed on the stage, mixing drinks while he watches the dancers dance. They shake his bottle, and he goes home to have Lily pop his cork.

Soon enough, Leo gets tired of just looking. He wants to touch. And he does. The first time he cheats on Lily is with one of the dancers, a quick hand job in the backroom. Next, it's oral sex with a regular patron of the dinner theater after Leo's late-night set.

It isn't until two years and eight or nine affairs later that Lily discovers Leo's infidelity. She finds a dark purple lipstick smudge on the bottom of one of his shirts when she's doing laundry one day. Lily does not wear dark purple lipstick.

Lily confronts Leo, and he admits to his disloyalty. He fesses up, however, to only one episode, neglecting to mention his numerous other misdoings. He discloses the identity of his mistress, pointing to one of the dancers at the club where he works. Truth be told, he isn't entirely certain that it was in fact that specific girl's mouth that left the stain, but it is easier to swiftly point his finger at a particular person than to obviously deliberate on the matter.

Lily is dejected. Even though they are not married, she is hurt that Leo broke his unspoken vows. For a few days, she is unable to even look at Leo, and, after that, she is unable to ever look at him the same way again.

Because Lily believes that Leo cheated on her with a girl at the club, whether that is or isn't the case, Lily insists that Leo quit working there and find employment someplace else, preferably where he won't be beguiled by naked dancers or sultry women of any sort.

Leo honors Lily's request and quits his job at the club. He does so decisively, without giving the management any notice more advance than a phone call twenty minutes before the next shift he was scheduled to work.

He beats the pavement, avoiding any business likely to goad his libido. Leo's self-imposed search criteria are pretty restrictive. No bars, clubs, lounges, or casinos. He does not leave himself with many options, since these types of establishments are the pillars of Vegas' commercial landscape.

Leo ends up with an unlikely job at a public library, shelving books and updating the card catalog. Employed there for no more than five months, he is fired for inappropriate conduct at work. One of the librarians caught him having sex with a coed in the stacks, which was definitely something not in his job description. While the library administrators are able to keep this incident out of the news, they are not able to prevent gossip. And it is through gossip that Lily learns of the reason for Leo's dismissal. She overhears two college students talking to each other as they are waiting in her check-out lane.

"Did you hear about Jessica?" the young fellow asks his shopping companion.

"No," the young gal replies. "What happened this time?"

"She banged some older dude at the library," the fellow continues. "He was some type of menial employee, not a real librarian or anything... So they're doing it, right there in the library, and the librarian catches them! Fires the old guy on the spot. Tells Jessica to leave before she calls the cops."

"No way... That's pretty hard to believe, even for Jessica... I don't believe it... It's probably just a rumor."

The young gal may not be able to believe it, but Lily is. She immediately infers that the old guy in the story is Leo. Some rumors aint that far from the truth, honey.

Ashamed, belittled, and hopeful that it was an isolated occurrence, Lily does not question or accuse Leo this time. Nor does she question or accuse him the next time. Or the next time. Or the time after that.

The fact that Leo thinks he is getting away with something makes his adultery even more appealing to him. Sneaking around makes him feel dirty and depraved, and he likes feeling that way. He likes it a lot.

As Lily gets older and her female façade starts to fade, her daughters' boons begin to flourish. Lily is starting to wrinkle and sag, while Tina and Robbie are starting to firm and swell into luscious curves.

Though Leo had helped Lily raise her daughters as a father would, he is reminded of the fact that there is no blood between him and them as he watches them mature. Things that were once inanities are now something else. Hugs, jokes, little fights, and open bedroom doors excite Leo in a way they never did before.

Leo is cautious around Tina and Robbie, always afraid he'll involuntarily make a wrong, or right, move. But it, it, becomes harder each day. The temptation is too great. So he starts spending more and more time away from home, and more and more time in the arms, crotches, mouths, and other ovals of other women.

As for Lily, she is left listless and alone.

Night after night, she waits for Leo to come home to her, to make love to her, to be hers. Night after night, she knows that he won't come home pristine, that he won't make love to her, because there is no love left to make. Night after night, she knows he is not hers.

Lily is not blind. She merely chooses not to see.

Above all else, what Lily chooses not to see is that her fate is her own fault. After all, she'd known about Leo's reputation, his penchant for pleasure, before she left to be with him. Since she was aware that he'd dipped into dozens of Yinzers in Pittsburgh, she should have expected that he'd go hog-wild in a more glamorous city. She should have known that she could never be enough for him.

This story has no definite end. It plays out like this until Leo has fucked nearly every woman in Vegas, possibly beyond. It stops some time just before Lily's daughters reach the age of consent, just before they're fair game.

The only conclusion it reaches is this: It was a mistake to leave a man like Bender, a man to whom sex simply did not matter that much, who would have never disgraced or deserted Lily by having untold affairs, who would have rather been in a stale relationship with her than in a brisk relationship with anyone else.

No, Lily should not have left him.

But none of these were lives that Lily ever lived. They were but transient thoughts, passing through her mind as casually as the funeral home guests who pass before her eyes at the close of this evening. Effortlessly, without ceremonial dismissal, they shift(ed) out of focus, onward to an existence on the fringe of Lily's perceptual framework.

Before this point in her life, it had been easy for Lily to reach each of her scenarios' conclusions that leaving to be with Leo would have been a mistake. Looking to all that could have gone wrong, remaining with Bender had clearly been the best of Lily's options, something she justified in terms of averting myriad disastrous outcomes.

And all the good that had happened over the years would never have come about had Lily lived her life with Leo. If Lily had joined him in Las Vegas, Leo might never have founded his company and found his great success. If Lily had extracted her daughters from Pittsburgh, Tina might never have become concerned with wet weather conditions, the focus of her present graduate studies in environmental engineering; and Robbie might never have found the print column in a Pittsburgh newspaper, which had been the impetus for her to pursue journalism as her major in college. If, then. If, then. The decision to leave would have resulted in a butterfly effect far too convoluted for Lily to comprehend at this, or any, moment.

Now in wake of her husband's death, however, Lily reconsiders whether she had, in effect, done the right thing. For had she acted differently all those years ago, she would not be seated here today. Bender's death would not have been at her hands. And she would not be haunted for all of eternity by the ghosts of what she'd done.

~ 11 ~

"What's that in your hand, Mum?"

Lily is sitting in the corner of the couch, and Robbie is sitting beside her. Lily's legs are crossed, and her right hand rests, closed, on her right knee, flicking up and down in an irregular motion.

She does not hear Robbie's question at first, so Robbie asks it again: "What's that in your hand, Mum? Hello? What's that in your hand?"

Lily hears her daughter this time and glances sideways at her. She turns her eyes away from Robbie's face, and Robbie reaches out her dainty hand, wrapping it around her mother's clenched fist.

"Can I see?"

"Oh, don't worry about it," Lily says, churning her wrist so that her fist is a pestle against the mortar of Robbie's palm.

"Now I'm totally interested in what you've got there, and why you're holding onto it so tightly," Robbie says as she squeezes her mother's hand.

Lily turns to look at Robbie again. Robbie flashes her famous smile, and softly speaks, "Let me see."

Just like always, Lily gives in to her daughter: "Okay."

Robbie removes her hand from Lily's and sits back in anticipation.

Lily's tight grip goes limp. She rotates her wrist so that her palm is facing upward. She unfolds her fingers to expose the folded-up strip of crinkled paper she is holding.

Robbie quickly pinches the paper from her mother's hand and unfolds it.

Her eyes narrow as her cheeks rise. A girlish grin curls at the corners of her mouth.

"Is this what I think it is?" she asks. "It's…"

"A recipe," Lily replies without waiting for Robbie to complete her sentence.

"Not just any recipe, though, huh?" Robbie asks. "This is *the* recipe, isn't it?"

"Yes, it is," Lily replies with a smile of her own.

"But why do you have it now?" Robbie pushes. "Why today?"

"I need it," Lily states with simplicity.

Although she does not ask, Robbie wants more information. She tilts her head like a puppy begging for a treat, and Lily reads the angle of her face.

"I have to go to the grocery store tonight," Lily offers.

"Shopping?" Robbie asks. "Want me to come with you?"

"No, that's okay," Lily responds. "I just need to use it as a shopping list. I always forget something and end up having to go back to the store to get it.

"And I want to be ready for tomorrow."

"Tomorrow?" Robbie repeats as she reads the details of the recipe. "What's tomorrow?"

"Tomorrow is the day I teach my girls how to make Grandma Roberta's chocolate pizzelles," Lily says with a slap on Robbie's leg.

"No way?" Robbie screeches. "It's about time!"

That was two months after Robbie's 14th birthday.

Lily was 45 years old at the time.

Lily had decided it was time to share the recipe with her daughters after she'd come into an unexpected inheritance a few months earlier. Her windfall had inspired her to pass some things on to her children while she was still alive, so that she didn't take everything with her to the grave.

A few months ago, Lily had received a certified letter in the mail from the escheat department of one of the city's lesser known banks. The letter was addressed to Roberta, but Lily opened it to see what it said.

As the letter read, the bank was contacting Roberta regarding an account in her name that had been inactive for over fifteen years. The bank was reaching out to her to ask her to claim the funds before they were turned over to the state, as mandated by the state laws governing estates.

The account referenced in the letter contained $2,498.16, making the letter a sight for Lily's sore eyes. She'd expended every penny of her inheritance many years before the letter arrived, and that $2,498.16 sure would come in handy.

And, it tickled Lily's heart. It was as if she had received a gift from her grandmother from beyond the grave, like her grandmother was still in her life, taking care of her and helping her out of a fiduciary bind.

Lily called the account manager at the bank, to alert him of Roberta's death and to find out what she, as Roberta's heir, had to do to claim the money. The manager gave her careful instructions, which included a request for a copy of Roberta's will, or any other similar document, naming Lily as heir or executrix.

Lily's mind raced when she heard this request. Her grandmother had died so very long ago, and Lily didn't know if she still had a copy of the will. She'd circulated through countless rounds of housecleaning over the years, getting rid of this and that, here and there, every now and then, to thin out the excess clutter in her home.

Had Roberta's will been one of the documents Lily got rid of? Was the proof Lily needed to claim the funds decayed and disintegrated in a landfill somewhere? Was it recycled into letterhead, toilet paper, or disposable coffee cups?

There was only one way for Lily to find out. She'd have to look for the will in the few places where she kept what paperwork she'd held onto. It was a necessary step to obtain money that rightfully belonged in her pocket.

There was no sense of organization to how and where Lily stored documents in her home. In the basement file cabinet, where she first looked for Roberta's will, Lily found warranty information and owner's manuals for different appliances and electronics around the home, as well as some of Bender's paystubs from prior employers and artwork from her daughters' toddler years.

In the bottom drawer of the china cabinet in the dining room, she found more toddler artwork, tax returns from a few of the past several years, service papers pertaining to various repairs on her and Bender's cars, copies of her grandmother's death certificate, and receipts for large household purchases.

It was in the attic that Lily found Roberta's will. And that's not all she found.

Searching through a pair of large storage boxes, Lily found an accordion folder with a label that read "Young Lily." She'd found it before she found the will, so she set it aside, intent on exploring it after she finished with the boxes.

And once she found the will, she shoved it under the right thigh of her crisscrossed legs and took to inspecting the contents of the "Young Lily" folder.

She had, of course, seen this folder before and thumbed

through its contents—such as when she extracted her birth certificate in order to apply for the marriage license that bound her to Bender. But it had been years since she pulled open the accordion. Now, as a mother, she figured she might be able to dissect it with a new perspective, that maybe she would greater appreciate remnants of her youth now that she had children of her own.

This was, for the most part, the case.

When she saw her tiny footprint on a hospital record, she smiled a smile that only a mother could smile—a smile that was entirely detached from hours of labor and painful delivery; a smile that reflected and refracted memories of a similarly-sized foot poking and prodding inside her distended pregnant belly, perhaps kicking one hard and final kick to rupture her placental sac and cause a rush of amniotic waters; a smile at thoughts of her own daughters' footprints and of the purplish-black ink stains that held to their new skin for days after the prints were taken.

Her certificate of baptism, her immunization record, a tracing of her hand drawn and decorated to look like a turkey—these things, too, made her think of her own children. Elementary school report cards, awards and ribbons of accomplishment—Lily was actually amazed by the fact that she was once a child. It was hard for her to imagine that she was ever anything different than what she was at that moment.

Next, Lily found three sealed envelopes in the backmost sleeve of the folder. One by one, she opened them.

The first contained curls of hair, and a note indicating that the hair was from her first haircut as a baby.

The second contained a rotten nubbin of a tooth, probably the first she'd lost as a young child, she reckoned.

The third did not contain anything that carried traces of

Lily's DNA, though it did hold something that pertained to her identity.

What was inside was a two-page legal document Lily had never before seen. Cursorily skimming over the text, it was evident to Lily what these pages were. The document was her Certificate of Adoption, which entrusted Roberta with parental rights.

Lily had always known she was adopted. For as long as she could remember, she knew that the woman she called "Grandma" had signed some papers giving her parental rights and control. And when she told people that her grandmother was like a mother to her, she was telling a very loaded truth, since Roberta had been her mother for all intents and purposes, including legal ones.

But what Lily didn't know for most of her life, what she was to discover only now, years after her grandmother died, was *when* Roberta actually adopted her.

She began reading the thick boilerplate and legalese on the thin paper. A few lines in, her heart fluttered as her eyes did a double-take of the date inserted into a standard clause. She could not believe what she saw.

Lily had always assumed her grandmother adopted her after her mother left. She had assumed Carla abandoned her and Roberta picked up the pieces. But the date on the page before her did not correspond with these assumptions.

The Certificate of Adoption was dated less than one month after Lily's birth.

So Lily hadn't been adopted at age 3 or later. Roberta hadn't picked up whatever pieces Carla dropped when she left town with her lover. She'd held those pieces from the very beginning.

Lily had been adopted as an infant—more or less at birth for actuary purposes.

In an instant, it hit Lily that her life had been a lie, not one of fabrication but one of withholding information. And why, she wondered, had this information been withheld? Had it been in an effort to protect her?

Lily sat there and considered her life. She remembered asking her grandmother where her mother was and why she had left her. She remembered feeling unwanted and unloved. She remembered feeling rejected.

These were the feelings that shaped so much of who Lily allowed herself to become. She was a person who wanted love, but who refused to give anyone the chance to abandon or reject her. That's why her only true friend had been her grandmother—her grandmother, the person who accepted and adopted her when her own mother no longer wanted her.

That's why, in her younger years, she'd used men for sex and nothing more, why she refused the idea of a romantic relationship for so long—if she did not make a meaningful connection with a man there would be no ties that he could sever.

And that's why she ended up with Bender, because, even if only for a moment, how ever fleeting, he had made her feel wanted and loved, despite her faults and failings. Fear of having him leave was what made her forgive the physical abuse, what caused her to rush into a premature marriage. Insecurity backed the human devices she had employed to appease him.

Considering how Lily ended up, from what could Roberta have possibly been protecting her? Wasn't it something Lily had a right to know? And, if she had known, was it possible that she might have actually endured a better fate?

Thinking she was abandoned at age 3 made Lily come to the conclusion that it was she who was being rejected—some characteristic, something she had or hadn't done, some shortcoming, some misgiving had caused her mother to leave and not take her with her.

Maybe it was her personality, her appearance, her voice. It was something about *her*. Her mother rejected *her*. Her mother abandoned *her*.

But, hmmm, if Carla had given up parental rights at Lily's birth, then it wasn't *Lily* who was being rejected. It was her existence. And her existence was something she could not be held accountable for. It was something that was not her fault. She had never asked to be born.

Wouldn't it have been better for Lily to believe that her mother never wanted a baby, rather than believe that her mother never wanted her?

Why had Roberta played her hand the way she did? Lily was three when her mother left, and she had only faint memories of her. Why had Roberta chosen to lie about Lily's adoption date instead of telling a different lie?

Roberta could have told Lily that her mother left at birth. She could have told her that her mother died, or pretended that she herself was Lily's mom. But she didn't choose any of these lies. Instead, she told the one lie that ended up hurting Lily worse than any of the others could have. She let that poor girl believe she was abandoned without thought or fight.

The truth of the matter was something that Lily would never learn. The truth of the matter was that Roberta was not trying to protect Lily. She was trying to protect herself.

Remember, Roberta was the one in control. She was the one who had the final say in what happened to her child's child—and it was her decision to adopt Lily.

At the bottom line, Roberta adopted Lily because she wanted to—no matter what words or examples she used to justify it, her real reason was a selfish one. Simply put,

Roberta wanted a second chance. She wanted to do good by Lily since she'd failed so epically with her own child. And simply helping Carla raise Lily would was not enough, she also had to irrefutably own her.

But, of course, that's not how she explained her decision to Carla. Instead, she called on logic and empathy, neither of which were her strong suit.

She stressed that, while she had been opposed to the idea of putting her daughter's daughter up for adoption, she was not against adopting her herself. It was an outside adoption that she wanted to avoid, not one within the family, not one that would make Lily's life more manageable.

Roberta had been a single mom as well, so she knew a thing or two about the hardships associated with the post. And those hardships would only be harder for a teen, or so went the selling points she pitched to Carla, which were as follows:

Inconvenience. This was the most practical point Roberta made. Since Carla was still a minor, she lacked the legal capacity to make certain decisions for herself and, therefore, also lacked the capacity to make decisions for her child. It would be more convenient to assign parental rights to Roberta, as age was not a hurdle she had to overcome.

Inexperience. Carla was still a child herself. A child raising a child is like the blind leading the blind. Roberta's older age, presumably, came with wisdom. More level-headed and informed, more practiced at the parenting game, Roberta would be the better person to care for, and make life-impacting decisions regarding, Lily.

Indignity. When a teen mom enters a room, there's always someone who shakes his head or whispers some crude comment under her breath. Some of that could be avoided if Roberta conducted parental business in lieu of a teenager.

Indifference. This wasn't one of Roberta's points. This was Carla's response to Roberta's reasoning. Carla was indifferent. Because her mother made a good argument and she didn't want to raise the child herself, Carla deferred to her mother's decision and signed Lily over to Roberta within weeks of her birth. Carla had wanted to give the babe up for adoption anyway—so if Roberta wanted her, she could have her.

But, over the years, something happened that Carla did not expect. She fell head-over-heels in love with her daughter.

It didn't happen overnight. It wasn't as if Lily burst out of Carla's womb and struck her with a mothering stick. It took time—time for the sleepless nights, diaper rashes, and spittle to become less meaningful than the smiles, coos, and warmth of baby-soft flesh.

By the time Lily was 1, Carla was hooked, and she was grateful that her mother didn't allow her to give her child away to a stranger. Carla even went so far as to speculate that this too had to have been one of the reasons Roberta adopted Lily—she thought that maybe Roberta kept Lily because she knew that Carla would want her one day.

And that's exactly what happened. Carla did end up wanting Lily. But when Carla wanted her, she could not have her. Roberta saw to that.

Lily's memories of the day her mother left—of her mother prying the car key out of her hand, of her silent exit, of her driving off, and of her abandonment—those memories are just that. They are Lily's memories and nothing more. They are only as sharp and accurate as one's memories of something that happened at such a young age can realistically be.

Limited. Isolated. Detached. Blurred. Lily's memories

were not of a full picture, but just of the picture's most vivid parts. What things Lily could not remember were the things that might very well have mattered most to her in the long run.

Carla did not choose to leave Roberta's home. She was forced out. When she confronted her mother and told her that she was a lesbian and that she was involved with Jill, Roberta effectively disowned her. She told Carla that she wanted nothing to do with her and demanded that she move out and never return. This was the price that Carla had to pay for being honest with her mother and for being true to herself and her partner.

Carla did not choose to abandon Lily. She was forced to leave her behind. After Roberta made it clear that Carla had to leave, Carla said she was going to take Lily with her. But Roberta would not allow it. It was Roberta, not Carla, who had legal custody of Lily, and she was not going to surrender that control. If Carla took Lily, Roberta warned, that would constitute kidnapping. So Carla had no choice but to leave Lily. This was the price that Carla had to pay for trusting her mother to look after the best interests of her and her child.

These are the truths that hid behind the date on Lily's Certificate of Adoption. And it was from these truths that Roberta sought to protect only herself.

Roberta did not want Lily to know that it was she who made Carla leave, and that it was she who prevented the natural relationship between mother and child. She did not want Lily to blame her for these things or hold her accountable for the choices she made.

It was all about being the good guy, about having Lily look up to her and consider her a savior, seeing the sacrifices she made without ever realizing the burdens she put on others.

If there was to be a bad guy in this story, Roberta was determined that Carla would play that role. Carla wasn't there to stand up for herself, so she was the perfect scapegoat.

Indeed, Roberta's plan worked out well. Lily deeply loved her grandmother and was committed to her until the day that she died. What's more, Lily had always felt indebtedness towards Roberta, a sense of owing her something for her stepping up and taking the reins. And this was the icing on Roberta's cake, the glutinous glucose glaze atop her unjust dessert.

And even after Roberta died, Lily's love and gratitude lived on. Roberta remained the savior, seated high on a pedestal though buried deep in the ground. When Lily found her Certificate of Adoption and discovered her real adoption date, she never once considered that Roberta concealed the truth for any reason other than for Lily's protection. Lily trusted that, for whatever reasons she withheld the truth, Roberta had done the right thing. Roberta could do no wrong, and if she thought it best to keep the date a secret, then keeping it a secret was the right thing to do. If anything, Roberta became more the martyr for keeping her lips sealed.

God bless Grandma Roberta for keeping this skeleton locked in the closet for so many years! God bless Grandma Roberta for biting her lip to save Lily's face! God bless Grandma Roberta for this, and God bless Grandma Roberta for that...

Bless Grandma Roberta if you will, because the truth would surely damn her. Damn her for never letting Lily know that she'd always had the one thing she'd been in search of for countless years. Damn Grandma Roberta for letting Lily believe she was unwanted when she'd been wanted all along.

The scores of men with whom she'd had casual sexual encounters, the one man for whom she settled—Lily had accumulated her collection to obtain self-validation and acceptance by others. Sure, she may have gone about it the wrong way, but it was her way. And although she never found lasting validation and acceptance, at least her experiences temporarily amused her and distracted her from the confusion going on around her.

Granted, there's no way of knowing if Lily's life would have been so different had she known these truths from the beginning. She may have still lived the life she'd lived. But, at the very least, she would have lived it making more informed decisions.

Discovering her real adoption date in her 40s had no profound effect on Lily's existence. Simply knowing the date, without the facts adjoining it, did not bring Lily confidence, clarity, or catharsis. But it did bring her something.

After Lily was done reading her Certificate of Adoption, she folded it and put it in the envelope. As she tucked it back into the "Young Lily" folder, she had a revelation: Some stories are better left untold, some cats need to stay in the bag so that they don't get out and scratch someone; and if an outstanding person like Roberta could find reason to be silent, then silence is sometimes needed.

God bless and God damn Grandma Roberta for posthumously teaching Lily this lesson, for it was this lesson that proved to be the most valuable of Lily's findings. When she exited the attic, she carried it with her, along with Roberta's will, which enabled her to claim to the $2,498.16 in Roberta's untouched bank account.

But long after the $2,498.16 had come and gone, this lesson still lingered. Of all the things to which Lily was heir, only this lesson perpetually vested.

Without formal decree, Lily had inherited her grandmother's ability to keep a secret.

Maybe, in time, she'd pass this skill on to her own daughters as well. But, for the time being, passing on Grandma Roberta's chocolate pizzelle recipe was legacy enough.

~ 12 ~

"I guess we're even now," Lily thought to herself as she sat on the cold slab of poorly painted concrete that jutted out from one of the four cinderblock walls that confined her.

The walls were covered with graffiti and smears of what was either dried fecal matter or brittled menstrual bleedings. The smell of the dank little room was sickening, and it gave Lily a headache, or made her preexisting headache worse. Whatever.

She'd asked for water a few hours earlier, and was mocked for so doing. She was told she could drink from the sink at the back of the room. But when Lily saw the sink, there was no way in hell she was gonna drink from it.

The sink was part of a larger standing bathroom unit. It sat adjacent to the tank of a toilet. Both fixtures appeared to be made of stainless steel, or some cheaper equivalent, though the steel of neither had done its job of resisting stains.

A thick bronze moss clung to the toilet bowl and sink basin. Out of curiosity, Lily tapped her foot against the toilet handle, to see if flushing would stir the muck loose from the bowl. But it didn't. It simply made the slime quiver and sway back and forth like a thousand tiny fins of algae.

The force of the flush on the unit's shared plumbing dislodged something from the drain hole in the sink. It burped up a thick black clot, which Lily understood to be a matted wad of afro-weave.

Lily had never been the most fastidious of housekeepers, but she was used to nothing this putrid.

Another thing that Lily had never been was vindictive.

She wasn't too familiar with spite, revenge, or vigilante justice. But she knew well enough that it had been action on at least one of those iniquities that landed her in lockup.

Alas, luckless Lily learned too late in life the importance of keeping a secret, and ended up paying a hefty price for her ineptitude. The cost was her freedom.

Telling the truth did not set Lily free. It sentenced her to life in prison.

No doubt about it, it was for her own transgression that Lily was arrested and hauled off to Allegheny County Jail. But she couldn't help but think that she would not have been there had it not been for a cycle of torment set in motion many, many years before the series of events that directly led to her incarceration.

All those years ago when Lily had her one-time, late-night affair with Leo, there were two wrongs she committed. The first was having the affair. The second was telling Bender about it.

Lily had expected Bender to be incensed by her admission, to react with some outlandish outward expression of outrage and abhorrence. But he hadn't acted as she expected. His response was something far more subtle.

After she told him about the affair, Bender lost all faith in Lily—though it's unclear how much faith he'd had in her to begin with. But regardless of whether it had been an atom or a ton, every bit of faith was lost. From then on, Bender never trusted Lily again.

Bender's lack of trust quickly evolved into distrust and suspicion. Within days, he was no longer merely disappointed by Lily's betrayal; he expected her to betray him again. And, if she did, he was determined to catch her.

But he wasn't going to leave it to chance. He wasn't going to sit back and wait for Lily to slip up or make a confession. Tossing out unsupported accusations, relying on circumstantial evidence or speculation—these sedentary stuffs would not suffice. If he were to do this, he was going to do it right. Rather than being inactive or reactive, he would be proactive. He would take preemptive measures to catch Lily red-handed and obtain concrete confirmation—that way Lily couldn't weasel her way out of the truth.

As for what constituted betrayal, Bender broadened his definition. He sought to obtain not only evidence of adultery, but also evidence of any other type of wrongdoing.

If Lily were to lie to Bender about her whereabouts, her plans, or the amount of money she spent, he would catch her.

If she were to neglect a parental responsibility, forget to do a chore, or pay a bill late, he would catch her.

If she were to leave a "t" uncrossed, fail to dot an "i," or use the last piece of toilet paper without replacing the roll, he would catch her.

If she were to do anything, anything at all, Bender would know about it.

Of course, Bender was not omniscient by virtue. All-knowingness was not his birthright from God. So he had to come up with manmade, external ways to glean proof.

There are several different terms that could be used to describe how Bender went about his mission. Some would call it tracking. Others would use words like covert operation, undercover investigation, or sting. Others yet would coin it paranoia at play.

And all of these terms are accurate, or at least partially correct. He employed elements of each of these tactics to keep tabs on Lily as best he could.

To track her movement inside, and to and from, the home, Bender religiously set up tell-tales. These "tell-tales" were things he placed in certain locations or configurations, the movement of which indicated some activity on Lily's part.

For instance, before going to bed for the night, Bender would place a piece of clear tape on the inside of the front door, across the narrow gap where the door met its frame. When he woke up the next morning, he'd check the status of that piece of tape. If it was broken, dislodged, or missing, it told him a tale—it told him that the door had been opened. And since there was no reason to believe his daughters would open the door late at night, it told him that Lily had been the one to break the seal.

Though the piece of tape on the front door was what he most frequently used, he utilized other tell-tales as well: a twig in the catch of the porch gate; a discarded soda bottle or tobacco can in the car console that had to be moved in order to properly shift gears; an accessory such as a scarf or a hat placed on the same hook as Lily's coat, that'd fall out of place when she grabbed her garb; a pebble in one of Lily's shoes; a book or magazine thrown atop her purse, where it lay beside the living room couch; etc., etc., etc., the list goes on.

He'd place her favorite liquors behind bottles of boozes she didn't much like. Because she never left the house without applying a thick coat of black eyeliner to her bottom lids, he'd rearrange her makeup drawer in the bathroom so that the black pencil was at the bottom of a mess of other face paint.

And then there were the inventories he kept only in his mind (he dare not leave a paper trail). He'd take mental note of the mileage on the car, the number of beers in the refrigerator, the amount and denominations of money in Lily's wallet, the last channel watched on the television, the last number dialed on the phone—etc., etc., etc., yet again.

Surveillance and surprise inspections were tricks he also carried in his bag, though he pulled them out less often than those mentioned above. From time to time, he'd tell Lily he was going somewhere—to work, to the bar, to visit a friend, or to go for a walk. But when he left the house, he'd double back.

Maybe one day he'd park the car down the street, just out of view from the front porch, and sit and keep watch, looking to see if Lily left the house or if anyone else approached the front door. On another day, he might go to a bar or the park for a short while and then come home earlier than he told Lily to expect his return. He'd say he forgot his wallet, that the scene at the bar was subpar, or that there were too many teenagers misbehaving at the park.

Bender did this non-exhaustive list of things for seventeen years, during which time he never caught Lily doing anything all that foul. Sometimes she'd drink a few beers and watch late-night television, or her purse would be moved, or Irene's number would appear to've been dialed on the phone. But these things alone weren't enough to cause Bender to confront her—they weren't coupled with any indication that she'd snuck out of the house or done anything other than simply exist. If he gave her guff about such menial things, he might compromise his entire operation, and he certainly didn't want that.

Years. Seventeen years. He kept tabs on her for seventeen years, though he never obtained any damning information. Never. Not once.

Anybody else who gave that much time and energy to a mission that yielded no results would have probably put the whole thing to rest or concluded that there was no reason to remain on the lookout. But not Bender.

He was dead-set that Lily was up to something—and he downright knew that if he were to stop watching her, it would be at that exact moment that she'd do something ghastly. So he kept up his game. He kept setting up his tell-tales, counting this, observing that, dropping in—etc., etc., etc., for a third time.

There was something else to it too. Tracking Lily gave Bender a purpose, something to do. It was a way for him to whittle away time, a diversion while time whittled away him.

And, actually, he was pretty good at it. The fact that he didn't catch Lily in flagrante delicto didn't mean that Bender was doing something wrong. It meant that Lily wasn't doing anything wrong. There was nothing for Bender to catch.

In another time and place, under different circumstances, Bender could have put his skills to better use. If he hadn't had a criminal record of his own, if he'd been more willing to learn or undergo formal education and training, if he hadn't smoked so much pot, he could have had a very successful career in law enforcement, investigation, or military service. He could have been a detective, an FBI agent, or a navy SEAL.

Oh, how many tragedies he could have averted! How many lives he could have saved! He could've worn badges and ribbons, received acclamations and praise. He could have made the world a much better place. The streets could have been safer, the future more bright.

But Bender—Ben, dear—never aspired to be the good guy. He wanted instead to be the bad boy. And, wow, did he play the part well!

In that vein, he would have made for a similarly successful criminal overlord. He could've been a hit man, an ad hoc bounty hunter, or a drug kingpin. But he chose never to pursue such widespread corruption. He sought only the demise of one person, one woman, whom he called wife, though he more often than not called her by other names.

He hunted only one pig. He dedicated himself to trailing the ooze of but one slimeball, laying bare one lone cunt. There was just one lump of coal he wanted to burn. Lily, sweet Lily, the loser he'd never let win—she would not get the better of him, not again.

Nor would she ever get a clue. Bender was meticulous in covering his tracks, and Lily's ignorance was a measure of his success. Despite the length of Bender's operation, Lily never figured out what he was doing. She never realized how closely she was being watched and studied.

It wasn't because she was an idiot—even though Bender called her by this name from time to time, he knew she was not dumb. She just never picked up on the signs. In part, it was because she wasn't a paranoid or suspicious person by nature, so she had no impetus for concern. But, in larger part, it was because Bender's methods were ingenious, both in simplicity of design and in mindful execution.

Bender set up his tell-tales in such a way that they told their tales only to him. He would put them in place after Lily went to bed, and would examine and remove them before she awoke.

Because his tell-tales were nothing more than careful reconfigurations of everyday items, no red flags were ever raised—though, had something ever been questioned, it could very easily have been explained.

Why was a book on top of Lily's purse? Who'd put a scarf by Lily's coat, or been messing around in her makeup drawer?

Lily had kids—two daughters, no less. Tossed aside books and pieces of clothes? A compromised makeup drawer? Par for the course.

What couldn't be blamed on the kids could be attributed to Daddy Bender or Mother Nature. That discarded bottle

or can in the car was the result of Bender's oversight. The
bottle of scotch that stood in front of Lily's favored vodka
had quenched Bender's thirst. And it was Mother Nature
who put the pebble in Lily's shoe or gently blew the leaf into
place at the gate.

The only thing that Bender would have had a hard time
explaining was the tape on the door. But, he figured, if he
had to explain that, Lily would have something greater
to explain. If she found the tape there, she'd have to have
reason for being at the door in the middle of the night—and
she could have no good reason for that. So if it came down
to balancing his act against hers, the scales would tip in
Bender's favor, since a watchful eye is less offensive than a
wandering body.

There was an added prong to Bender's strategy that made
it difficult for Lily to uncover his undercover work. He not
only employed covert measures to keep tabs on Lily, he used
overt ones as well. He questioned her daily about her plans
and asked her to give him details of where she was going and
where she had been.

She was required to put appointments on the calendar
and consult him when drafting a shopping list. If possible or
practical, at least one of their daughters was to be her
companion, or chaperone, whenever she left the house.

When Lily ran into an unexpected delay, she was
obligated to drop everything and notify Bender—whether
that meant using the phone at the doctor's office to alert
Bender of her postponed exam, or pulling off on the side of
the road and stopping at a payphone to give Bender a traffic
report, among other things.

And then there were the unexpected delays Lily had to
obviate—like turning away from an extensive conversation
with an old friend she ran into at the grocery store or

bringing the kids home hungry to avoid long lines at the drive-thru.

With these requirements came an equally stringent set of rules. Money was granted more as an allowance than as a right, and unnecessary expenses and excursions were frowned upon, to say the least. Unless she got case-by-case approval from Bender, Lily was to have no guests in their home other than Irene. And as alcohol had always been her aphrodisiac of choice, Lily was not permitted to go to bars or parties without Bender, or to consume booze outside of the home in any setting where Bender was not at her side.

In light of all these restrictions, Lily never suspected that Bender had any other checks and balances in place. And, in light of what she had done, she never challenged Bender's blatant decrees.

As the saying goes, hindsight is 20/20—and Lily's perfect vision of her past was that she had been imperfect. Could Bender ever forgive her for what she'd done? She didn't know. But one thing was certain: She could not forgive herself.

No matter what was going on in their marriage, no matter how cruel or vicious Bender had been to Lily, no matter how unsatisfied she was in the bedroom, there was absolutely no reason for Lily to do what she had done. Nothing could justify her cheating on her husband.

The ring on her finger—that tattoo on the small of her back—was supposed to mean something. It called for fidelity, which she so flagrantly flouted.

Whatever problems she had, she should have otherwise addressed before stepping outside the boundaries of marriage. If it was sexual gratification she wanted, she should have jumped her husband or taken matters into her own hands, or fingers. Even a battery-operated lover would have been a more dignified alternative to adultery. If she was sick and tired of the degrading names and blames, she should have dissolved the marriage rather than defy it. Separation, divorce—these too would have been nobler alternatives.

But she took the most loathsome route and acted in a way repugnant to the fundamental concept of marriage. She disrespected herself, her husband, a holy sacrament, and a legal institution.

Lily ceded to the fact that she had done an unquestionably bad thing and that there was nothing she could say or do to vindicate herself or diffuse the situation. She had done something that she could neither remedy nor revoke.

She was stunned that Bender didn't beat the hell out of her when she made her confession. And, after the initial shock wore off, she was equally as stunned that he didn't pack up and leave. In cheating, she'd given him good cause—an opportunity, a free pass—to abandon her and end their marriage.

Bender, however, did not take advantage of the opportunity before him. He did not use that free pass. He stuck around and stuck it out—though by no means should the words used here be construed to suggest that Bender took the high ground. It was just that the ground he took was higher than the bottom of the barrel, which was where Lily'd wound up.

Nonetheless, because he took a higher ground, Lily was beholden to her husband. She was thankful that he didn't leave her when he very well could have, and very possibly should have.

The best way for Lily to express her gratitude was through obedience, which seemed to be the thing Bender craved most. So when he laid out his set of ridiculous requirements, rules, and restriction, she obliged posthaste.

Life lived by prescription—an exacting toll, perhaps. But Lily owed Bender, and this was how he chose to collect.

Lily had to kiss Bender's ass because she'd sucked Leo's dick.

Kissing Bender's ass, of course, is a metaphor. Lily did not physically place her lips on Bender's backside. Just like how she was not sentenced to life in prison in any literal sense. That, too, is a metaphor—an allegory for something else.

The only prison in which Lily ever found herself was a figurative one. Her life itself was the prison, a hodgepodge of rules and tell-tale traps, of guilt and obligation, from which she could not escape. Her crime had been adultery, and she'd signed her own warrant when she disclosed to Bender what she had done. She lost her freedom that way, the freedom to live an ordinary life or be autonomous in any way.

And it was all because she couldn't keep her mouth shut.

Now, as per Lily's stint in jail, that is no metaphor. That actually happened. She was, in fact, arrested and taken to jail at one point in time—in the wee hours of the morn following her 50th birthday, to be exact. And how she ended up there is quite a story indeed.

She broke the law, obviously. But before she broke the law, she broke one of Bender's rules, and it was the latter that led to her capture.

Despite a few observations, Lily's 50th birthday was not the ceremonious occasion she'd hoped it would be. The highlight of her day was lunching with her daughters, each of whom was more than less grown and in college, and both of whom took time out of their busy schedules to meet up with Mama for Chinese food and homemade brownies. Robbie had baked up a double batch and decorated them with squiggles of pink and green frosting.

The only birthday cards Lily had received had been received over the few days prior to her birthday. The first card came from Irene, who'd mailed it from Mallorca, the last leg of her seven-months-abroad leisurely travels. It was a humorous card, or at least it was supposed to be, comparing women to red wine—"Both get finer with age," the inside touted.

The second card came from Cookie. On its front, there was a doe-eyed puppy wearing a ribbon as a collar. It opened to a straightforward message—"Happy Birthday to a Very Special Girl"—signed with Cookie's love in red marker. It was the type of card clearly intended for a child, and Lily found it extremely touching.

The third card was more extravagant and mature. Thick, matte navy blue cardstock bedecked with a glossy, gold, and grand calligraphic "50" on its obverse, its inside message was frank. It read: "With each new decade comes new joys and new concerns. At 50, give yourself the gift of a healthy colon. Call today to schedule a colonoscopy."

This card came from Lily's health insurance company. And, even though she wondered if her premiums would have been a little cheaper had the company mailed her a simple form letter rather than something so ornate, she shoved the card under a magnet on the refrigerator door, to be displayed alongside her two other lonesome birthday greetings.

Lily looked forward to placing a fourth card on the refrigerator. If her 50th birthday was to be like her most recent handful of others, that card would come from Bender, bestowed to her on the evening of her birthday proper.

Some time ago, after presenting one too many unsuccessful presents to the women in his life, Bender realized that he wasn't the best gift-giver. He didn't know how to shop for his wife or daughters, and his efforts repeatedly resulted in failed offerings that went unused or unappreciated. He'd wasted a lot of money, so cards became his gift of choice.

To sweeten the pot, he'd insert some cash between the sappy sheets of sentiment when gifting to his daughters. Giving cash to Lily, however, was too crass, so, in lieu of money, he substituted some other pageantry, the nature of which depended on the holiday in question.

For Lily's birthday, it had become Bender's practice to take her out to dinner. They'd toss on their fancy pants and hit an upscale eatery, where they'd arrive early and he'd place the card in front of her as they enjoyed pre-dinner cocktails at the bar.

Such a nicety may seem out of place in this narrative, but it's not. Lily and Bender were together for over 28 years. That's roughly 10,220 days—more if you account for leap years, and even more if you add the earliest days of their courtship into the equation.

28 years. 10,220 days. 245,280 hours. 14,716,800 minutes. 883,008,000 seconds.

No matter how you slice it, only the slightest fraction of their time together bears repeating—and what facts and theories make the cut are merely matters of accounting.

10,220 days. Between the two of them, they consumed an excess of 50,000 cups of coffee; somewhere around 33,500 tablets of acetaminophen; no less than 15,000 pounds of meat or other healthy proteins; and a minimum of 1,308,160 ounces of alcohol.

245,280 hours. They burned upwards of 25,000 gallons of gasoline in their various vehicles; changed approximately 13,200 diapers; spent more than 3,000,000 minutes watching television; and each walked an average of 35,770 miles in as many as 100 different pairs of shoes.

But neither Bender nor Lily ever took the time to crunch these numbers. Very few people ever do—other than statisticians, statesmen, and the occasional author.

When people look back on their lives, or on the lives of others, it isn't the big numbers that stand out, unless, of course, the big numbers refer to sums of money. But, less those sums of money, the big numbers represent nothing more than common patterns, everyday habits that have become so infused in our daily lives that they no longer have any real meaning, let alone deserve to be tallied.

What stands out are the smaller numbers, and the words and feelings associated with them.

14,716,800 minutes. Between the two of them, they shared one wedding ceremony in the park; and welcomed into this world two children, who pooled together six religious rights of passage, four proms, two high school graduations, one National Merit scholarship, and letters of admission from eight different colleges, inter alia.

883,008,000 seconds. They decorated 28 Christmas trees; went on 19 vacations; purchased three automobiles outright, and leased two others; attended 11 pro football games as a couple; and sat for seven family portraits.

These small numbers are counts of the things people want to remember but tend to easily forget. They are of joys too often taken for granted in life, which fall to the shadows when held up to another set of small numbers.

Those other small numbers are counts of the things people don't want to remember but can never forget. They are of the grim, of suffering, heartache, and sadness, which are the binding on the books of the greatest stories ever told.

28 years. 10,220 days. 245,280 hours. 14,716,800 minutes. 883,008,000 seconds.

pig

Between the two of them, they endured several noteworthy plights, some small numbers of some not so small things: one miscarriage; one broken arm; two arrests and temporary incarcerations; two dead dogs; one failed band; one fallen bandmate; one act of adultery; one act of vengeance; two, if not three, broken hearts; and one untimely death.

And there was more.

Lily had been given at least 20 hurtful nicknames; two black eyes; 13 other scrapes and bruises; and one very shitty birthday present.

Ah, birthdays, yes, birthdays! Back to those joyful things. Back to Lily's 50th and the very shitty present it brings.

Her birthday fell on a weekday, which meant that Bender worked. He was on the clock until 4:30 p.m., which suggested his return somewhat later than 5.

Lily readied herself for a night out on the town.

Gauzy black pants with much sway, a tight-fitting black top with a sheer overlay—the ensemble she selected was unseasonable perchance, but it flattered her body and fit circumstance.

She sat on the sofa, wearing this and a smile. But little did she know, she'd sit there for a while.

First came 5, then 6, then 7, then 8. But still no husband, no Bender, no date.

Lily twiddled her thumbs and mussed with her hair. She tried not to worry, to fret, or to care.

Enough was enough when the clock struck 9. Fed up, let down, she went for the wine.

First came one glass, then two, three, and then four. Reason had already left her, now rhyme too was no more.

It was after 11:30 when Bender got home. He found Lily

239

drunk on the couch, still waiting for him, vacant look on her face, glossy eyes staring straight ahead at her goblet of red wine.

"Why are you all dressed up?" he asked.

"Don't you know what today is?" she returned.

"Yeah, it's Thursday," Bender said as he took off his coat and threw it on the couch.

"That's not all, Bender," Lily frowned. "Today is my birthday… Well, it was my birthday. There's not much left of it at this point."

"Yeah, we'll celebrate this weekend," he coughed. "That's what I was planning on doing anyway. I mean, today's Thursday, Lily. You know I go to Joe's every Thursday."

And Bender did go to Joe's every Thursday. He went there weekly without fail to take the karaoke stage. Still at 60, Bender sung his heart out at karaoke. Still at 60, Bender had rockstar dreams.

Those Thursdays at Joe's were very important to him—so important that he wouldn't miss a night, not even to celebrate his wife's 50th birthday.

"Are you kidding me, Bender?" Lily asked. "I'll only ever have one 50th birthday. Joe's has karaoke every Thursday night."

"Drop it, Lily," Bender said, adjusting his focus on Lily. He too was drunk. "I said we'll celebrate this weekend."

"No, that's not good enough," Lily said as she jumped to her feet. "You may not want to celebrate my birthday today, but I do."

She picked up her purse and a thin shawl she'd selected to compliment her outfit.

Walking out the door, she turned to say the words which

she'd later regret: "I'm going to the bar down the street. Don't wait up."

"Lily," Bender shouted, as he watched his intoxicated wife slide into the car, "you know I don't want you going out to the bar alone!"

But Lily did go to the bar alone. It was a local dive, located on the same street on which they lived, a little less than two miles away. Lily decided to drive, rather than walk, because it was a little cold that evening and she didn't want to catch a chill.

There's a joke floating around in the mass market about a lady who walks into the bar—something that starts with "Did ya' ever hear the one about the drunk lady who walked into the bar alone on her 50th birthday?"

Lily never heard this joke. No. She was the one who spurred its creation.

When a girl turns 21 and goes to the bar on her birthday, everyone buys her drinks and cheers. It's okay when she gets shit-face drunk, because she's new to the game.

When a woman turns 30 and goes to the bar on her birthday, everyone buys her drinks and tells her how good she looks for her age. It's okay when she gets shit-face drunk, because she's still young.

When a woman turns 40 and goes to the bar on her birthday, a few people buy her drinks and a few others toast her milestone. It's okay when she gets shit-face drunk, because she's on the brink of being considered "old" for the first time.

When a woman turns 50 and goes to the bar on her birthday, well, that's another thing. There are few, if any, cheers or toasts. She's the only one who buys herself drinks. And, it's not okay for her to get shit-face drunk. She's 50, and she should know better than that by now.

When Lily turned 50 and went to the bar on her birthday, that's pretty much how things went.

She walked into the bar, sat down on a stool, and was immediately defeated by her surroundings. As alone as she'd felt drinking at home by herself, she felt even more alone in a bar filled with others.

There were a few older men drinking by themselves, but Lily didn't identify with them—even though that's the exact boat she was in. She was a little younger and a lot more attractive, but, just like them, she was out at the bar, alone, looking to drink her troubles away.

Several sets of young men and women filled the tables and booths on the far end of the bar. If given the choice, Lily would have chosen to identify with them. But she wasn't given the choice, as none of them gave her a second look or a second thought. She was at least 20 years older than the lot of them, which meant she'd be more of a mother figure than a drinking buddy or piece of tail.

The only person to talk to her was the bartender, when he took her drink order.

"A large draft," she said with a smile. "Today's my birthday."

"Happy birthday," the bartender replied as a matter of course. "That'll be $3."

Lily drank her beer and ordered another. By the time she was on her fourth draft, less than 45 minutes after she'd arrived at the bar, she was feeling pretty good about at least one of the situations she was in.

She'd stuck it to Bender after all these years. She'd broken one of his rules and showed him that he was not her boss. At 50, she was old enough to look after herself, answer to no one, and do as she pleased. It was a rebirth of sorts. And it was baptism by beer.

Just as she had these revelations, she had another as well. Those youngsters who'd paid her no mind were now looking her way, giggling and chuckling—and she knew they were giggling and chuckling at her.

They'd seen how much she drank, and how quickly she'd drunk it. They saw how pitiful and alone she was, making conversation with nobody but the bottom of her glass. She was all dressed up with nowhere to go, a joke to them in every sense of the word.

But, really, they weren't laughing at her. Not at all. One of the fellows had spotted a sign above the bar that read: "No shirt, No shoes, No service. No bra, No panties, No problem." That's why they were giggling and chuckling, why they were looking her way. It was that ridiculous sign and the conversation that ensued.

Drunk Lily hadn't seen the sign though.

Lily decided to leave the bar. She chugged what was left of her beer and grabbed her purse. Keys in hand, she didn't know whether she was going to head to another bar or go home. She'd make that decision based on the direction she drove once in the car.

Lily got behind the wheel, put the key in the ignition, and started the car. Foot on the brake, she shifted the car into drive. She hadn't even pulled out from her parking spot, drove no more than two feet, when she heard sirens wail and saw flashing red and blue lights.

"Shit," Lily said, taking notice of the squad car beside her.

She put her own car in park as the officer climbed out of his.

His approach was slow. He circled the car twice before coming over to Lily's window, which she'd already rolled down.

"Been drinkin' tonight?" he asked behind the flashlight he pointed in her face.

"A little," she answered. "It's my birthday."

"Well, birthday girl, get out of the car," he instructed. "Let's just see how much 'a little' is."

Lily had wanted attention on her big day, but this definitely was not the type of attention she'd had in mind. The officer asked her to walk in a straight line, track the movement of his finger from side to side, and put her index finger on her nose.

She failed each of these field sobriety tests and was arrested on the spot.

Lily was handcuffed and delicately placed in the back of the police car. The officer didn't have a breathalyzer unit on hand, so he set out to take her to the hospital for a blood draw to determine the level of alcohol in her blood.

As the policeman drove the car down familiar streets, Lily pleaded with him. She asked him not to arrest her, to just drop her off at home. She reminded him that it was her birthday and vowed to never drink again.

But all the officer did was giggle and chuckle. And this time, the giggles and chuckles were directed at her. This time she was, indeed, the joke.

The plea which got the greatest laugh was when she asked the officer if she could call her husband.

"Please, sir," she said to the policeboy who was at least ten years her junior. "Please, sir, please let me call my husband. He'll be really worried. He'll be so mad. I need to call him to let him know about this."

"Honey," the officer said with a grunted laugh, "he already knows."

"How?" Lily asked.

"He put a bolo out on you."

"A bolo?"

"Yeah, a bolo."

"What's that?"

"Bolo... B-O-L-O," the officer spelled it out. "Bolo, be on the lookout... He called the cops on you, babe. He called and told us to be on the lookout for a blue Ford sedan with a very drunk woman driving. Gave us your license plate number. Told us exactly where to find you too.

"He ratted you out."

"No, not Bender," Lily said, tears pooling her eyes. "He wouldn't do that to me, not on my birthday."

"Well, he did," said the officer. "You must have done something to really piss him off."

Somewhere out there, at that exact moment, there was a woman being raped—maybe a lesbian teen at a party, who was just being herself. And at that exact moment, there was a woman being beaten—maybe because she forgot to latch the child gate or her husband'd had a bad day. But neither the rapist nor the attacker was brought to justice that night. It was Lily, sweet Lily, who was captured and cuffed, for driving under the influence—for driving two feet towards a straight shot destination less than two miles away.

Lily chose silence for the rest of the ride. At the hospital, a clumsy phlebotomist poked at her arm three times before Lily spoke again. "Enough," was what she said. "You're hurting me. Stop. If you haven't gotten blood yet, I must not have any to give."

So without her blood being drawn, Lily was cuffed again, delicately placed in the back of the squad car again, and taken to jail, where she was tossed into a cell in which she'd spend the remainder of the night and much of the next day.

"I guess we're even now," Lily thought to herself as she sat on the cold slab of poorly painted concrete that jutted out from one of the four cinderblock walls that confined her.

But even for what?

Was this Bender's act of revenge against the fact that Lily had once been instrumental in his own time in jail? Was it retaliation for her act of adultery? Or was it simply his way of enforcing his rules?

Lily hoped that it was for the last of this list—for if it had been for either of the two other reasons, that meant Bender had lied dormant for many, many years. And, to Lily, it meant that the worst was yet to come.

If he could sit on something for so long, wait for over a decade to deliver a punch, what else did he have in store for Lily? She did not want to know.

But she knew one thing: The next time he delivered a punch, she'd punch back.

Late the next afternoon, Lily was ROR—another acronym with which she was not familiar. It stood for "Released on Recognizance," which meant that she was released from jail without bail, on the promise that she'd show up for her court date.

And, as promised, she did show up for her court date, ten days later, at which time she surrendered her rights to a fair trial in exchange for the prosecutor's proposal of ARD. ARD—yet another acronym.

ARD. Accelerated Rehabilitative Disposition. The judge explained it to Lily as a luxury offered to first-time offenders that gives them a parole-like alternative to jail. The bailiff who stamped her paperwork, however, had a more apposite explanation. He described it as the laxative of the Pennsylvania judiciary—a way for the state to shove a huge pile of shit through the judicial system with one hard push.

Lily's ARD program involved attending six weeks of classes on substance abuse and road safety. She was court ordered to go to nine Alcoholics Anonymous meetings, pay a fine in excess of $1,500, and submit to random drug and alcohol tests at the discretion of her case manager.

She also lost her driver's license for a period of one year. Under general ARD provisions, she would've only gotten a one-month suspension, but her refusal to have her blood drawn confounded this variable. Even though Lily, arguably, had good reason to object to the unskilled nurse's mistreatment of her veins, state law mandated a one-year suspension upon any refusal.

From the moment Lily was released from jail to Bender's last day on earth, Bender repeatedly told Lily that he'd called the police on her for her own good. He claimed that she'd been drinking far too much in recent years, and that getting behind the wheel of a car drunk had taken things to a new extreme. Calling the cops on her, he said, was the one way he could get her to stop before things got any worse.

On its face, this argument made a great deal of sense. But sense, like beauty, is only skin-deep.

Bender was the goose to Lily's gander, the pot to her kettle. She'd done nothing more than what he'd been doing at least once a week for more than two-thirds of his life. In fact, she'd done far less.

Without question, what she did was wrong. Very wrong. But Bender was not in any position to point his fingers at her.

And maybe that absurdity is why discussion of Lily's arrest didn't take place all that often.

Sure, it was discussed, at great length, the day that Lily got home from jail, when she asked him how he could do such a thing to her and stressed how absurd his reasoning was.

But neither Lily's tears nor her words could penetrate the superficial sense of Bender's argument. He refused to recognize that the house in which he lived was constructed entirely of glass. So Lily stopped trying to convince him, and the topic of her arrest became a seldom visited one.

It just was what it was.

It was something that happened.

Both Lily and Bender wanted to move on.

Moving on was harder for Lily to do, in an unembellished, physical sense. For years, she'd abided by Bender's rules about where she could go and what she could do. Now she had legal restrictions circumscribing her life as well, the most significant of which was her suspended driving privileges.

The loss of those privileges made her all the more Bender's ward. Since she was not permitted to drive, she had to ask Bender to take her places. To the grocery store, to a doctor's appointment, to those court-ordered classes and meetings—to any and every destination over the course of a year, Bender was to be Lily's escort and ride.

And she had to do things according to his schedule, which meant she could do very little while he worked during the day and she'd have to miss out on Thursday night AA meetings so that he could sing karaoke at the bar.

When Bender was unavailable to give, or uninterested in giving, Lily a ride, she had to take the bus. Public transportation is no big deal—for people who are used to using it. But for someone who has driven wherever she pleased for 34 years, who has only ever used public transport during vacations in other states, it's a pain in the ass. Taking to buses so late in life isn't something that people typically do, and it's hard to teach an old dog new tricks.

Nonetheless, Lily acclimated to her new set of rules,

which, mind you, were rules in addition to those Bender already had in place. Bender still required Lily to put things on the calendar and check in when she was out. He still did not allow houseguests without preapproval and still did not allow Lily to attend certain social events.

He still set up his tell-tales and still kept tabs on Lily as best he could—and the law was on his side this time around.

While Lily was limited more so than ever in what she could do, there was one cherished freedom that she still had. Her ARD program couldn't take it away from her, and Bender had been kind enough to respect this one right.

Her rooftop retreat.

In all the years that Bender set his tell-tales in place and restricted Lily's activity outside of the house, he never interfered with her rooftop retreat. He didn't track her movement to and from the roof and he never dictated, or even suggested, that she refrain from visiting her safe spot—not before she was arrested, and not after.

Lily deserved one safe haven, Bender supposed. He had his music to turn to, even if only in the form of karaoke at bars or scream sessions in the basement, and he had his visits with Bob, so she too should have something.

A trip to the roof was a pretty harmless thing—he figured there was little trouble she could get into, or cause, up there.

He was, however, quite wrong.

~ 13 ~

An electronic bell chimes over the speakers, generated from some box out of sight and out of mind.

It chimes again.

The door at the back left corner of the room opens and a small crowd of people push in. They're entering through one door so that they can exit through another.

Lily catches a glimpse of Celia and turns her head away. She wants no longer to be reminded of a past so far out of her reach.

Leo kneels down in front of Lily and scans the entire space around her, taking in all that he can until he can take it no more. After a moment of silence, he speaks.

Tears wetting his eyes, he says, "Until tomorrow, my Flower."

"Until then," his Flower says back.

He stands up and takes a few steps away from Lily. He is wobbling a little, so he stops in his tracks. He reaches his arm out, calling his wife to his side. Celia rushes over and gives him a loose hug, from which neither she nor Leo let go. Her arm around his waist, his arm on her shoulders, they follow the stream of human traffic out of the room.

Lily is actually pretty astounded by the amount of people she sees leaving the funeral home. She'd been astounded by the volume of guests all day, and by their nature as well.

If the success of one's life is to be measured by the turnout at his or her final farewell, then Bender had lived a mighty successful life. He may have never achieved rockstar fame, but his viewing brought out a lot of fans.

Lily hadn't counted the number of different people who showed up, and she is not going to start now. But she guesses it was somewhere in the ballpark of 200.

Two-hundred people! She finds it hard to believe that Bender knew that many people. But, she realizes, they probably weren't all his friends. She'd seen quite a few people who she is certain that Bender did not know. Those people were her friends and acquaintances—and some random anonymous alcoholics—who must have come out not to view Bender's coffin but for Lily's sake.

So, sure, yes, between the two of them, a gathering of 200 people is no surprise. And it warms Lily's heart to think that there were those who came out for her sake alone.

But if there had been 200 people here throughout the day, only a few remained now. As a final collection of visitors makes its way to the door, Lily decides it is time for her to leave too.

She grabs her purse, slides it over her hardened fist, and moves to the hallway.

She can hear her daughters sobbing in the larger room, which is now empty but for them and death. She walks past the room with her eyes fixed straight ahead. She maintains tunnel vision so as to respect her daughters' rights to a private viewing, and so as to prevent herself from viewing the lacquered box in which her husband now rests.

The tunnel of her vision is grotesquely long. It takes her more time to walk the path to the door than she wishes it would. To her, it feels like a funhouse trick, an expanding hallway that only grows longer when you think you've reached its end.

As she trudges the seemingly endless course, she feels lightheaded and sick to her stomach, her heart, and her soul.

"You've made it this far," she tells herself, "just a few

252

more feet to go. Then you're in the clear."

She's reflecting on the fact that she's made it through this entire day without spilling her secret, without opening her hand to reveal what's inside.

It very well could be that it is the weight of these things that is holding her back and preventing her speedy progression down the hallway. The weight of her secret, combined with the weight of the paper, is possibly too much for her to carry anymore.

Oh how her body aches! But she can't let go. Not yet.

Let go. "Let go." Those two tiny words mean more to Lily than anyone else will ever know. They're the last two words Bender said to her before he died, a crucial element of the story she has not told.

Though she's told no one what happened, she's played it out innumerous times in her head.

And now she plays it out again.

~ 14 ~

They'd fought that night, the night that Bender died.

The fight started in the living room and ended on the back lawn. Between those two points, there was a lot that went down. A lot. Everything, in fact.

But there's no putting the cart before the horse here. Their fight actually began a day before it ended, allowing their contentions to ferment over that brief period of time.

It all started when Bender came home early one afternoon. Lily was sitting on the couch reading a book as her homemade lasagna baked in the oven.

"You're home early," she said when he walked through the front door.

"Yeah," he said in return, "I didn't go to work today."

"Well then, where the hell have you been?" Lily asked with a spirited smirk.

"The same place I was two days ago, and last week," Bender told her.

"I've been seeing someone," he added.

"What?"

"An oncologist," he clarified as he walked to the kitchen. "I have cancer."

Lily's book fell to the floor, followed by her feet a few seconds later.

"What?"

She ran to the kitchen.

"I have cancer," he said again. "I just thought you'd like

to know that I'll be dead soon… So what's for dinner?"

"What?"

"Stop asking that, Lily," Bender commanded.

He opened the oven door to see what was inside.

"Lasagna, sweet! You gonna make garlic bread too?"

"What?" Lily asked for the fourth time. He'd told her to stop asking that question, but she couldn't think of anything else to say.

Bender didn't answer her. He grabbed a beer from the refrigerator and walked past her, back to the living room.

Lily followed.

He sat down on the couch and popped his beer open. He sipped from the can as if he hadn't just said what he'd just said.

Lily sat down beside him. She watched as he took another sip. She still couldn't think of anything else to say. So she said nothing, sitting by her husband's side in stunned silence.

She'd been stunned not just by his words, but also by the way he'd delivered them. He'd been so casual, so nonchalant, about it, as if the information was a dismissible, everyday fact, not like the shocker it was.

Nearly 30 years ago, he'd revealed his true age to Lily and told her about what happened to make him move out of his apartment—he had approached these topics with more carefulness and compassion than the grave matter at hand.

Those other topics had been such meaningless things! They didn't merit such care. A topic like cancer did. But Bender didn't want to give cancer the care it demanded. He'd decided that it had already taken too much from him.

She was waiting for him to say something. But he just sat there drinking his beer.

The silence was too much for Lily to take, so she spoke again: "Please, Bender. Explain."

"There's nothing to explain, Lily. I have cancer. That's it."

"But what does that mean? What are you gonna do? What happens next?"

"What happens next?" Bender laughed. "What happens next is I die."

"No, I mean, where do we go from here?" Lily asked. "How are they going to treat it?"

"They're not," Bender said as he pulled the can away from his lips.

"Wh—," Lily caught herself before she articulated the "—at." Instead, she asked, "Why?"

"It's stage four, Lily. I'm pretty much already dead."

"Don't say that," she moaned. "There's got to be something they can do."

"It's already in my lymph nodes… Or at least that's where it was last week. By now it's probably in my bones too, or wherever it goes next… It's metastatic. I have no chance."

"But what about chemo?" Lily persisted. "Radiation?"

"Come on, Lily," Bender said as he glanced at her. She hadn't realized it until now, but this was the first time he looked her in the face during their conversation.

"All those things do is buy time," Bender continued. "And the time they buy isn't worth the cost… At least not to me. Maybe treatment would get me a couple more months, but I'd spend those months puking my guts out, lying in bed. That's not what I call life, Lily.

"Unfortunately, it's not the kind of cancer they can

prescribe medical marijuana for. If I could score some good weed, that'd at least give me a reason to live. But, eh, without that, what else do I have to look forward to?"

Bender had meant that bit about weed to be some type of joke. But Lily wasn't laughing.

"You have two daughters, Bender. Don't you want to give them more time with their dad?"

"No," Bender said without pause. "I want to give them memories of me being me. I want them to remember a strong dad who loved them, not a sick old man.

"I'm not even going to tell the girls about this. And neither are you. I don't want them to know."

"But don't you think they deserve to know?"

"No, Lily. They deserve better than that."

"But don't you think they'll find out?"

"Not unless one of us tells them… And, like I said, I'm not going to—and neither are you. You owe me that much, Lily."

"But if it's only gonna get worse," Lily started, "won't…"

"No, Lily," Bender said to stop her from asking whatever she was about to ask.

"The oncologist gave me one month, max," Bender reported, "and that was last week. I figure I've only got a couple more weeks left. I'm just gonna wait it out.

"What's probably gonna happen is that my organs will start shutting down, and hopefully my lungs will go first. That way I'll just stop breathing, maybe die in my sleep… That's how I want to go—naturally, right here at home. I don't want to spend my last days alive in some hospice or hospital. I'm an asshole, I know that. But not even an asshole like me should have to go through torture like that."

"But…"

"Please, Lily, just stop. It's my decision, not yours. This is what I want."

And Lily did stop, at least for the moment. She sat there and said nothing more.

"So," Bender grinned, "you gonna make garlic bread or what?"

Lily hadn't planned on making garlic bread, but she had to now. She had to obey her husband, and had to honor this dying man's request. So to the kitchen she went.

As she worked on dinner in the kitchen, she heard Bender flick the television on. He was watching a sitcom, laughing and snorting as if nothing was wrong.

They ate their dinner with little verbal exchange. This was how they usually ate together. Their silence usually meant nothing, but it meant everything during this meal.

Lily could barely eat—she was too full of questions. She did little more than play with her food, pushing it around her plate with her fork. Every once in a while, she'd take a small bite, so that she had something in her mouth that prevented her from speaking when she knew Bender did not want to converse.

It wasn't until Bender was done eating that Lily addressed him. As she stood to clear the plates from the table, she picked up somewhere around where she'd left off: "There's still more I want to know."

"Like what, Lily? What do you want to know?"

"Well…," she thought for a moment, "You said it's in your lymph nodes now and it's spreading. What kind of cancer is it? Where did it start?"

Bender was reluctant to reply. Now he was the one

playing with his fork. He'd picked it up unwittingly and was moving it back and forth between his right thumb and middle finger like the sputtering propeller in the wingfan of a failing jet plane.

"It started," Bender started, "in my mouth. I have oral cancer, cancer of the mouth."

Why was Bender reluctant to offer this reply? Because he'd always had a filthy mouth and that filthy mouth caught up with him in the end.

It was Bender's filthy mouth that made Lily notice him in the first place. It was Bender's filthy mouth that insulted Lily every day of their life together. And it was into that filthy mouth that Bender inserted wads of chewing tobacco for more than 50 years.

How humbling, nay humiliating, that Bender's filthy mouth should get the better of him!

The word "irony" is one of the most misused words in the English language. And use of that word here would only demonstrate that fact. It is not ironic when a lifelong tobacco user is diagnosed as having cancer. Nor is it "coincidental," which is another commonly misused word.

What it is is incidental. Just ask the Surgeon General.

Every saleable container of tobacco is required by law to have a warning label which states, in one way or another, that use of that product may cause cancer. While not every tobacco user will end up having cancer and not everyone with cancer was/is a tobacco user, there's a damn good reason for those labels.

But even more than being incidental, it's something else: It's sad. It's just plain sad.

And "sad" is the only way that Lily chose to see it. In her head, under her breath, behind closed doors, Lily had cursed

Bender thousands of times for the foul things he'd said to her over the years, but she'd never wished for anything like this.

Lily's next question for Bender was how he found out that he had cancer. He explained that he went to the dentist a month ago because he had lumps throughout his mouth. He'd thought it was gum disease or ulcers, but his dentist knew it was something else and referred him to a specialist without even doing a brush biopsy.

Lily went on to ask Bender more questions for the next hour or so, and he answered them all. It wasn't a fight, more like an inquisition—and it was one of the more civil discussions they'd ever had. It only lasted so long because of the contemplative recesses and intermittent beer breaks.

Bender was the one to conclude this chapter of their conversation, after answering a dozen of Lily's questions.

"Look, Lily," he said, "I can't talk about this anymore right now. I'm gonna go get changed and head out to the bar to sing. We can talk more about this tomorrow if you want, but I can't keep at it tonight. I need to take a breather."

It was time again for Lily to obey her husband and to grant this dying man his wish. So she stopped asking questions, for now.

When he went out that evening, Lily tried to keep herself busy around the house. She washed all the dishes and mopped the floor. She did a few loads of laundry and tried to get back to reading her book. She put a cake in the oven and played a few hands of solitaire.

But nothing she could do could keep her mind busy. She could not stop thinking about Bender, cancer, and Bender's cancer.

Around 11 that night, she decided to go to bed. She took four over-the-counter sleeping pills, even though the bottle suggested a dosage of one. Sleep was something she would not have to feign that night—within 20 minutes, she passed out on the bed.

She woke up early the next morning. Bender was lying beside her in bed. He was usually the first to wake up in the morning, so she wasn't really used to seeing him there. He looked so peaceful, Lily thought with a smile. But that smile went away as quickly as it came. It was replaced with panic.

Peaceful. Peaceful! She wondered if he was actually at peace—if he was dead, if he'd died in his sleep like he wanted to, like he expected he would. She thought of shaking him or calling out his name, but she knew better. He might wake up and attack her if she tried something like that. So she had to figure out something else to do.

First, Lily pulled the blanket down from Bender's chest and watched closely, to see if it moved up and down to indicate breathing. But she couldn't quite tell.

Next, she tickled his cheek ever so softly. His hand flew up in the air towards his face, and Lily moved her hand out of the way just in time. He scratched his cheek, grunted, and rolled over. Ah, man alive, Bender was not dead, just fast asleep!

Calmed, cooled, and collected, Lily crawled out of bed. She grabbed a quick change of clothes from her closet and headed to the bathroom to get dressed, making as little noise as possible so as not to wake Bender.

In the bathroom, she rushed through the process of readying herself. Since she wasn't dressing to impress, she decided not to apply a full face of makeup, but instead to just slap on some eyeliner. It took her a while to find her eyeliner pencil, which was buried at the bottom of the drawer.

Lily ran downstairs, into the dining room, where she slid into her shoes. As she turned to walk away, she felt a sharp pain in the arch of her right foot.

"Son of a bitch!" she exclaimed, before taking the shoe off and turning it upside down. A tiny piece of gravel spilled out. She massaged her arch a little and then put her shoe back on her foot.

To the living room, she went next—to collect her coat and purse. Her coat was beneath Bender's, so she had to rehang his after putting on her own. She placed the three magazines that were lying on top of her purse on the coffee table, fanned out for display.

When she pulled the front door open, it seemed to open with more resistance than usual and she heard a strange noise—something like a pop, or a tear, a crinkle of sorts. She'd have to ask Bender to take a look at it later, she thought.

As she exited the porch, a twig fell from the gate latch. She narrowly escaped tripping over it. "That would have been just what I needed today," she mumbled on her way to the car.

Inside the car, she noticed an empty soda bottle in the center console. She couldn't believe Bender'd been so thoughtless, leaving a bottle in a place where it would clearly have to be moved in order for the next driver to shift gears.

And this was all the mind that Lily paid to the little hitches that got in her way that morning. She thought nothing of them. She made no inferences, asked no questions. If anything, it was just a weird start to her day— or, maybe, a slow start to a day that'd drag on forever.

Her mind was too preoccupied to give these tiny details any more attention. She had a bigger mission for the day. She was headed to the library.

To the library. She was going to the library to conduct research on oral cancer, cancer of the mouth. The idea to do this had hit her yesterday, when Bender talked about the pointlessness of treatment and the expiration date that'd been placed on his life.

She'd decided she wasn't going to settle for those conclusions the way he had. If there was information out there that suggested that treatment might somehow work, if there was some medical article or research study that showed he had a fighting chance, she was going to find it and present him with facts and figures that would give him hope and save him from death.

But just because a person wants to find facts and figures that support a certain conclusion, that doesn't mean those facts and figures actually exist. It took Lily several hours at the library to realize this.

She'd pulled out numerous books, referred to articles and spun through rolls of microfiche, consulted the librarian, then some, then some, and then some more. The sources pretty much all said the same thing: Bender was screwed.

Given the stage to which Bender's cancer had already progressed, considering the other facts and factors he'd shared with her, Bender was already living on borrowed time. Survival rates in the single digits. Lives extended but a few weeks or months. There was nothing to support any conclusion other than the one Bender'd already reached.

Lily decided next to look to survivor stories, self-help books, and inspirational texts. The information they contained was far more promising—but it was worthless in Bender's case.

Those materials may have been intended to bring hope, but they brought Lily nothing but despair—despair because they did carry messages of hope, messages of the sort Bender did not want to hear.

Some people do find God late in life, when they're sick or condemned—but only if they choose to look. And Bender had made no such choice.

Lily knew how Bender's mind worked, for the most part. He wouldn't want to hear spiritual mumbo-jumbo or new age mantras. He liked cold, hard facts. And the cold, hard facts were clear on this matter.

Lily had lost all track of time at the library. It wasn't until she heard nearby church bells ring that she realized it was 6 p.m., and that she'd been at the library for nearly nine hours. She'd put in more than the average work day of research without even knowing it, and without finding anything sound to present to her husband.

Notwithstanding the results of her studies, she printed out a few articles and checked out a few books—at the very least, these things would be proof of her whereabouts for the day, and, at the very most, they'd give her something to discuss with Bender.

Lily left the library and returned home. When she walked in, around 7, she found Bender lying on the couch watching television. He looked tired and agitated. He looked sick and old.

"Hey," he said.

She was alarmed that he didn't ask her where she'd been.

"Hey... I was at the library," she asserted.

"Okay."

It was unlike him to not press her for more information.

"I was doing some research," she began to explain. "I wanted to know more. I read a lot of stuff that says you don't have to give up, stuff about not losing your will."

She knew this line of reasoning wouldn't work, but it was the best line she had and it was worth trying.

"Lily," he said, sitting up, "I don't want to hear it."

"But, just listen. Why not try treatment for a week or two, see how it makes you feel, if they think it's working. Then, once you try, you can decide for sure."

"I've already decided, Lily. You won't change my mind. You can't save me, babe—I'm already dead."

Bender rubbed his fingers and thumb over his eyes. He sniffled and coughed, then reached into his pants pocket and extracted something.

Lily's jaw dropped.

"You've got to be fucking kidding me!" she shrieked, as she watched Bender open his can of chewing tobacco, scoop out a gob, and insert it into his cancer-ridden mouth, between his cancerous gums and cancerous cheek.

"What?" he asked, tossing the shiny can onto the coffee table in front of him.

"You have cancer, Bender," Lily said, as if she needed to remind him. "You have oral cancer. And you're still chewing? Don't you think you should stop?"

"Stop? Why would I stop now? There's no point in stopping now."

Bender was laughing.

He was actually laughing.

"Don't you think it'll just make things worse?" Lily asked.

"Worse?" Bender laughed, again. "You know what, Lily. You asked me a ton of questions yesterday, but there's one you didn't ask… You didn't ask me how I'm doing. You didn't ask me how I feel. So, ask me Lily. Go ahead. Ask me how I feel."

Lily didn't speak.

"Ask me, Lily!" Bender shouted. "Fucking ask me how

I'm doing. Fucking ask me how I feel. Do it."

Lily didn't speak.

"Ask me, Lily! Now!"

Lily knew she had to ask, so that things didn't get any worse than the worse they were already getting.

"How are you Bender? How do you feel?"

"I feel like shit, Lily," Bender said. His voice was rough and mean, but there were tears in his eyes.

"When my head doesn't feel like it's gonna explode, I'm so dizzy I can't walk," he continued. "My neck feels ten times its regular size. And you wanna know what else, Lily?"

"What?"

"I shit my pants today. I fucking shit my pants today. I'm a grown man, and I shit my pants today. It just came out of me. I didn't even feel it coming on.

"And there was blood in it—clots of dark blood. I don't know what that means, but it can't be good."

Lily's eyes started to tear up as well. She hadn't thought to ask him how he was doing—and, even if she had thought to ask, she never expected to hear things like this. Her heart ached.

"My body feels like someone beat me with a hammer. I lose my breath doing nothing, when I walk up the steps, when I stand up. I can't even make myself stand up without losing my breath.

"And that's just my body, Lily. What the hell do you think my mind is going through? I'm gonna die. I'm dying. I'm not cool with that. I don't know what death is, what's gonna happen to me, how much more I'm gonna have to suffer, where I'm gonna end up.

"Is there a heaven, Lily? Is there a hell? Where am I

gonna end up? And what about all the horrible shit I did to you? … I'm thinking about that, too. I'm wondering if I'm gonna have to pay for it. I'm wondering why I ever did it in the first place, if I'm paying for it now.

"So, that, Lily, *that* is how I feel," Bender concluded. "You really want me to add nicotine withdrawal on top of all that? … Get real."

Bender stood up and walked out of the room. He went into the kitchen to get a beer and prepare a plate of leftover lasagna.

Lily stood in the living room and thought about what Bender had just said. She hadn't considered how nicotine withdrawal would take a toll on him. All she'd considered is how the cessation of carcinogen use might buy him more time. She thought it could only make things better, not make them worse.

She was, of course, wrong—in an empirical sense. The amount of nicotine he could use in the amount of time he had left to use it was so minimal in comparison to what he'd used throughout his life. The damage had already been done. Stopping his tobacco use at this point in time would be like using a cocktail umbrella in a rainstorm. It wouldn't make a bit of difference.

But Lily was unable to frame things this way. She believed in the sanctity of the spirit from the initial moment of conception to the final moment of death—and if there was any way to save even a second of life, Lily was gonna do whatever she had to do to save it.

She looked down at the coffee table and noticed that he'd left his chew there. She picked up the can, put it in her own pocket, and went up, up, and away—to her hiding spot on the roof, to hide from Bender both her self and his chew.

On the tiny roof space, she removed the can of chew from

her pocket and stared at it, spinning it around like a wheel in her hand. It looked like a hockey puck. Lily smiled. She was reminded of that urinal cake Bender put in his mouth the first time she ever saw him. And she was reminded of other things, of good and bad moments they shared—of a life lived together, with plenty of ups and downs. It'd been a bumpy ride, but it was a trip worth taking, if for nothing but the incredible scenery along the way.

She'd been up on her rooftop for a little less than two hours when she heard the attic door open. Bender made his way up the stairs and to the pane. Lily clasped her hand shut when he opened the window.

He didn't have to ask her what was in her hand. He already knew. It was his, and he wanted it back.

"Give it to me, Lily," he ordered.

"No," she growled back.

"Lily, I'm not kidding. Give it to me… Now!"

"No."

"Lily. Don't be such a bitch. Give me my chew."

"No."

What Bender did next caught Lily off guard.

He climbed out the window and onto her roof space. He'd never done this before, and she never expected he would. He was, after all, deathly afraid of heights.

"Okay, Lily, that's enough," he said, kneeling down beside her and reaching for her hand.

But before he could make contact with her hand, Lily took action. She tossed the chew can upward and outward away from her body. It flew through the air like a tiny Frisbee, a disc at the ancient Olympic games.

Bender turned his head and watched as it landed in the backyard.

"You fucking pig!" Bender yelled.

And he did more than yell. He sprang forward and sunk his body into hers. He grabbed her by the neck and crashed her head into the exterior brick wall behind her.

This was the first time Bender laid hands on Lily since the night that Fox died.

This was the first time Bender laid hands on Lily since Lily decided that, the next time he delivered a punch, she'd punch back.

And this was the first time that Lily did, indeed, punch back.

Though, it wasn't a punch, per se. It was more like a karate chop. She stiffened her hand flat and straight and delivered a heavy, forceful blow straight to Bender's neck, which caused him to fall backwards.

He gasped. She'd knocked the wind out of him, both by the strength of the whack she delivered and by the fact that she delivered it at all.

He was lying on his back like a turtle on its shell, struggling to right himself so that he could come at Lily again.

"You're gonna pay for that, Lily," he said as he turned himself over. He got up on his knees and grabbed Lily's leg.

This was the second time Bender laid hands on Lily since the night that Fox died.

This was the second time Bender laid hands on Lily since Lily decided that, the next time he delivered a punch, she'd punch back.

And this was the second time that Lily did, indeed, punch back.

Though, it wasn't a punch, per se. It was a kick. She stiffened her other leg flat and straight and delivered a heavy, forceful kick straight to Bender's chest, which caused him to fall backwards.

The strength of Lily's second retaliatory move had been even greater than that of her first. When she kicked Bender, when he fell back, he didn't land flat on his back. There was an arch to how he fell, one that sent him farther backward.

He still had a hold on Lily's leg.

Instinctively, she started kicking that leg, jerking it, to get free of Bender's hold on her. And this movement only added to Bender's movement, more force acting against him, more momentum in the wrong direction.

Pushing. Backwards. Sliding.

Sliding turned into rolling.

He still had a hold on Lily's leg.

Rolling turned into stillness.

Their bodies were positioned like a capital "T," if read from the attic window. Bender was lying flat on his back, parallel to the sill of the window, and Lily was the stem that jackknifed him.

But they weren't positioned near the window. They were quite far away, as fate would have it.

"I'm gonna fall," Bender cried out.

All the backwards motion—the falling, the sliding, the rolling—landed Bender on the edge of the rooftop, with the majority of his body across the storm gutters, which were already bellowing and buckling at his weight.

It was his grip on Lily's leg that kept him from falling off of the roof completely. Lily's leg was the only thing keeping him alive.

And then he let go.

He let go of Lily's leg.

Lily immediately scooted back further onto the rooftop, to get more solid grounding.

And just as immediately, she dove forward again.

She grabbed Bender's left arm with both of her hands while the gutter beneath him finally gave way and fell to the ground.

His body fell too, left dangling from the side of the house, held in place by Lily's slipping grasp.

Lily's chest and stomach pressed against the smooth slate. She tried to dig her feet—her breasts, her elbows—into the surface, to resist the downward pull of Bender's body.

"Let me fall, Lily!" Bender shouted.

"No!"

"Let me fall," he instructed.

But Lily could not do that. She could not give up on a life when there was a chance to save it.

"No," she wept.

"Lily, come on," Bender begged. "You can't save me. You're not strong enough. Just let go."

"No!"

Her body was slowly inching forward, downward. Her arms were burning, aching, getting weaker.

The weight of the world was not on her shoulders. It was in her hands.

"Lily, please!"

Bender swatted his free arm in the air, trying to beat her hands off of his arm. His efforts made him even heavier.

"Lily," Bender said for the last time ever. "Let go."

"I won't," she bawled. "I won't let go."

And she meant it.

~ 15 ~

Lily is at the funeral home again, for the second day in a row.

She is very disoriented. She does not remember leaving last night, or what happened after she left.

She's not sure how she got back here today.

The last thing she remembers is walking down this same hallway—to leave. And now she's walking down it again. But this time, she's walking in the opposite direction.

She's walking to, not away from, the action.

It is the morning of the funeral. Most, if not all, of the people who had visited yesterday are here again today. They are all gathered in the large showing room.

Lily knows that it is time for her, too, to go to that room. She must finally face the truth, and meet reality head on.

In her hand, she still carries that folded piece of paper. She hugs it with her palm—holding on to it with all her might. Perhaps it will give her the courage to do what she must now do.

She is at the doorway of the showing room, where scores of people are standing. She can barely see beyond the crowd to discern any particular faces or to see the casket.

What she hears is mostly silence, interjected only by the warm voice of the priest who is standing in front of the audience.

She steps forward to enter the room and is struck by an incredibly odd sensation.

She tries to walk closer to the front of the room, but

it's difficult for her to make her way through. She tries to squeeze between people at the back of the assembly. She quietly asks to be pardoned. But no one budges. The people are not moving. It's as if they are deaf, as if they can't hear her. She cannot pass.

Lily feels anxious. She is frustrated. Confused.

She turns and runs out of the room. She runs down the hallway, toward the smaller room—the sitting parlor.

When she arrives at the smaller room, she is not surprised to see that it is empty. She expected that it would be, since everyone else is in the other room for the ceremony.

She looks to the corner of the room, to the couch where she sat yesterday.

The couch, however, is not there.

It never was.

What is there is an easel. And it props up something.

She walks over to examine it.

The easel is propping up a large photo collage, which contains dozens of photos.

Lily's head feels light. So light. Her heart is pounding.

The collage chronicles her life, Bender's life, and her and Bender's life together. There are photos of her as a child, photos of her with Roberta, even photos of her with Carla and Jill. There are photos of Bender as a boy, of him with his parents, of him with the different bands he fronted over the years.

Several of the photos are of Lily and Bender together—a photo of their wedding in the park, of them on trips they took to the beach.

But most of the photos are of the entire family—of Lily, Bender, Tina, and Robbie.

Christmases. Easters. Birthdays. Vacations.

Random photos.

Happy faces.

Smiles.

Lily's eyes are moving rapidly from one image to the next. Her breathing is quick and shallow. She is frightened.

At the bottom of the collage, there is an empty space. It is obvious that a photo had been placed there and then removed later.

Lily's right hand tingles with pins and needles, as if it had fallen asleep and only just now woken.

She draws her closed hand to her chest, sweeping it across her breasts and over her heart.

And then she opens it. With her other hand, she extracts the piece of paper and unfolds it.

She looks at what she's holding.

It's the missing photo.

A family photo—of Lily, Bender, and their daughters. It was taken last Christmas, when they all went out for a night at the theater to see a holiday performance.

She flips the photo over, though she's not certain why.

On the back, there is a message scrawled in green ink: "We're with you always."

Lily feels her body swaying. Her head is spinning. She can't see straight. She can't think straight.

All of her senses are affronted in an instant. She smells the stench of 13,200 dirty diapers and the aroma of 25,000 gallons of gasoline. Her stomach is filled with 7,500 pounds of rotten meat, and her feet are blistered from walking 35,770 miles.

She's high from 25,000 cups of coffee, and drunk from 654,080 ounces of alcohol. She feels the pleasure of 75—no, make that 77—throbbing cocks inside her; the pain of two babies bursting out of her vagina, and of one dying in her womb.

Sadness. Disgust. Embarrassment. Guilt. If only she'd been a wee bit stronger…

Twenty hurtful nicknames. Two black eyes. Thirteen other scrapes and bruises.

A body full of broken bones. Bloodied. Dying. Dead. One untimely death.

One untimely death.

The only secret sweet Lily has been keeping is from herself.

She feels the bulk of Bender's body pulling on her arms. She feels her own body slipping. She's falling down. She's falling down with him.

When she told Bender she wouldn't let go, she meant it. She didn't let go.

The weight of the world was in her hands, but her arms were too weak to lift it. So she just held steady and let it happen. She let him bring her down with him—one time too many.

One untimely death. Lily's.

The night that Bender died, Lily died too. And it's only now that she realizes it.

She runs back to the other room, where the mourners are walking in procession past not one but two caskets. One casket is Bender's. The other is Lily's. This is her funeral, too.

"NO!!!!!" she screams.

But no one hears her.

Just like no one heard her yesterday.

All those conversations she thought she was having? She never had them. By all means, they took place—just not with her.

Those guests who casually dismissed her, who murmured under their breath, who made hollow remarks and offered empty condolences? Ah, that's just the funeral home experience, the grieving process!

When Jimmy Hayes apologized for using the word "ghost," when he talked about not knowing what to do without Bender? He wasn't talking to Lily. He was talking to Leo.

That conversation with Cookie in the bathroom? That was nothing more than the idiosyncratic chatter of a developmentally disabled adult who talks to herself quite often.

When Leo talked about how Celia was baggage? He was talking to Jimmy Hayes. Just some good old fashioned guy talk, the kind of shit guys say when there aren't any women around.

What about everything else that happened with Leo? Hadn't he stood by her last night? Hadn't he told her he missed her? Didn't he kneel down before her?

No. Lily was not the object of these actions. The collage was.

It was recognition of Lily's death that brought Leo back to Pittsburgh. But he couldn't handle being in the same room as her dead body for very long, so he stationed himself by the collage and looked at photos of her when she was living. When he knelt down, he knelt to get a closer look at those photos. When he spoke, he spoke to those photos, not to Lily, whom he couldn't have known was right there with him.

But how did Lily get that photo in her hand? How could she have removed it from the collage?

Come on, Lily didn't do that. She didn't remove the photo. Tina did. She and Robbie selected their favorite family picture and placed it in the casket with their mother—in her hand, something tangible she could hold onto to remind her of happy times with her family.

All this while, Lily only heard what she wanted to hear, only saw what she wanted to see. She believed what she wanted to believe.

Maybe there was a part of her that knew she was dead this whole time. Maybe it was that part of her that made her refrain from lengthy conversations, eye contact, and physical interaction. Maybe that part of her was protecting the rest of her, or was just sitting back waiting for her to put two and two together.

Whatever it was doing, it gave her time—time for her to review her life's most vital moments.

They say that when a person dies, her life passes before her eyes. But nobody talks about the pace at which that happens, the setting where it takes place, or the overall method of accounting. And perhaps they don't talk about these things because there is no universal rule.

The way that Lily's life passed before her eyes allowed her to feel alive for a little longer than she was, whether because that's the way it's meant to happen or because that's the way she wanted it to happen. Regardless, this is how it happened. For someone else, it may be a much different experience—or not.

There is no way of knowing.

But that's beside the point.

This is Lily's story, not someone else's.

Cover Art:

Catwoman

by

Jenn Wertz

Jenn Wertz is a musician, writer and accomplished visual artist best known as an original member of multi-platinum recording artists *Rusted Root*, having enjoyed success with the band from 1990-1995, and again from 2000-2007. *Rusted Root* has several gold and platinum recordings including "When I Woke," a double platinum LP which featured the hit "Send Me On My Way," and has enjoyed a prolific touring career. Her artwork is mixed media, using abstract photographs, oil paint, and wax encaustic. She makes her home in Pittsburgh, Pennsylvania with her young son.

SBR
Martin

Sarah Beth (Rem) Martin, penname sbr martin, was bred, born, and raised in Pittsburgh, Pennsylvania, where she continues to live and work as a writer, journalist, and mother.

Martin is an alumna of The Ellis School, the University of Pittsburgh, and the University of Pittsburgh School of Law. Her writing has received recognition through awards, invitation to the New York Conference on College Composition and Communication, and citations in scholastic works and legal texts. Her journalism experience includes projects with AOL's Patch Network and CBS Local Media Pittsburgh.

A quarterfinalist in the 2012 Amazon Breakthrough Novel Awards, *pig* is her second book. Her first book, *in wake of water*, was published in October 2011 by The Artists' Orchard.